"My Turn," She Said.

He gave her the soap and stepped beneath the cascade. She washed him, his muscles twisting and rippling beneath her touch, flowing into his shoulders and arms powerful enough to dig her out of a deadly trap and bring her into the sunlight.

She turned him gently. When she saw the bruises on his back, she was afraid to touch him. She remembered the moment when he had put his body between her and the rockfall. As lightly as breath, her fingers settled on a bruise.

"Does that hurt?" she asked.

"Nothing hurts when you touch me."

"You put yourself in danger . . . protected me . . ."

"Of course," he said. "You're my woman. I'll always protect you."

Dear Reader:

There is an electricity between two people in love that makes everything they do magic, larger than life. This is what we bring you in SILHOUETTE INTIMATE MOMENTS.

SILHOUETTE INTIMATE MOMENTS are longer, more sensuous romance novels filled with adventure, suspense, glamor or melodrama. These books have an element no one else has tapped: excitement.

We are proud to present the very best romance has to offer from the very best romance writers. In the coming months look for some of your favorite authors such as Elizabeth Lowell, Nora Roberts, Erin St. Claire and Brooke Hastings.

SILHOUETTE INTIMATE MOMENTS are for the woman who wants more than she has ever had before. These books are for you.

Karen Solem
Editor-in-Chief
Silhouette Books

Lover In The Rough

Elizabeth Lowell

Silhouette Intimate Moments
Published by Silhouette Books New York
America's Publisher of Contemporary Romance

Silhouette Books by Elizabeth Lowell

Summer Thunder (DES #83)
The Danvers Touch (IM #18)
Lover in the Rough (IM #34)

SILHOUETTE BOOKS, a Division of Simon & Schuster, Inc.
1230 Avenue of the Americas, New York, N.Y. 10020

ISBN: 0-671-47538-X

First Silhouette Books printing January, 1984

10 9 8 7 6 5 4 3 2 1

to my editor
Patricia Smith

who with intelligence, humor and tact
ensures that I don't stray from
the primrose path

thanks

Chapter 1

"Ms. Farrall," asked the photographer, "do you want the white jade dish next to the baroque pearl cluster or the ivory sculpture?"

Reba Farrall walked gracefully over the dry streambed toward the photographer. Angular gravel grated beneath her flat-heeled sandals. She stopped behind the photographer, bent and looked through the camera lens. Absently she pushed aside wisps of honey-blond hair that had escaped from the casual knot she wore on top of her head. She straightened and flipped through the papers on her clipboard, trying to look professional and competent when all she wanted to do was steal away for a few minutes and cry.

"Group eight?" asked Reba, her voice higher and harsher than its normal contralto.

"Yes," said the photographer, consulting her own clipboard.

Reba looked back at the precious objets d'art resting on the ledge of natural marble. Pale marble walls rose on either side of the dry streambed, walls polished by water and time into flowing curves and hollows. Bands

of cream and pale yellow, gold-grey and eggshell wove
through the walls, giving depth and subtle texture to
the satiny stone. Above the marble rose steep, deeply
eroded hills of vermilion and black and chocolate,
volcanic rock so new that the sun hadn't had time yet to
bake out the intense colors.

Mosaic Canyon's contrast in textures was fascinating.
Polished marble walls that would be the envy of any
castle were juxtaposed against the jagged debris of past
volcanic explosions. Bent, broken, canted on edge, the
banded marble strata were almost shocking in their
smoothness. The subtly untamed stone was an excellent
foil for the tranquil, highly civilized curves of the white
jade dish. The baroque pearls, however, didn't quite
fit. As for the arching, intricately carved ivory
bridge . . .

"Do the dish alone on the marble. Try the baroque
pearls in one of the hollows," said Reba, pointing to
one of the many holes that pocked the marble, creating
natural handholds and footholds up the face of the
eight-foot wall. "I think the ivory bridge will do better
contrasted against the darker mixture of marble and
volcanic rocks in the streambed."

The photographer's assistant arranged the jade and
pearls and ivory, adjusted the lighting and stepped
aside. The photographer squinted through the lens,
readjusted the white parasols and reflective panels and
began to shoot.

Reba watched with a patience that went no deeper
than the mist of perspiration on her skin. She knew that
her desire to lash out at the people around her was
irrational. The photographer was excellent. The guards
were as unobtrusive as men carrying guns could be.
The two insurance agents had stayed out of the way.
The various assistants and gofers had been more help

than bother. Except for Todd Sinclair, everyone was doing exactly what was expected. And, in a way, so was Todd. He was being every bit the crass boor that he had been while his grandfather was alive.

With a silent cry Reba turned away from the sight of the beautiful objets d'art that Jeremy Bouvier Sinclair had collected during his long lifetime. A month hadn't given her enough time to adjust to Jeremy's death. Even at eighty he had been erect, alert, his eyes bright and quick. In his precise, elegant French, he had introduced her to a world that she would never have found alone.

The half-century gap in their ages had not prevented a mutual understanding that was as rare as the materials they worked with. Never having known a father, Reba had given Jeremy a daughter's love. He had returned that love, taking a parental pride and pleasure in her growth from a rootless young divorcee to a sophisticated, accomplished collector of natural objets d'art. He had given generously of his immense knowledge of gem minerals, cut gems and art created from precious materials. He had taught her everything and accepted nothing in return but her delight when they found something exquisite to add to his collection.

When it had come time for Reba to make her own way in the world that he had opened to her, Jeremy had given her his blessing. His unqualified confidence in her skill, taste and honesty had gone out along the gem grapevine. In a milieu where a person's integrity was his only bond, Jeremy's support had been a priceless asset . . . but still not a tenth so valuable to her as his love.

And now he was dead.

"Ms. Farrall?" said the photographer in the voice of someone who has repeated a question several times.

"Should we go back to the mouth of the canyon for the Green Suite? I don't think those shades will do well against the marble. Perhaps the salt flats or the dunes?"

"Hey, sweet stuff," called Todd before Reba could answer. "Wake up! The lawyers are gone. There's nobody here to impress with your great grief for the old goat."

Reba looked at Todd with golden-brown eyes that were as clear and hard as the cinnamon diamond Jeremy had given her for her thirtieth birthday. The ring glinted fiercely as she clenched her fist, then relaxed it. Today was the last day that she had to put up with Todd Sinclair, yet it wouldn't be the last time that she would wonder how a gentleman like Jeremy could have given rise to a toad like Todd.

Ignoring him, Reba turned to the photographer. "The dunes, I think." She looked at her watch. "Take a break, everyone. We'll meet at the dunes in half an hour."

She waited while people packed up equipment and began walking back toward the mouth of Mosaic Canyon. When the last person vanished around a bend in the canyon's marble walls, she closed her eyes and fought the welling tears. She had more work to do. The terms of Jeremy's will dictated the sale of his collection. She would do as he had asked. She would even accept the five percent commission—then she would use it to pay for publishing a full-color book containing photographs of his collection as it had been while he was alive. The book would be her memorial to him, a celebration of Jeremy Bouvier Sinclair's taste and unerring judgment.

But first she had to get through this day as she had gotten through every other day since Jeremy died, by not giving in to the despair and emptiness inside her. She turned and put her cheek against the marble wall, enjoying its coolness. Even in April, Death Valley was a place of dry winds and barren mountains black against the cloudless cobalt sky.

She hadn't wanted to come here. The very name had set her on edge. Yet, once here, she couldn't help but respond to the fierce, naked land. There were no plants to mask the infinitely subtle variations of color and texture that marked the passage of geological events and eras. Minerals both common and rare were jumbled together, colors and textures juxtaposed in a haphazard way that told much about the violent geologic history of the valley. Earthquakes, molten rock flowing thickly, seas and lakes alternating with grinding drought, floods eroding mountainsides, strata of rock sinking, rising, bending, breaking; it was all here, written across the hard surface of the earth.

The land had been here so long and human life was so brief, a glitter of gold dust riding a restless wind.

Reba heard footsteps and spun around, angry that her solitude had been spoiled. Todd Sinclair was picking his way along the streambed toward her. His city shoes and sidewalk gait looked awkward in the primal land.

"What do you want?" she asked, her voice clipped and cold.

"Same thing you gave old Jeremy," said Todd, trying to close the distance between them as quickly as he could.

Pebbles rattled beneath his feet, threatening to trip him. He swore and slowed down. Reba made a sound of disgust and moved to walk around him. He stepped to the side, cutting her off.

"C'mon, sweet stuff," he said, smiling and reaching for her. "They're all gone. No need to pretend you don't want it as bad as I do."

Reba stepped back with quick grace, only to be

brought up short against the marble wall. She looked at
Todd and felt nauseated. Tall, dark, handsome, rich.
The perfect prince. And she'd just as soon kiss a toad.
"I'm through being polite, Todd. I'm through ignoring
all your sleazy double entendres and 'accidental' paw-
ing. All I want from you is a guarantee that you'll never
touch me again. Is that clear enough or would you like
it notarized with copies to your lawyer?"

"Too bad, baby. I want to know what the old goat
thought was good enough to be worth five percent of
$7.6 million. And don't worry," he added, grabbing
her. "If I like it, I can afford it now that he's dead."

Reba straightened her arms and shoved suddenly,
using every ounce of her strength. Todd wasn't expecting her to resist. He staggered backwards two steps and
sprawled on his rear in the gravel. He scrambled to his
feet, swearing.

"That's it, Farrall. I was going to be nice about it, but
it's time somebody taught you that a whore's place in
this world is on her back!"

Reba spun around to run up the canyon, only to
collide with something warm and hard. A man. His
presence shocked her into utter stillness. She had heard
no one approach, seen no one—but there he was, as
unyielding as the canyon wall. He lifted her, turning to
put her behind him, then faced the furious Todd.

The stranger said nothing. He merely stood, waiting,
as calm and unbending as the black mountains.

Reba stared at the man's back, too surprised even to
speak, caught by the impressions of the instant—the
hard warmth of his hands, his easy strength as he had
lifted her, the brilliance of silver-green eyes. He was
not as tall or as heavy as Todd, but the stranger had
moved with a muscular grace that spoke of power and a
rare coordination. There was also an indefinable assurance about him that was like nothing she had ever seen.

Todd took two steps toward Reba before he stopped. Though angry, he was no fool. He looked at the stranger. "This isn't any of your business," snapped Todd.

The man said nothing, did nothing, simply stood and waited with a patience that was frightening.

Todd took one more step forward, saw the smooth change in the stranger's stance and backed up quickly. With a crude oath, Todd turned and stumbled back down the dry streambed, pausing only to call over his shoulder, "The whore isn't worth it!"

The man watched until Todd was out of sight, then turned toward Reba. She stared at him, caught by the color of his eyes, a pale, shimmering green that was startling against the sun-browned darkness of his face. Crisp black hair curled out from beneath the rim of a dark western hat. A thick sable moustache contrasted with the fine sculpting of his lips. The short-sleeved khaki desert shirt he had tucked into his faded jeans did little to conceal the male strength of his body. From a loop on his wide leather belt hung a geologist's hammer, blunt on one face and shaped like a pick on the other. Though he could have used it as a weapon against Todd, the stranger hadn't even put his hand on the tool.

"Thanks," Reba said. "You saved me a run through the rocks."

His smile was a slash of white against the tanned darkness of his face. She revised her estimate of his age downwards. She doubted if he were over thirty-five. Hard years, though. His face made that clear, as did the physical assurance that had routed a man younger and larger than he.

"The next time you need to be alone," he said, "you might try the valley. It's so quiet there you can hear grains of sand hiss down the slipface of a dune." His deep voice had a gentle western drawl overlaid with harsher accents she couldn't identify. "And," he added dryly, "it's not as easy to be trapped out in the open."

"How did you know I wanted to be alone?" Reba asked, pushing a wisp of hair behind her ear. The cinnamon diamond flashed and burned with each movement of her hand.

"The same way I knew that you weren't just playing hard to get with loverboy. Body language doesn't lie."

"Like you standing there, just waiting for Todd to move, so confident you didn't even touch the hammer on your belt."

His light green eyes narrowed as he reassessed her in a single, comprehensive look that noted the eggshell silk of her blouse, her russet shorts, her Italian leather sandals, the vibrant cinnamon diamond ring on her right hand, and most of all the curving woman's body conditioned by a lifetime passion for gymnastics.

"He doesn't know you very well, does he?" said the man softly.

"No."

"And he's not likely to," added the man, a statement rather than a question.

"Not if I can help it," she agreed, feeling more at ease with the stranger than she had with any man but Jeremy.

The man's smile flashed suddenly beneath his midnight moustache, transforming the harsh planes of his face into less intimidating lines. "There's another way out of the canyon, if you're game."

"How did you know that Todd's the type to ambush me on the way out?"

"Same way I knew I wouldn't have to use the hammer on him. Instinct."

"And experience in a few rough places?" said Reba lightly, somewhat shocked by the casual way he had spoken about using a hammer on Todd. If she'd had any doubt that the stranger was as hard as he looked, that doubt was gone.

The man measured her for an unsmiling moment, then nodded abruptly. "A few. Still want to come with me?"

"Yes," she said quickly, surprising herself. She was usually wrapped in layers of professional reserve, armed and armored against life's emotional ambushes. Jeremy's death had changed that, fracturing her careful facade like a gem struck by a careless stonecutter. The stranger's quiet strength drew her as surely as the naked beauty of the land.

The man watched her for another instant, black eyebrows raised in silent query. He turned away without saying anything, walked three steps and disappeared around a bend in the marble wall. She followed, then watched with admiration as he went up the polished marble wall as though it were a staircase, moving from handhold to foothold with an easy rhythm that told of years spent in rough country. It answered one small mystery—where he had come from so suddenly. His speed and silence were impressive.

Reba removed her sandals, knowing that their slick leather soles would not help her climb the marble. She slipped the sandal straps over her left wrist and waited until the stranger reached a wide ledge where the marble gave way to steeply slanted layers of volcanic rock. She took a few deep breaths as though she were preparing to execute a gymnastics routine, measured the footholds available and began her ascent. She let the spacing of the hollows determine her rhythm. Only the last part was difficult; she was seven inches shorter than the stranger's six feet and there were no hollows for the last four feet of the wall.

"Hold up your arms," he said.

She did. He bent and wrapped his hands around her arms. There was a brief sense of hard, callused hands followed by a surge of strength. He lifted her up the last few feet so quickly that she had no time to object. He steadied her, took the sandals and knelt to put them on her bare feet.

Reba made a startled sound as his fingers closed around her calf and the arch of her foot. Caught off balance, she braced herself with a hand on his back, feeling the shifting resilience of his muscles beneath her palm. A warm hand held her foot, brushing away sharp bits of rock before he strapped on her sandal. He moved so quickly, so surely, that by the time she realized she should object to his touch, the moment for objection had passed. In a rather dazed silence, she watched him buckle the second sandal.

"That's the worst of the climb," he said, standing up in a single smooth motion. He assessed her confusion, smiled slightly and nodded. "Loverboy was wrong about that, too."

"What?"

"You aren't a whore. Whores are used to being touched by strangers." He turned and began walking along the ledge.

Reba stared after him for a few seconds before she followed, wondering how much of Todd's tirade the stranger had overheard. She flushed and then went pale, remembering Todd's accusations. Emptiness settled in her. More than ever she missed Jeremy's presence, his faith in her as a person worthy of friendship and love. No one had treated her like that before she met Jeremy—not her mother, not her husband. No one.

Tears burned behind her eyelids, blurring the rough trail. Impatiently she rubbed her eyes. Not yet. Tonight, after the last photograph of Jeremy's collection was taken and the last person left for Los Angeles, tonight she would cry.

She realized that the stranger had turned and was waiting for her. She knew that those silver-green eyes hadn't missed her brief tears. With a defiant lift to her chin she walked toward him, pulling her professional composure around her like an opaque shell, concealing her emotions inside.

He hesitated for a moment, as though he would speak or hold out his hand to her, but did neither. Instead, he turned and walked soundlessly through the crumbling volcanic rocks. She followed, moving carefully, sensing his attention on her during the roughest parts of the trail and his approval when she negotiated the tricky spots with a poise that came from hours spent on a balance beam. She said nothing, though, nor did she meet his eyes again. She couldn't bear to think of anyone overhearing Todd's crude accusations.

As Reba walked, the silence and primal beauty of the canyon seeped into her, easing her feelings of anger and humiliation and emptiness. Curiosity grew in her as she watched the stranger's unconscious grace of movement, his silvery eyes constantly appraising the cliffs and rocks, his alertness to every shift of sound. He was like a wild animal, intensely aware, moving powerfully and silently over the harsh land.

He stopped to wait for her by a stratum of black rock thrusting out of the land.

"Precambrian," he said, pulling out his hammer and striking the stone. It gave off a hard, almost crystalline sound. The hammer left no mark. "One of the oldest rocks on earth. There was no life then, nothing but water and rock, lightning and wind. After a few billion years, single-celled life caught on. Algae. Not much as we measure life, but damned powerful just the same. The algae gave off oxygen as a byproduct, same way we breathe out carbon dioxide. They divided and multiplied and finally polluted the atmosphere with oxygen so badly that they killed themselves off."

"Polluted?" Reba asked, startled.

His lips curved. "By their standards, yes. But they left behind a fantastically rich environment for life as we know it. Oxygen-breathing life."

"'*Plus ça change, plus c'est la même chose,*'" she said, her voice soft.

He smiled crookedly as he translated in his deep voice. "'The more things change, the more they stay the same.' Exactly. Four billion years and nothing much has changed, not really." He tapped the rock again, listening to the flat ring of metal on stone. "Sometimes I wonder what will follow us."

"The way we followed the algae?" she asked slowly, staring at the incredibly ancient black rock. Billions of years . . . life growing, dying, changing, and time curving, beginning everything anew, lives and deaths balanced as harmoniously as the crystal lattice of a flawless diamond. Nothing lost, not really, not utterly. Life and death were part of the same continuum, different facets cut on the face of time.

Without realizing it, Reba let out a long sigh. The icy knot that had settled in her stomach the night Jeremy died began to loosen. To stand here, to see time solidified in ebony stone and hear it described by a deep, gentle voice made her feel less terribly alone.

"The thought of extinction doesn't bother you?" he asked, his voice soft, his eyes as transparent as the sky, watching her.

"There's only change, not extinction," she said slowly. "Birds were once dinosaurs."

His laugh was as surprising as the fire inside a black opal. "I should have expected to meet another geologist here."

She shook her head, making sunlight twist and gleam in her thick honey hair. "Just a reader of natural history," she said, remembering the years of her marriage when her professor-husband laughed at her for wasting time reading about 'cold science' when he was handing the living worlds of romance languages to her. Cramming them down her throat, to be precise. By the time she was divorced she read and understood Spanish, Portuguese and Italian, and was wholly fluent in French.

But she hadn't enjoyed any language until she met Jeremy. He had refused to learn the language of his English father, a man who had seduced and abandoned his mother. When Reba first saw Jeremy, he was at a service station trying to explain what had gone wrong with his car. As the mechanic spoke no French, Jeremy's explanation was of the hand-waving variety. She had volunteered a translation—and for the first time in her life she had understood the thrill of speaking more than one language. When Jeremy had answered her in his pure Parisian accent, she had a visceral sense of the beauty of the French language as a form of communication rather than a series of academic exercises.

"And a linguist," said the stranger.

"What?" she said, startled by the parallel between her thoughts and the man's words.

"A reader of natural history and a linguist, *n'est-ce pas?*" He smiled at her surprise. "My accent isn't as refined as yours, but most of the Frenchmen I've dealt with weren't from the Sorbonne."

Reba lifted her hand to capture a stray wisp of hair as she studied him, suddenly wondering where he had been and what he had done. She saw his glance shift from her eyes to her ring and then back again.

"He gave the diamond to you, didn't he?"

"He?" she said, startled that the stranger had accu-

rately identified a gem whose gold-orange-brown color
was so unusual that few people even knew diamonds
came in that shade. "Who?"

"The man whose sheets loverboy is dying to sleep
in."

Reba's hand dropped. She stepped backwards, angry
and oddly hurt. "It wasn't like that with Jeremy."

He measured the change in her with cold, quick
intelligence. Then he nodded. "But he did give that
ring to you."

"What makes you so sure?" she asked, her voice
tight, her eyes searching his.

"Cinnamon diamonds are usually too dark or too
pale, lacking distinction. Yours is very rare, very
beautiful, the exact color and brilliance of your eyes.
Only a man who was . . . *close* . . . to you would give
you such a gem. He must have looked a long time for
it."

Reba's throat tightened, remembering Jeremy's
words as he had given her the ring. "Seven years," she
whispered. "He looked for seven years."

The stranger's hand moved so quickly that she didn't
have time to step back. Surprisingly gentle fingers
brushed away strands of hair that the dry wind kept
blowing across her face. "It was worth every minute,"
he said, looking from the ring to the clear cinnamon
depths of her eyes.

"That's what Jeremy said." Her voice broke as
sudden tears magnified the beauty of her eyes. She
blinked and looked away, unable to bear the stranger's
penetrating gaze. Brilliant tears clung to her lashes but
did not fall. She looked at her watch. "I have to be at
the dunes in fifteen minutes."

A long finger tilted her chin up. "Are you sure you're
feeling tough enough to face down loverboy?"

She met the stranger's transparent green eyes without flinching. "He's the least of it," she said, thinking of Jeremy and the cold emptiness of loss. "But yes, I'm ready. I have no choice."

He held her glance for a long moment before he nodded. "All right."

He turned away and walked around the ancient bed of black rock. She followed, her attention divided between the rough land and the hard-faced man with the gentle voice and hands. She had met many men in her travels as a collector, men who were polished and men who weren't, men who had graduated from the great universities of the world and men who had graduated from the school of mean streets, but she'd never met anyone like the man who walked in front of her. His combination of intelligence and toughness was new to her, as unsettling as the strength and gentleness that characterized his touch.

She followed him around the rumpled chocolate tongue of an ancient landslide and found herself looking out over the valley. He had brought her to a point just below the tiny dirt parking lot at the head of the Mosaic Canyon trail. There were only two cars left in the lot, Todd's Mercedes and her own BMW coupe. She looked, but saw no sign of Todd.

"Waiting up the canyon no doubt," said the stranger.

"Yes," sighed Reba, no longer surprised when his thoughts paralleled her own. She rubbed the back of her arm over her forehead, wiping away beads of sweat. "I hope he cooks."

"Not in April. July, though." He smiled grimly. "In July it's so hot that the soles of your feet burn and blister right through your boots. The Outback is like that, sometimes."

"Lightning Ridge," she said, and felt absurdly pleased when he gave her a startled glance.

"How did you know?"

"Most people would think this was either topaz or zircon," she said, looking at the diamond on her hand.

He shrugged. "It has too much dispersion to be anything but a diamond."

"Which proves my point," said Reba. "You know gems. And to gem people, the Outback means only one thing. Opals. You don't strike me as the type to waste your time on anything but the best. That means black opals, and that means Lightning Ridge. There's also the fact that you look"—she hesitated—"well, rough enough to survive the black opal mines."

"Oh, they're not that bad," he said, smiling down at her. Then his mouth changed, hard rather than curving, and his eyes became the color of hammered silver. Whatever his memories were, they weren't pleasant. "The diamond strikes in South America are worse."

Reba's eyes widened. She wanted to ask a hundred questions but doubted that he would want to answer. South American diamond strikes were like the Vietnam war—the men who had seen the most were the ones who talked about it the least.

"Are you going straight to the dunes?" he asked.

"Yes."

"Are you going to be out in the dunes the rest of the day?" Silver-green eyes measured the angle of the sun as he spoke.

"Probably."

"Are you carrying water in your car?"

She shook her head. "In April, I didn't think I'd need it."

"You always need water in a desert." He reached behind his belt and unhooked the canvas-covered canteen he carried there. He pulled a leather thong from his pants pocket and rigged a sling for the canteen. "Take this."

Reba licked her dry lips as she looked from the canteen to the hard face of the stranger who was offering her the only water in miles. "But what about you?"

He shrugged. "Like you said, it's April. Besides"— he smiled gently and touched her still-wet lashes with his fingertip—"you need it more than I do right now."

"I—" Her breath rushed out and for a moment all she could do was stare at the man's oddly colored eyes. Pure, almost transparent green with a silver shimmer. "I'm glad I don't have to find a gem to match your eyes," she said musingly. "It would take a lifetime."

When Reba heard what she had said, she shook her head and laughed helplessly. "Forgive me. I'm not usually so, so *unwrapped.*" She looked away from his unique eyes and shook the canteen briskly. Full. She unscrewed the top, drank quickly, put back the top and handed the canteen to him. "That should hold me. Thanks."

Without looking away from her eyes, the stranger removed the canteen top, drank deeply, sealed the canteen and gave it back to her. For an instant all she could think of was his lips touching where hers had so recently been. The thought sent an odd feeling through her. She tried to look away from his eyes but could not.

"Mint," he murmured. "Nice."

"Mint?" Then she realized that she must have left the taste of her favorite candy on the rim of the canteen. "Oh . . . mint," she said. She laughed and held her hands up to her flushed cheeks. "My God, what you must think of me!"

He took off his hat and ran his fingers through his thick black hair. "I think you can drink out of my canteen any time," he said, chuckling.

Reba caught herself wondering if his hair felt as

springy-silky as it looked. He smiled down at her suddenly, as though he knew what she was thinking and it pleased him. She took a shaky breath. He had the most unsettling effect on her of any man she had ever met.

"I'm going to be late," she said quickly. She turned away, then looked back. "Thanks for helping me."

His smile widened. "If you hadn't been wearing those silly sandals I'd have let you run loverboy right into the rocks," he said, looking down at the smooth curves of her legs, at their feminine strength and grace. "You're in a hell of a lot better shape than he is. No wonder he couldn't wait to find out if you'd feel half as good as you look."

"Do you ever have an unspoken thought?" she asked tartly.

"All the time," he murmured in his husky drawl, looking at her mouth, at the outline of her breasts beneath the clinging silk blouse, at her bare legs and the smooth feet he had brushed off and fastened into delicate sandals. "You'd better go before I start thinking out loud."

She tilted her head to the side as she looked up at him. "Aren't you afraid I'd run you right into the ground?"

His slow smile sent warmth curling through her. "Want to try?"

For a wild moment she wanted to do just that. Then sanity returned. But he had seen the moment of wildness in her, and responded to it with a ripple of movement that reminded her of the change that had come over him when Todd looked as though he would fight. Muscles taut yet relaxed, silvery eyes intent, body poised for whatever might come, the stranger waited for her to decide.

Reba closed her eyes and shivered, suddenly not trusting her own reactions. The weeks since Jeremy's death had shredded her usual control, threatening to reveal her most private feelings. And this rough stranger had the uncanny ability to touch those feelings. No matter how gentle the touch, it frightened her. She hadn't been this vulnerable since she was a child. She didn't like it one bit.

When she opened her eyes, the stranger was watching her. The intensity of a moment ago was gone, replaced by a gentleness that was almost tangible.

"He's dead, isn't he? The man loverboy wants to replace."

"Yes. A month ago."

He lifted his hand, then let it fall without touching her. "The first weeks are the worst," he said simply.

"I hope so," she whispered. "I can't live like this, with my skin inside out, every nerve exposed."

"You're still fighting it. When you stop fighting you'll begin to heal."

"Yesterday I would have said *'Never!'* But today, when you showed me a rock as old as time . . ." Impulsively Reba touched his cheek with her fingertips, a light brush of warmth. "Thank you."

She turned around and walked quickly to her car. She turned back once, realizing that she still was holding his canteen. There was no one behind her. He had gone as silently as he had appeared. If she hadn't felt the weight of his canteen in her hand, she would have thought she had dreamed him.

Were there any lingering doubts about the stranger's reality, though, Todd's presence at the dunes would have removed them. He hung around the edges of the activity like a sullen cloud looking for a place to rain. Reba stayed out of his way. The third time she casually evaded Todd's attempts to get her alone, she remembered the stranger's words: *It's not as easy to be trapped in the open.*

Reba waited patiently while the photographer rearranged the last pieces of the Green Suite on the lip of a dune. The descending sun threw out long, crisp shadows, emphasizing ripple marks in the sand. Cut stones and gem crystals in matrix gleamed against the umber sand, tints and tones and every possible shade of green. Emeralds cut and in matrix, tsavorite cut and in matrix, peridot and diopside and corundum, topaz and diamonds scintillating; a stunning crystal shaft of Brazilian tourmaline that gave new meaning to the word *green.*

A smile curved Reba's lips as she looked at the tourmaline. That, at least, was one thing time could not take from her—the only thing that she had left of her childhood, half-ownership of the China Queen, an abandoned tourmaline mine in the Pala area of San Diego county.

The mine had come down to her from her great-great-grandmother. The terms of her will stated that it was to go to the oldest girl in each generation on her twenty-sixth birthday. That had worked well until her mother was born, one half of identical twins. The birth had been accomplished in the backseat of a car. By the time her grandmother and the twins were in the hospital, no one knew which girl had been born first. So her mother got half of the mine and her aunt got the other half. The aunt had married an Australian and vanished into the Outback, taking her half of the mine with her.

Once, Reba had dreamed of opening the China Queen and finding fabulous treasures overlooked by earlier miners. Sometimes she wondered if that fantasy hadn't been what urged her onto the gem trail with

Jeremy, a dream of treasures come true. But as for the mine itself . . . it remained merely a childish fantasy. The costs of mining were staggering and the mine itself sagged under eighty years of neglect. She hadn't been to the China Queen since she was a child.

"Ms. Farrall? We're ready to leave if you are."

Reba looked up at the owner of the patient voice. "Sorry," she murmured. "The Green Suite always sets me to dreaming."

The photographer grimaced and watched the last of the precious specimens being packed away in their individual cases. "It gives the insurance people nightmares. They can't wait to get back to L.A. and steel vaults. That guy hanging around a few dunes over isn't doing anything for their nerves, either."

Reba turned and saw a man standing outlined against the late afternoon sky. Lithe, relaxed, radiating strength even in his stillness, unmistakably the stranger whose canteen now bumped companionably against her hip. "Tell the guards to relax," she said. "That man has seen moré rare gems than a tour guide at the Smithsonian."

"Tell it to Mr. Sinclair. He's been trying to talk the guards into running the guy off."

"Death Valley is a national monument. He has as much right to be here as we do."

"That's what one of the guards said. Several times." The photographer shrugged and turned away. "I'll call you when I have today's proofs."

From the top of her dune, Reba watched as the group of people slowly fragmented and retraced their hollow footprints back out to the road. She looked over her shoulder, expecting to see the stranger. The ridge was empty of all but wind. When she turned back she saw Todd struggling up the face of the dune, determination in every stride. She turned and lightly ran down the back side of the dune. By the time Todd reached the spot where she had been, she was several dunes away, moving with an ease that he couldn't hope to equal.

Sound carried very far in the desert but meaning was quickly lost. She was just as glad. She didn't need to know precisely what names Todd had called her.

Though Reba was headed toward the spot where the stranger had been, she didn't see him. She climbed several more dunes before she turned and looked back. All she saw was Todd struggling in the crimson sunset light, moving slowly away from her toward cars that looked no bigger than one-carat stones scattered along the narrow road.

She waited until she saw Todd get into his car and drive away. It was almost cool now, the temperature descending with the sun. Slowly she turned in a full circle. Nothing moved but her shadow and the wind. There was no one in sight, nothing near her but softly folded dunes glowing in the rich evening light. All around her was silence and beauty.

The western mountains were glittering mounds of black crystal suspended against a ruby sky. The eastern mountain peaks were a transparent, icy pink, fractured into spires and pinnacles that scintillated in the twilight. Every color had a gemlike clarity and radiance, as though she were suspended in the heart of an immense black opal with darkness all around a fiery center of life.

She didn't know when she began to cry. At first it was a gentle rain. Then it became a torrent that shook her mercilessly, bringing her to her knees. She tried to stop sobbing but could not. The nerve and discipline that had carried her through the month was dissolving away, leaving only icy loss and scalding grief. She sank

to the sand and wept helplessly, holding onto herself
like a child.

Dimly she was aware of the stranger's hands lifting
her, strong arms folding around her, pulling her across
his lap and rocking her slowly, his deep voice murmuring comfort against her hair. She tried to talk, to tell
him about Jeremy, but all she could say through her
tears was, "I l-loved him and now he's d-dead."

"Pauvre petite," he said gently, his voice a velvet
warmth against her hair. *Poor little one.*

The familiar French phrase stripped Reba of her last
defenses. With a broken sound she put her arms around
the stranger and gave herself over to grief. His fingers
slid through her hair, easing out the carved ivory comb
that held her hair coiled on top of her head. Her hair
fell in heavy waves over her shoulders and his arms.
Slowly he stroked her hair and her back, holding her
against his hard strength, comforting her.

After a long, long time her tears were spent and she
could breathe without sobbing. He wrapped his jacket
around her and gently bathed her face with water from
the canteen. In the moonlight his eyes were molten
silver, his expression dark and unreadable. Common
sense whispered that she should be frightened; she was
alone in the dunes with a rough stranger whose name
she didn't know. Yet as she looked up at him she felt
only peace, his warmth seeping through her.

With a small sigh Reba rested against his chest, too
spent to hold herself erect. His arms tightened around
her, silently supporting her. Strong fingers slowly
rubbed up her back and neck, loosening muscles that
had been knotted for weeks. She murmured and
sighed, relaxing. Gradually, strength returned to her,
as though she were drawing it from him.

"Better?" he asked softly.

She nodded, sending moonlight sliding through hair that looked more silver than gold.

He stood, pulling her up with him, holding her until he was sure she could stand. "I'll walk you to your car."

"You don't have to," she said. "I can manage now." But her voice was hoarse with crying and her face was as pale as moonlight. "Really, I can."

"I'm sure you could," he said, "but you don't have to."

He took her hand and led her toward the rising moon. As they walked through the black and silver land there was no sound but the whisper of sand sliding down the steep face of a dune. Neither of them spoke, not wanting to disturb the sable silence.

When they reached her car he turned toward her. His fingers eased through her hair, seeking the warmth beneath the cool silk. He tilted her head back, letting moonlight pour over her oval face. Slowly he bent to take her lips, giving her long seconds to evade his kiss.

She felt the gentle cage of his fingers, saw his wide shoulders eclipse the moon, heard his breath sigh out when her eyes closed, accepting his caress. His kiss was a gentle warmth moving over her mouth, a sweet pressure that she couldn't deny. Instinctively her lips softened, surrender and invitation at once. He kissed her with a gentle restraint and thoroughness that made her moan.

And then he changed, his arms closing around her while he kissed her with a hunger as deep as the night, his hard edges melting and flowing over her until she fitted against him perfectly. With a small sound she clung to him, shaken by his heat and the velvet demands of his tongue, responding to him as she had never responded to any man.

When he finally lifted his mouth she was barely able to stand. He looked at her for a long time, breathing deeply, his body hard and very male. His voice was husky, almost harsh.

"If you loved him, he died a lucky man."

He turned and walked into the night, vanishing into the moon shadow of a dune, leaving his jacket wrapped around her and his hunger burning in her blood.

Chapter 2

THE OBJET D'ART WAS A SMALL SHOP, ONE OF MANY along Rodeo Drive. The shop was heavily but discreetly guarded with the latest in electronic alarms. Not for Reba the ugly black wires and bars of a pawnshop. Her business was guarded by nearly invisible optic fibers and hairfine wires that were embedded in the heavy glass door and exterior eye-level windows. The windows themselves were beveled, as gleaming as the materials they enclosed.

Today she had set out a few pieces from the Green Suite, mineral specimens and magnificent cut gems placed on clear pedestals or nestled in artful folds of silk. The lighting was high intensity, from unexpected angles, sending coruscations of color across the black matte silk that was Reba's trademark.

She wore the same silk herself, a simple long-sleeved blouse and matching slacks. High-heeled black sandals added inches to her height, as did the shining, dark honey mass of hair piled above her pale oval face. Two perfectly matched black opals burned darkly against her earlobes. The only other jewelry she wore was the ring Jeremy had given to her. The ring hadn't left her hand since her birthday almost twelve months ago.

But as she looked at the diamond's cinnamon brilliance it was the stranger, not Jeremy, who filled her thoughts. Even after ten days, the memory of being held like a child and then kissed like the last woman on earth sent unfamiliar sensations shimmering through her.

"Every shade of green there is," said Tim.

"Not quite," she said absently to her assistant. "There's a silver-green that—"

Reba made an impatient sound and pulled her mind back to the present. She didn't even know the man's name, nor was she likely to. He had vanished as completely as yesterday's sunlight. If only he would vanish from her memory, too. But he wouldn't. He had helped her begin filling one kind of emptiness, only to leave another kind in its place, a yearning as intense as it was irrational. How could she miss something she'd never had?

"When is the first appointment?" asked Reba in a clipped voice.

Tim flipped through a notebook. "Eleven."

"Who is it?"

"Todd Sinclair."

Reba grimaced. "What does he want?"

"The Green Suite."

"He'll get it the same day hell freezes over."

Tim looked up, his brown eyes shrewd and appraising. "You mean you've decided?"

With an effort, Reba curbed her impatient response. It seemed like half the world was after her to decide which two parts of Jeremy's collection she would choose as her own. Individual collectors, museums, newspapers, magazines, lawyers and Todd Sinclair had badgered her since the moment the will became public

knowledge. People who had never known her—and
who never would, if she had any say in the matter—
speculated privately and in print as to the exact nature
of her relationship with the deceased Jeremy Bouvier
Sinclair. Protégée, certainly, but something else, perhaps? Something more *intimate?* And which part of
her, er, *mentor's* collection would she keep? Would she
go for money or sentiment?

Tim held up his hands as though warding off blows.
"Don't hit me, boss. I'm just like the rest of the world,
eaten up with curiosity."

Reba gave the compact young man an exasperated
look. Tim was invaluable to her, an accomplished
gemologist with an instinctive feel for fraudulent
stones. His easygoing manner concealed a shrewd grasp
of the gem trade and human nature. Best of all, he was
utterly in love with his wife. He treated Reba the same
way he did the gems that passed through his fingers—
appreciation, respect and a total absence of desire to
possess. In the two years he had worked for her, a
brother-sister camaraderie had grown between them
that was as great an asset to her as his unquenchable
humor.

"I'm keeping the Green Suite," she said.

Tim shouted exultantly, then looked vaguely sheep-
ish. "I just made a thousand bucks," he explained.

"Who lost?"

Tim smiled maliciously. "A bastard called Sinclair."

Reba's lips curved into an unwilling smile. "Don't
count it until Todd pays you."

"Oh, he'll pay," said Tim, "if I have to hammer it
out of him a dollar at a time. He was so damn sure you
were going to take the Ace of Diamonds. Or is that
your second choice?"

She shook her head. "It's beautiful, but it's just a big
diamond."

LOVER IN THE ROUGH   35

"Just a—boss, that just-a-diamond is worth 1.85 million dollars at last appraisal, and that was two years ago! You could sell it, invest the money and spend a lot of time clipping coupons."

"I'd rather earn my money. Old-fashioned, I guess."

Tim looked at her closely. "You don't want them saying that you cozied up to Jeremy for his money, right?"

"Leave it alone, Tim," she said in a flat voice. "When people ask, just tell them that the Ace was a bit garish for my taste."

He touched her hand quickly. "Sorry, Reba. I know what Jeremy meant to you. It's just that he was such a sonofa—" Tim coughed. "He was hell on wheels with everyone but you."

"I spoke French," she said, her voice softening as she remembered Jeremy's delight in his native tongue.

"So did I," grumbled Tim.

"With an atrocious accent," she pointed out.

"Details, details." He flipped his notebook shut and put it in the pocket of his fawn wool suitcoat. "What's your second choice?"

"That's what I like about you," Reba said tartly. "You take a hint."

"Uh-huh. Give."

"More bets?"

Tim smiled.

"The Tiger God," she said, giving up.

"The what?"

"The tiger's-eye carving."

"Oh . . ." He swore softly. "How did she know?"

"Who?"

"Gina. She bet that you'd take that statue."

"How much did you lose?" asked Reba indulgently. Gina was the receptionist/bookkeeper/secretary for the Objet d'Art. She was also Tim's wife.

"Oh, it wasn't exactly the kind of bet that anyone loses," he said, smiling wolfishly.

Reba smiled in return, hoping that Tim didn't see the icy emptiness in her. What would it feel like to be so close to someone that there were no losers, only winners? What would it feel like to hold someone, to die "the small death" in a lover's arms and awake reborn each morning? What would it feel like to know that someone gave the last ultimate damn about you? Next to that, the rarest gems were a less than a handful of sand hissing down the slipface of a dune.

"Reba, are you all right?"

"Fine," she said dully. "Just a headache." And memories that haunted her relentlessly, sand dunes and moonlight and the heat of a man whose name she didn't know. "I'm going to sort through the photos of Jeremy's collection. When loverboy comes, bring him to my office."

"Loverboy?"

"Sinclair," said Reba, frowning at the slip. Only one person had called Todd Sinclair "loverboy."

Tim gave her a speculative look. "Did Sinclair give you a bad time in Death Valley?"

"Not as bad as he got," she said succinctly.

Tim smiled. "I wish I'd been there. He's overdue for a session in the woodshed."

"Nothing that violent happened to him, I'm afraid," said Reba.

But it could have if Todd had taken one more step. The memory of the predatory change rippling through the stranger's body both frightened and reassured Reba. It had been a relief to know that a man would help her rather than take advantage of her relative weakness as Todd had wanted to do. Even when she was utterly helpless with grief, the stranger had done no more than hold her while she came apart in his arms.

"I think I'll take a late lunch today," said Tim casually.

Tim's usual lunch was eleven to twelve. Todd was coming at eleven.

"That's not necessary," said Reba.

"I had a late breakfast." Before she could object further, he asked quickly, "Want Gina to do a press release about your choices?"

"Poor Gina. She gets stuck with everything."

"She loves it. Really. In fact, if you need someone to do words for your book about Jeremy's collection, you might think about her." Tim watched Reba with intense brown eyes that did little to conceal his interest in her answer.

Reba tilted her head to the side and absently tucked a stray lock of hair back into the coil on top of her head. "I like it," she said finally, decisively. "Yes. We'll have to hire another bookkeeper, though. Gina shouldn't work too hard in her condition."

Tim looked startled. "She told you she was pregnant? She only told me last week."

"My eyes told me, Tim." Her eyes and the possessive way Tim stroked Gina's slightly thickened waist when he thought no one was looking. "Don't worry, I won't tell anyone, though why you'd want to keep it a secret is beyond me. If I were Gina, I'd be taking out full-page ads in the L.A. *Times.*"

"You ought to get married," said Tim, smiling and serious in the same moment.

"I was."

He looked startled.

"It was a long time ago," she said indifferently.

"What happened?"

"I grew up. He didn't want me to."

"I'm sorry," said Tim uncomfortably.

"I'm not. He was a lousy husband but a fantastic

French teacher. Without him, I'd never have known Jeremy."

The phone rang. Tim picked it up, listened, then covered the mouthpiece. "Sinclair," he said curtly. "He wants to see you now."

Reba shrugged. "All right. At least you'll be able to have lunch at the usual time."

Tim put the receiver to his ear. "We can squeeze you in if you can be here in ten minutes." He hung up before Todd could say anything.

"That was remarkably rude," observed Reba, trying not to smile.

"Thank you. I hope he gets a ticket on the way over."

"No such luck. God watches over fools and drunks."

"Which category is Sinclair in?"

"Both."

Reba went into her office. The first thing she saw when she opened her office door was the eighteen-inch piece of crocidolite that had been mined in Cape Province, South Africa. A German carver had taken the exquisite specimen of tiger's-eye and transformed it into the likeness of a man.

The Tiger God stood in an attitude of lithe relaxation, naked but for the solid gold longbow slung over his shoulder. He held a golden arrow loosely in his hand; the triangular arrowhead contrasted with the muscular curve of the thigh it rested on. His eyes were narrowed, slightly slanted, pure gold. The statue had been carved so that the mineral's subtle bands of color ran diagonally, giving the man an arresting appearance of being poised between stillness and rippling strength. Light shimmered across the surface of the Tiger God's masculine body, a seamless blending of every tone between rich gold and luminous brown.

But she had not chosen the statue merely for its

power and extraordinary beauty. She had chosen it because the Tiger God's magnificent physical self-confidence reminded her of a stranger and a sable night and a kiss that had told her how much of a woman she might be in the right man's arms.

Reba heard the distinctive buzzer that sounded in her office every time the front door of Objet d'Art opened. Her office door had a one-way mirror in it that allowed her to see out into the shop while retaining complete privacy. She looked out and saw Todd's broad figure coming toward her. With a muttered curse she put the Tiger God on her desk, sat down and released the electronic lock on her office door. Automatically, the door swung open a few inches. She would see that it stayed that way the whole time loverboy was in her office.

"I'm sick of this jerkaround, Farrall," said Todd, throwing himself into the chair opposite her desk. "Start selling the damned collection. The rest of the old goat's estate isn't worth the lawyer's fees to straighten it out. I need the money and I need it now."

Reba folded her hands and leaned back in her chair, giving Todd a cool look from beneath long lashes. She studied him in silence until he shifted and swore harshly. The smell of alcohol and long nights washed over her.

"Slow horses and bad cards?" she asked indifferently.

Todd flushed, telling how accurate her observation was. "Shut up!" he said thickly.

Reba watched Todd with eyes as hard as the diamond in her ring. Experience had taught her that Todd handled liquor as badly as he did cards. It had been Jeremy's standing order that his bodyguards refuse to admit his grandson if Todd had been drinking. A year ago Todd had attacked his grandfather in a drunken rage. The thought did nothing to calm the anger that had turned Reba's usually feminine mouth into a hard line of distaste.

"Don't sit there looking so proud and perfect," Todd snarled. "You're nothing but a cheap trick the old bastard picked up off the street."

The buzzer sounded again, telling Reba that someone had come in the front door. She couldn't see who it was. Todd's bulky shoulders cut off her view into the store. Probably Gina, back from her appointment.

"Say something, damn you!"

"Make up your mind," Reba said in a flat voice. " 'Shut up. Say something.' Take your pick. I can't do both."

"Why, you snotty little bitch!" he shouted, lunging to his feet and reaching across her desk, trying to grab her.

Reba slipped through his fingers with a grace that only enraged him further. He shoved the desk hard, trapping her against the wall. The Tiger God swayed. She grabbed it. Even as she realized that the statue could be a weapon, she regretted having to use its polished beauty on something as sleazy as Todd Sinclair.

Tim burst into the room, a blackjack in his right hand. "If you touch her I'll break your neck!"

"You'll have to stand in line," said a voice from behind Tim, a voice that was quiet and cold.

Both Tim and the drunken Todd froze, pinned by the promise of violence in the voice. Reba felt like laughing and crying at the same time. She wanted to call out to the man but she still didn't know his name.

The stranger entered the room with a silent, predatory stride. He grabbed Todd, pivoted smoothly and slammed the larger man against a wall. Todd swore and shook his head, suddenly sober and more than a little afraid.

"I won't break your neck right away," continued the stranger in his soft, deadly voice. His hands were a steel vise clamped on Todd's throat. "First I'll break your fingers. Then your thumbs. Then every bone all the way up to your shoulders. One by one. By the time I get around to breaking your neck you'll thank me for it. Hear me, loverboy?"

Todd made a strangled sound that could have been yes.

The stranger turned his head and looked at Reba. The harsh lines of his face changed. "Did he touch you, *chaton?*"

She shook her head, unable to speak for the emotions seething through her, emotions triggered by the deadly stranger and the soft French word that meant both kitten and a set stone, things small and precious and vibrant with life. *Chaton.*

The stranger turned back to Todd. "Keep pushing, loverboy. You'll get there."

Fingers dug into flesh with cruel skill. The stranger pivoted again, then released Todd with a force that sent him staggering through the open office door. The man watched in silence until Todd blundered through the shop and out the front door. Then, with his back still toward Tim, the stranger said coolly, "Unless you're planning to use that blackjack, put it in your pocket."

Tim looked at Reba.

"It's all right, Tim," she said quickly, not looking away from the stranger, as though she were afraid he would disappear as unexpectedly as he had appeared.

The stranger turned around to face Tim, waiting for the younger man to decide. Tim gave the man a long, assessing glance, then slipped the blackjack into his back pocket with an easy gesture that suggested the weapon could reappear very quickly.

As the blackjack disappeared, the stranger's posture shifted subtly, relaxing the disciplined readiness of his body. "Why don't you introduce us, Tim?" he said, gesturing to Reba. An odd smile curved lips that were no longer thin and hard.

Startled, Tim looked at the stranger. "Hey, you told me she knew you!"

"She does," said the man, laughing softly. "She just doesn't know my name."

Tim looked at Reba in disbelief.

"I'm afraid he's right," she said. "It's a long story. . . ." Her voice trailed off.

Tim made an exasperated noise. "Reba Farrall, meet Chance Walker. Chance, Reba. Now would one of you two kindly tell me what the hell is going on?"

Chance smiled, ignoring Tim. "Hello, Reba Farrall," said Chance in his deep, intriguingly accented voice. He pulled Reba's desk back into place with an easy motion, then plucked the Tiger God from her grasp. He turned the statue over in his hands, admiring the play of light across its surface. "Would have been a shame to bend this over loverboy's thick skull."

Reba laughed a bit wildly. "I thought the same thing when I grabbed it."

Chance looked at her, missing nothing from the shimmer of dark blond hair to the sensual curves lying beneath black silk. "You're like the night," he said quietly, "made to wear black. Beautiful *chaton*."

Reba felt the compliment radiate through her, changing her. She had never considered herself pretty, much less beautiful, but when Chance looked at her, she felt she was the most exquisite woman ever born. Tiger God smiled at her with sensual fire in his eyes.

Tim cleared his throat. Reba realized that she had been staring at Chance. Reluctantly, she turned to Tim. "Chance—that is, Mr. Walker—"

"Chance," corrected the Tiger God firmly.

"Chance," she murmured, savoring the unusual name.

Tim cleared his throat again.

"Chance discouraged Todd once in Death Valley," said Reba quickly. "Afterwards, Chance let me . . ." Reba looked helplessly at Tim, not knowing how to explain that she had wept out her grief for Jeremy in a total stranger's arms. "I was missing Jeremy. Chance . . . understood. Oh, damn," she said suddenly, impatient with evasions. "I crawled into his arms and cried like a baby! He was very patient and gentle about it, more so than I deserved."

Tim looked dubiously at the man who had efficiently, ruthlessly reduced a large meaty drunk to a sober mound of hamburger. "'Gentle,' you say. 'Patient.' Yeah, sure. Glad I didn't meet anyone as gentle and patient as Chance while I was working my way through school tending bars."

"That where you learned about blackjacks?" asked Chance.

"Yeah."

"Some bartenders prefer a gun."

"A blackjack is more selective," said Tim dryly.

Chance nodded, approving the younger man. He glanced at Reba. "Is he yours, *chaton?*"

The question was so soft, so unexpected, that it took a moment for Reba to realize its meaning. "Tim? Mine? Good God, no! He has a wonderful wife."

Chance turned and held out his hand to Tim. "Glad to meet you, Tim. And bloody glad you're married."

Tim laughed abruptly. "So am I. I'd hate to get between you and something you want."

"Tim!" said Reba, shocked at Tim's blunt assessment of Chance Walker.

"That's all right," said Chance. "I like a man who's smart enough to come in out of the rain."

Tim grinned and shook Chance's hand. "Glad to meet you, Chance. You're the first man I've seen who might give my hardheaded boss a run for her money. *Bonne chance,*" he said, mangling the French words almost beyond recognition. At the pained look on Reba's face, Tim translated quickly, "Good luck." He hesitated. "Did I just make a bilingual pun?"

"No. My brother was the one called Luck." Chance's face was serious, his silver-green eyes narrowed against memories that didn't please him.

"Was?" asked Tim.

Chance said no more. Tim didn't ask again. There was something about Chance Walker that flatly discouraged questions.

The buzzer sounded. Tim looked through the shop and saw a petite, red-haired woman waiting patiently at the front door. He hurried forward, grinning like a kid.

"His wife?" asked Chance as Tim left.

"Yes. Gina's a gem," said Reba. "She only has one failing," added Reba wryly. "She makes every other woman around her look like a three-legged giraffe."

In two gliding strides, Chance was so close to Reba that she could feel the warmth radiating from his body. "Not every woman," he said, smiling.

Reba looked up at him, remembering the moment she had been wrapped in his arms and his male heat had made her want to melt and run like gold in a jeweler's crucible. The feeling had haunted her at unexpected moments, sending sensations through her that made her quiver invisibly, as though fine wires were tightening deep inside her body.

She had never felt like that in a man's arms before. She had married a man interested only in virginal responses. After the first few weeks of marriage, her husband's embraces had become infrequent, almost indifferent. Since her divorce she had dated many men but found none whom she trusted enough to respond to physically. She had begun to wonder if there were something wrong with her . . . until a single kiss from a stranger taught her more about being a woman than years of marriage had.

And for the life of her, she couldn't figure out why she responded so intensely to Chance Walker. She'd dated more handsome men, men with more wealth, more social grace and position, but it was only this rough stranger whose kiss had gone beyond her polished exterior to tap the molten core of woman beneath.

"What are you thinking?" Chance asked, watching the play of expressions across her face as he gently eased his fingers into her hair, caressing her cheeks with his hard palms.

Sensations shivered through her, making her breath catch. She considered evading his question with half-truths or simple silence. Then she decided that Chance Walker would hardly be shocked by anything she said or did. He was obviously a man who had seen and done it all. Several times.

"I was wondering why you're so attractive to me," she said simply.

His thick moustache shifted and gleamed in the office light as he smiled. "And you to me, *chaton.*"

She stared into the green-silver depths of his eyes, then his black lashes swept down. He took her lips with a devastating blend of hunger and gentleness. She felt the comb holding her coiled hair loosen and slide away, giving his fingers free access to the silky warmth of her unbound hair. The tip of his tongue traced her mouth, teasing her until she sighed and opened her lips.

He buried his fingers in her hair, his hands gentle but so strong that she could not turn her head aside. Half in protest, half in response, she put her hands on his upper arms. Hard, powerful, as inflexible as stone beneath her hands, his arms told her much about the hunger and strength and restraint of the man holding her. He could have crushed the breath out of her, forcing from her the kiss he so plainly wanted.

But he didn't. He held her as though she were infinitely fragile. He coaxed rather than demanded that she share his pleasure in being close to her. She had never been held like that, with absolute strength and safety.

When she felt the velvet roughness of his tongue against her own, her hands tightened on his arms. Tentatively, then with greater assurance, she responded, touching the smoothness of his lips, the serrations of his teeth, the sweet warmth of his tongue, all the fascinating textures of his kiss. She felt his body shift and tighten as one hand clenched in her hair and the other moved down her back beneath the heavy silk of her hair, molding her body against his for a long moment.

With tangible reluctance, Chance lifted his head. His arms shifted, cradling rather than caging.

"I'm too hungry to be teased," he said in a husky voice.

"I wasn't—" she began breathlessly.

"I know. But I was. I thought I'd kiss you once, just to see if it was as good as I remembered." His eyes followed the soft line of her lips. "It was better. So much better that I want more." He bent swiftly, taking her mouth in a fierce, penetrating kiss that made her cling to him for balance. "And then I want much more. I want to take off your clothes and shred them into pieces so small they would never be able to cover you again. I want to kiss you and feel you change beneath my mouth until you can't breathe for needing me. And then I want to cover you, all of you, with your hair like hot silk between my fingers."

Reba closed her eyes and trembled as a strange weakness claimed her, his words like fire inside her. She looked up at him with dazed cinnamon eyes, unsure of herself, almost afraid of him. "Chance—"

He kissed her gently, soothing rather than overwhelming her. "But I've shocked you and Tim enough for one day," he said, smiling down at her crookedly.

The world returned to Reba in a rush. She realized that she had been standing in her office with the door wide open, passionately kissing a man she barely knew. Scarlet stained her cheekbones.

"The door," she said, trying to step away from Chance.

"Tim closed it," said Chance, tightening his arms, holding her close. "A discreet young man, your Tim."

"Not mine. Gina's."

"A good thing, too," said Chance, biting her lower lip in a slow, gentle caress that made her weak all over again. "I'd hate to have to take such a nice young man out in the desert and lose him."

Chance was smiling but his eyes were cold silver.

"Tim's like the brother I never had," said Reba, holding onto Chance's hard upper arms, wanting him to understand. "That's all he is." Then she heard her own words and was divided between confusion and irritation. Why should she have to explain her friendships to Chance Walker? No matter how intense the feelings he evoked in her, she had known him only a short time. "Not," she added evenly, "that how I feel about Tim is any business of yours."

"You don't believe that, do you?" asked Chance quietly.

Reba stared at him for a long moment, eyes clear and hard. Then she shook her head slowly, sending dark blond hair whispering over her cheeks. "No, I don't believe that. But I'm *damned* if I know why. I don't know you, Chance Walker. And when I'm with you, I don't even know myself."

"You keep taking words out of my mind," he drawled. "Shall we get to know each other by playing Twenty Questions over lunch?"

Reba couldn't help smiling at the idea of sharing a child's game with a man called Chance. "All right. Me first, though," she added, gathering up her hair as she spoke and twisting it expertly into a coil.

"Why?" he asked, amused.

"You're bigger and a lot tougher than I am. I need whatever advantage I can get."

He put his hand on her cheek and looked at her searchingly. "Don't be afraid of me, *chaton*."

Sensing the vulnerability beneath his quiet words, she turned her face and kissed his hard palm. "I'm not afraid of your strength. It's your questions that I'm uncomfortable about." She smiled at his startled look. "Don't you have things you'd just as soon not talk about?" she asked, searching his clear, oddly colored eyes.

His hand moved from her cheek as his face changed, all expression gone. He was again a stranger, hard and utterly assured, invulnerable. "Did you have any particular area of questioning in mind?" he asked, his voice uninflected.

Chance's black moustache didn't disguise the harsh

lines of his face or the unflinching intelligence that appraised her. Compelling, dangerous, a Tiger God hewn out of uncompromising stone.

"No," she whispered.

Stillness pooled in the room for a long moment, then the coiled intensity slowly seeped out of Chance. He touched her cheek. "Yes, there are things I'd rather not talk about."

"And they're the only ones that matter, aren't they?"

"Do you have a jacket?" he said calmly. "There's a cool wind blowing outside."

Reba thought of repeating her question until she remembered his cold words to Todd. *Keep pushing, you'll get there.* She wouldn't push. Not yet. Pushing a man like Chance was not only dangerous, it was futile. She might as well go push a mountain. When he trusted her, he would talk freely.

That is, if a man like Chance Walker ever trusted anybody. But he had to, for without trust nothing was possible, not pleasure, not friendship and certainly not love.

With a feeling close to fear, Reba realized that she wanted to know all of those things with Chance, and more—things for which she had no names, only a hunger as deep as the one he had revealed to her when he kissed her in the moon shadow of the dunes. The thought of such *wanting* was a shock to her, and the implications frightening.

"I seem to have lost my comb," she said casually, but the hand holding her hair had a fine tremor in it.

Chance smiled and reached into the pocket of the tailored charcoal wool slacks he was wearing. He held out his hand to her. On his palm was the simple jet comb that had held her hair in place. "This one? Or"—he reached into the pocket of his pearl-grey chamois shirt—"this one?"

His left hand held the polished ivory comb that she had worn in Death Valley. She looked up at him, remembering the night and the dunes where she had felt safe enough to let down the barriers she held against the world and cry in his arms until she was too weak to stand. Then his kiss, and the world falling away as they held each other and discovered needs and possibilities she had never before known.

"The jet, I think," Chance said when Reba didn't speak. He fitted the comb into the shining mass of hair coiled on her head. He stroked her hair. "It's a shame to imprison such beauty. But there are compensations." His teeth moved delicately along the curve of her ear.

She closed her eyes and trembled at the sensations he caused, a tightness going from her throat to her navel and beyond. When the tip of his tongue moved intimately, learning every contour of her ear, she made an inarticulate sound. Her hands went to his arms, steadying herself in a world that had suddenly begun to turn swiftly around her, throwing her off balance. She felt the tremor that went through him, the heat and tension of his body as it moved against hers.

With a soft curse Chance held her at arm's length. "Lunch," he said in a husky voice. "Unless you're on the menu . . . ?"

"Why do I suddenly feel like I'm being stalked by a tiger?" Reba asked, laughter and something more serious rippling beneath her question.

He chuckled. His lips brushed her temple. "Are there any restaurants around that serve live Maine lobster?"

"You're very good at changing subjects, aren't you?"

Chance smiled down at her. "If you don't like lobster—"

"I love Maine lobster," she interrupted in an exasperated voice.

"So do I, and I haven't had any for seven years." He laughed at the curiosity that leaped in her eyes. "You'd make a wonderful cat," he murmured, "all tawny and supple, with a cat's full share of grace and curiosity."

"Flattery will get you."

"Get me what?"

Reba smiled like a cat and walked out of the office without answering.

Chapter 3

THE RESTAURANT WAS SMALL, UNOBTRUSIVE AND DEDI-
cated to the principle that customers preferred the
management to spend money on food rather than fancy
furnishings. As a result, Jaime's was unknown to the
tourists who sought out only the flashy and more
famous watering holes. The atmosphere in the restaurant was convivial, the selection of wines limited but
well chosen and the customers more interested in
conversation than in being seen and oohed over by
strangers. Jaime's had been one of Jeremy's favorite
restaurants.

"What is it?" asked Chance quietly, sensing the
change in Reba as she looked around the room.

"Jeremy loved this place," she said, her voice even.

"Do you want to go somewhere else?" asked
Chance, taking her hand in both of his.

"No," she said, feeling his warmth and hard strength
surrounding her hand. "Since Death Valley, it's been
. . . better. I can look at his picture. I can remember
things we did together and not cry every time. I think
I've accepted the fact that Jeremy is dead." She looked

at Chance. "Thank you. I was running blind before you found me in the dunes. It was only a matter of time until I tripped and broke my neck."

Chance lifted her hand to his mouth. His moustache stroked her palm like a silk brush. "You would have survived. You're stronger than you know."

Reba smiled slightly. Tears magnified her eyes. "Sure," she said huskily, "I'm a regular cat, born to land on my feet. You just happened to find me when I'd lost my balance."

A waiter appeared to show Chance and Reba to their table. Chance sat next to Reba, waved away the menus and ordered lobster for both of them. He looked at the wine list and then at Reba.

"No Australian wines," he said wryly. "Unless you have a better suggestion, I'll just close my eyes, point my finger at the white wines and pray."

"I have a weakness for Chardonnay," she admitted, reading the list quickly. She looked up at him from beneath thick, dark brown lashes. "Unless you'd prefer something sweeter?"

His slow smile made heat tingle through her. "What I want isn't on any wine list," he drawled softly, looking at her lips with hungry silver-green eyes.

"The Balverne Chardonnay," she told the waiter quickly, watching as the man tried not to smile and failed.

Chance laughed, a sound as soft and fundamentally untamed as his chamois shirt.

"Question number one," said Reba in a determined voice. "Where were you born and where have you lived since then?"

"That's two questions," he pointed out.

"Where have you lived since you were born?" asked Reba, smiling triumphantly at having squeezed two questions into one.

Chance saluted her silently, admiring her quick intelligence. "I was born on the New Mexico-Texas-Mexico border. No one knows for sure where we were when mother couldn't walk any further and lay down to have me beside the trail. Dad, as usual, was dragging her from one place to another on some damned fool treasure hunt and, as usual, his map was a smudged twentieth century copy of a seventeenth century liar's tale." Chance shrugged, but his eyes were the pale, transparent green of glacier ice. "New Mexico is listed as my birthplace on my passport."

Reba listened intently, watching the subtle shift of expressions across Chance's face.

"Eventually we went to Lightning Ridge. I don't remember much from that time. I was too young. But if I had a home, I suppose it was Australia. Whenever Dad failed in one part of the world, we'd go back to Lightning Ridge until we'd found enough opals to buy another bloody treasure map." He smiled grimly to himself. "There's nothing crazier than a Texan with a treasure map, hellbent on wealth. Unless it's that Texan's son, hellbent on proving himself a man."

"You?" she asked softly.

Chance shrugged. "I was thinking of Luck, but I suppose the description would have fitted me when I was fourteen."

"How old is Luck?"

He said nothing. Then, "Luck is dead."

Reba put her hand over Chance's. His fingers curled around hers, accepting her wordless sympathy.

"I was almost fifteen when he died," Chance continued in a voice that no longer drawled. "Luck was twenty-four, older but not smarter. He broke the first and only law of the South American jungle: *Never drink with a diamond miner.* When Luck didn't come back to camp one night, I went looking for him. I didn't find him, but I found the miner who had cut Luck's throat."

Reba waited, but Chance said no more.

"Afterwards, Glory—my older sister—sold the diamonds miners had given her and took me to Australia. Dad didn't want to leave Venezuela. He'd heard that there was an even bigger diamond strike in Guaniamo, a few miles over on a tributary of the Orinoco River. Glory didn't argue with Dad. She just bought our way out of the jungle and never looked back. We went to Lightning Ridge because that was the only place we'd been to more than once in our lives. She started up a small business hauling drinking water to the opal gougers."

"What did you do?"

"Gouged opals with the best of them," Chance said sardonically. "It gets in your blood worse than malaria." He put his hand under Reba's chin and tipped her head so that light flowed across the earrings she wore. "I could have been the one to tear these opals out of the earth," he said softly, "sweating and bleeding in a tight black hole so that you could wear gems to equal your beauty. But they don't equal it," he murmured, brushing her ear with his soft moustache, smiling as she shivered beneath his touch.

The waiter appeared with two platters. A scarlet lobster crouched on each large plate, surrounded by crisp vegetables and pots of butter as clear as amber. While the mouth-watering scent of lobster rose up to Reba's nostrils, the waiter poured a bit of wine in Chance's glass. He tasted the wine, nodded, then handed the glass to Reba.

"It was your choice, after all," he said, smiling. "You should have a chance to approve it."

She tasted the wine and turned to the waiter. "Yes, we'll take this one."

For a time there was only silence and the sounds of lobster shells cracking as both Reba and Chance pried out succulent bites of pearly flesh. Reba had discovered long ago that there was no prim, civilized way to eat whole lobster. For the duration of the meal, fingers were considered nothing more than especially useful utensils. She didn't actually smack her lips but she did lick her fingertips discreetly from time to time. Once she looked up and found Chance watching her.

"The next time we have lobster," he said, "we're going to be alone."

"Are my table manners that bad?" she asked, only half joking.

"No"—softly—"it's just that I'd like to lick your fingers for you."

Reba felt the new yet increasingly familiar sensation of heat and wires tightening inside her body. "Chance Walker," she breathed, "you are the most incredibly *unbridled* male."

His laugh did nothing to deny her words. "Finish your lobster. I enjoy watching an unbridled female eat."

"I'm not unbridled," she muttered, "and you haven't answered all of my first question."

"Peru, Venezuela, Alaska, Madagascar, Chile, Australia, Brazil, Northwest Territories, Sri Lanka, Burma, Colorado, California, Africa, Montana, Japan, Afghanistan, Nevada, St. John's Island, Columbia, Finland and the Veil of Kashmir. Some of them more than once and not necessarily in that order."

She gave him a narrow-eyed cinnamon glare. He smiled and took a sip of the pale gold wine.

"You asked where I've lived since I was born," he said reasonably, setting down his wine glass. "I admit I might have left out a place or two." He shrugged. "A few weeks here and there hardly count."

"What did you do after you left Lightning Ridge?"

"Which time? Seems like I've been leaving Lightning Ridge as long as I can remember."

"The time your sister took you out of the jungle."

"I gouged opals for awhile. Glory worked and tried to teach me that there was more to life than fighting and drinking and whores."

"You weren't even fifteen!" said Reba, appalled.

"I'd been doing a man's work since I was ten. I'd been man-sized since I was thirteen. But I grew up long before then," Chance said, his voice quiet and hard. "There's no such thing as a child in the jungle. Only survivors."

"Where is your family now?"

"Glory is married." He smiled slightly. "A prospector came to Lightning Ridge, took one look at her and swore he'd found the only woman he'd spend his life with. She laughed the first time he said it. Then she walked out with him into the desert. When they came back she was his woman. It was that fast"—he snapped his fingers—"and as permanent as the mountains. I never understood what came over either one of them, until ten days ago."

Reba looked up from her lobster suddenly, but Chance's face was turned so that shadows from the tabletop light concealed his eyes.

"My father," continued Chance, his eyes still hooded by shadows, "is somewhere in Africa, I think, looking for blue garnets."

"There's no such thing," said Reba, wiping her fingers on a napkin and pushing aside her plate. Not a scrap of lobster remained.

"You know that and I know that, but Dad? No way. He's got a map." Chance laughed harshly.

"Is your mother with him?"

Chance signaled the waiter to remove their plates.

Reba waited for Chance to answer, then realized that he wasn't going to. "Is that one of the things you don't talk about?" she asked quietly.

Chance paid the check in silence. When they reached her car all he said was, "Do you have to go back right away?"

Reba thought of what waited for her at the Objet d'Art—phone calls from museums and collectors and reporters hungry for a new lead on an old scandal— Jeremy and a woman fifty years younger. The thought made her mouth flatten and turn down. She had worked relentlessly in the weeks since Jeremy's death, weeks when Tim and Gina had urged her to take time off. Now, all Reba cared about was doing Jeremy's book and learning more about the baffling, fascinating man who stood very close to her, not quite touching her, waiting for her answer.

At the moment, there was nothing more she could do with the book. The man, however . . .

"Do you like the beach?" Reba asked.

"Is that one of your twenty questions?" Chance countered, smiling. Then, "I've spent so much time in the deserts of the world that water fascinates me. Even when I can't drink it," he added whimsically.

"There's a private beach nearby. Well, not really private," she admitted. "No beach in southern California is private enough to satisfy me. But you can sit there and listen to the waves without being surrounded by people."

"Sounds good," said Chance, opening the door to her red BMW for her. "I'm not used to being in the middle of two million people."

He tucked her into the car, settled himself in the passenger seat and turned to watch as she threaded the BMW skillfully through the heavy traffic headed toward the freeway.

"Nice," he said softly as she downshifted going into a curve and the car responded with a well-mannered growl of power. "I'd forgotten how much fun a smooth road and a good car can be. Where I've been, a twenty-year-old Land-Rover is the local equivalent of a limousine."

"Want to drive?"

"Maybe on the way back. Right now, I'm having too much fun watching you."

Reba glanced over at Chance quickly and saw that he meant what he said. She smiled at him, glad that he wasn't one of those men who had to be in the driver's seat no matter whose car it was. She had bought the BMW because it was a machine for people who enjoyed driving. There were flashier cars on the road, more expensive cars, more powerful cars, but there were few that could equal her car in sheer driving pleasure.

A few minutes later, having been ushered by a guard through an iron gate, she cruised the lot looking for the right place to park. Finally she pulled in between a Mercedes 450 SL and a glittering black Ferrari. Chance, who had said nothing when she passed up parking slots closer to the beach, looked at her inquiringly.

"First rule of southern California driving," said Reba. "Never park next to a car that's in worse shape than yours." She gestured to the expensive cars on either side of her. "This is one time I'm sure the people parked next to me will be as careful of their paint jobs as I am of mine."

"City survival skills," he said admiringly. "I'd never have thought of it."

Reba got out, unlocked the trunk and pulled out a faded beige comforter. Chance raised a dark eyebrow.

"Another city survival skill?" he asked. "Do you do this often?"

The cool distance in his tone made her turn and stare at him. "Do what?"

"Bring a man and a blanket to a *private* beach."

For an instant Reba was too surprised to react. Anger flushed her cheeks. She threw the comforter back in the trunk, slammed down the lid and spun around, obviously intending to get back in her car. Chance moved with startling speed, cutting her off by caging her against the side of the BMW. She faced him with narrow eyes. He ignored her efforts to push past him, keeping her prisoner with an ease that infuriated her.

"Let me go," she said curtly.

"After you answer my question."

"What in hell was your question?"

"If not Tim, then who?"

"Who what?"

"Who is your man?"

Reba stared at Chance, too surprised to speak.

"A woman like you just doesn't run around loose," he said, the words clipped, all trace of a drawl gone.

"This one does."

"Why?" he asked bluntly.

It was the question she hadn't wanted to answer. Anger helped, though. And she was angry. "No man has ever wanted me, *just me*. They always wanted other things. A perpetual wide-eyed student-virgin in my former husband's case. After him, most of the men I met just wanted a bedwarmer and ego builder. Nothing special about it. Any woman would do. Then later, after I had worked hard and Jeremy had taught me so much, there was a new wrinkle. Men wanted my connections or my money. Not just me, though. Never just *me*."

It wasn't an easy thing to admit. The anger and humiliation in Reba transmitted itself to Chance. His hands gentled, moving slowly over her arms, savoring her warmth beneath the black silk sleeves.

"I'm not like your ex-husband, *chaton*," he murmured. "I've never been interested in virgins."

Reba stared through Chance, refusing to see him, waiting only to be released.

"Look at me," Chance demanded in a rough voice. "Do you think I'm like the other men you've known?"

Her eyes focused on him, clear and hard. "No," she said coolly, "I don't. You don't seem to want any of the usual things from me. I doubt that your bed is ever cold unless you want it that way. You're too self-confident to need me to build your ego, and I suspect that there's damn little I could teach you about the gem trail that you don't already know. As for money—"

He stood very still, searching her eyes, his face tense. "As for money," he said harshly, "I have enough. Or don't you believe me?"

"I don't care," she said simply. "You didn't know who I was in Death Valley, and you wanted me then. That's why I trusted you so much, so quickly. You didn't know me but you helped me, held me . . . and then you kissed me. You wanted *me*. That never had happened to me before." She looked at his face, hard and very male, black hair like a sleek, softly curling pelt, his eyes a silver-green unlike any gem she could name, his mouth firm and yet so sensual it was all she could do not to stand on tiptoe until she could feel his lips moving across hers. She looked away. "I've answered your question. Now let me go."

"I can't," he said, bending down until his mouth was so close she could feel the warmth of his breath. "What happened in Death Valley was like walking down a dry streambed and finding a hundred-carat diamond blazing in the sun. The thought of you sharing that incredible fire with someone else made me angry." Chance laughed abruptly. "Let me rephrase that. Now that I know you, the thought of any man but me touching you makes me killing mad. It's not rational or polite or pretty. It simply *is*."

Reba looked up at Chance again. There wasn't anything in his eyes that comforted her now. Tiger God, burning bright. As she sensed the wildness seething beneath his control, something deeply buried in her stirred and stretched, awakening. When she spoke her voice was soft and very certain. "I don't want any man but you to touch me."

Slowly the tension left Chance's body. Muscles that had stood out against his soft shirt became supple again rather than rigid. Without holding her, he kissed her gently, brushing his lips over hers until her mouth softened and her breath sighed out. When his tongue touched hers, he made a sound deep in his throat. He pulled her close, holding her as though she were water slipping through his fingers and he must drink now or be forever thirsty.

When he finally lifted his mouth, both of them were breathing raggedly. "If you'll share your beach with me," he said in a husky drawl, "I'll promise to behave."

"You won't have any choice. The beach really isn't *that* private."

As he turned to get the comforter out of the trunk again, her voice stopped him.

"Chance . . ."

He looked over his shoulder.

"This is the first time I've come here with anyone."

"I know." He smiled crookedly. "I used to think that the old saying about green eyes and jealousy wasn't true. I was wrong. I just hadn't found anything worth being jealous of."

Chance opened the trunk, draped the comforter over

his shoulder and took her hand, lacing his fingers through hers. The subtle roughness of his palm, like his total alertness to movement around him, was a reminder of what his life had been like. He was a man who had lived and worked in harsh places. It showed in everything about him, even the texture of his skin. Yet for all that, there was nothing coarse about him. She had met men who had offended her with their crudeness, men who had never set foot on anything more uncivilized than a sandtrap at the local country club. Chance was not like that. Beneath his harsh surface he had the clean, brilliant strength of a diamond.

They walked a few steps before Reba remembered. "Shoes," she said quickly, heading back to the car, pulling him along behind.

Chance watched in silent amusement while she kicked off her high-heeled black shoes. "I was going to say something about them but you seemed to know what you were doing."

"You have a distracting effect on me," she said lightly, tossing her shoes in the trunk.

Smiling, he took off his own shoes and socks. Then he held out his hand. She laced her fingers through his again, amazed at how natural it seemed to be standing barefoot in a parking lot with him, holding his hand.

She led him past the rumpled main beach where women lay in scented oils and designer swimsuits, carefully made-up eyes closed against southern California's potent early spring sun. Children too young to be in school swooped and screamed with laughter, chasing waves and seagulls with equal abandon. The water was cold and unusually calm. Long, low waves curled over lazily, as though unwilling to make the effort to break with their usual thunder and flashing spray.

The tide was out, leaving behind a damp ribbon of packed sand. Chance followed Reba along the margin of the land and the sea, watching her gracefully find a way among the rocks scattered at the base of the headland that defined the north end of the beach. The headland had eroded into a series of fingerlike projections. Between the fingers nestled tiny, protected patches of sand no bigger than an apartment patio. Reba kept going until she found the miniature beach that was farthest away from other people.

"We'll have to keep an eye on the tide," she said as Chance spread out the comforter for them to sit on, "but we should get an hour of peace."

"That's why you come here, isn't it? Peace."

She looked past him to the immense sapphire sea shimmering beneath the sun. "I spend so much time with people," she said quietly. "When that and the noise and the telephone get to me, I sneak down here to be alone."

"Except today."

She turned to him, surprised.

"You're not alone," he said.

She smiled. "I don't mind. I have lots of questions to ask. Nineteen, to be precise."

"Sixteen," corrected Chance.

"Who's counting?" asked Reba innocently.

Chance groaned and sank down onto the comforter. He sat cross-legged, looking up at her. His thick moustache didn't disguise the essential hardness of his tanned face or the sensual sculpting of his mouth. Behind the startling silver-green of his eyes was a mind that weighed everything on a scale as old as life. Survival. Despite his expensive clothes and indulgent smile, he looked as though he had been born out of the restless movements of the earth. There was an intensity to Chance Walker that was compelling, a dynamic balance of opposites—distance and intimacy, danger and safety, excitement and release—that shifted with each moment.

He waved his hand in front of her face. "Hello?" he asked. "Did I suddenly grow horns and a halo?"

"If anyone could, it would be you," she agreed, sitting beside him. "What's your father like?"

"No bloody halo."

"That isn't what I meant," retorted Reba.

"What did you mean, then?" he teased. "Be specific."

"I'll use up too many questions that way."

Chance shook his head. "Clever little *chaton.*" He brushed his knuckles over her cheek. "Dad was born on a piece of west Texas dirt that couldn't even grow cactus. He started hunting treasures when he was six. He ran away from home when he was thirteen. He never went back. He's lived in more godforsaken places looking for more godforsaken treasures than any man alive."

"Did he ever find any?"

Chance's laugh was hard and unpleasant. "He lost the greatest treasure he ever found and didn't even know it."

The cold emotion in Chance's voice told Reba more than his words. Whatever Chance felt for his father wasn't love. For the space of several breaths Chance stared out at the sea, his eyes narrow and remote. Then he took Reba's hand in his as though he needed to feel something warm, alive.

"Between treasure hunts, Dad prospected for gold, diamonds, gem-quality quartz, uranium." Chance shrugged. "Whatever men would pay money to have."

"Another kind of treasure hunt," said Reba softly, thinking of her own prowling among various collections, seeking the one unique specimen that would literally be worth its weight in diamonds to the right customer. "The adrenaline is addictive."

"It's worse than any drug," he agreed.

"Have you made good strikes?"

His face changed. "A few," Chance said, his voice resonating with remembered excitement, memories of extraordinary pleasure lighting his expression. "There's nothing like it. *Nothing*. There's no risk too big, no work too hard, no sacrifice too great if a big strike is the reward."

Reba saw the change in him and felt something close to jealousy. It wasn't that she wished she had found gold or diamonds buried in the earth as Chance had. It was the passion and intensity of his response that made her jealous. She wanted to be able to captivate him that completely, to have him as hungry for her as he was for gemstone buried in the earth.

"You feel the same way about treasure as your father. Why do you hate him?" Even to her own ears, her voice sounded accusing.

Chance turned on Reba with a look that made her want to get up and run. "My father knew enough about minerals to tell gold from pyrite but he didn't know dirt from diamonds when it came to people. Luck was the same way. The strikes they made were stolen by gamblers and whores and gem buyers. Before I was old enough to fight back, Dad even gambled away money from my own small finds. He believed in honest card games almost as much as he believed in treasure maps and whores with hearts of gold. He never grew up.

"But I did," continued Chance in a hard voice. "I learned to tell an ambush from an accidental meeting. I learned that treasure maps are lies and that most gem buyers are crooks. I learned that any cards I don't buy and deal myself are almost certainly marked and stacked against me. I learned that whores lie down with men for money, not pleasure. I learned that you *never* trust anybody. I learned that information is all that separates men from sudden death. If you know something that gives you an edge, you bloody well keep it tucked.

"And most of all," Chance said, watching Reba with eyes like hammered silver, "I learned not to be like my father. I never married and dragged a good woman after me into some of the worst hellholes on earth. I never made my family go ragged and hungry to buy a fool's map. I never went off prospecting and left my seven-year-old son to watch his mother die of some jungle disease that didn't have a name or a cure."

For a time there was only silence punctuated by the harsh cries of seagulls wheeling overhead. Reba realized that she was shaking her head in silent protest at what the answer to her question had cost Chance. She didn't know she was crying until she felt a tear fall from her cheek. She looked down and saw her tears glistening on his hands.

"I didn't mean to frighten you," said Chance, his voice gentle again as he held her clenched hands between his. "Don't cry, *chaton*. I'm not angry anymore."

"That's not why I'm crying."

He tilted her face up until she had to meet his eyes. "Why?" he asked.

She took his hand and pressed her cheek against it, then she kissed his palm. "I can't bear to think of you being hurt like that," she whispered.

Chance drew Reba into his arms, holding her with a fierce tenderness that made her tremble. "No one has ever cried for me before," he said huskily, kissing her eyelashes where tears glittered. "Some tears taste very sweet."

Reba put her arms around Chance, holding him

tightly, feeling again the paradox of his hard body and gentle hands. His heart beat smoothly beneath her cheek. With each breath she felt his chest muscles shift beneath the soft chamois shirt. Gradually his warmth sank into her like sunlight, relaxing her until she fitted against him perfectly.

"Tell me about yourself," he said quietly. "I want to know what kind of woman cried for me."

"My life sounds very dull after yours."

She felt his fingers in her hair, pulling out the comb once more.

"Nothing about you is dull," he said, taking a handful of her hair and pouring it out of his palm like gold dust in the sun. He tipped back her head and kissed her slowly, deeply. "Tell me," he murmured finally, settling her across his chest once more.

"I never had a father. In fact . . ." Reba hesitated, then shrugged. Whatever she said could hardly shock a man of Chance's experience. "I think I'm a bastard."

"Love-child," he corrected easily, trying to erase the tension he felt returning to her body.

She laughed shortly. "Some love. Mother never told me his name. Sometimes I wonder if she even knew it."

"Don't, *chaton*. Not if it hurts you."

Reba rubbed her cheek against his shirt. "Mother raised me to be perfect. Other girls could get dirty, but not me. Other girls could get angry, but not me. Other girls could go to Christmas dances and kiss under the mistletoe. Other girls could date and have boyfriends and even neck in cars. Not me. Mother was obsessed with never giving the neighbors anything to talk about. Above reproach. That was it for her, the El Dorado and the Hope diamond in one."

"But you married," said Chance.

"My mother picked him out. I was too innocent at eighteen to know which end was up. He was my French professor at college. Old enough to be my father. I suppose that's what I wanted. A father. He wanted a little girl who would always look up to him. But girls have a terrible habit of growing up."

"Particularly bright little girls," Chance murmured, stroking her hair. "I'm glad you grew up, Reba."

"So am I. Mother wasn't very pleased, though. She hasn't spoken to me since the divorce. Seven years."

Chance shifted until he could look into Reba's eyes. "Why?"

"I was no longer perfect," Reba said evenly. "My mother never loved me, not really. She loved what she wanted me to be. And when she discovered that I was something else, she no longer loved me at all. It was the same with my husband. He loved one thing and I was another. No one ever loved *me* until Jeremy Sinclair."

The sudden tension in Chance's body lasted only an instant. "Tell me about him," said Chance, his voice neutral, his eyes hooded.

Reba hesitated, not knowing where to begin. "I met him by accident. I was getting gas one day when I heard these absolute fountains of French pouring out of the next car. I looked up and saw a white-haired man trying to describe mechanical problems in French to a very bewildered American mechanic who was about one-quarter Jeremy's age."

Chance made a startled sound.

"What?" she said, looking up.

"How old," he asked carefully, "was Jeremy?"

"When I met him? Seventy-three." For the first time since she had known Chance, Reba saw him totally off balance. "You didn't believe me when I said Jeremy and I weren't lovers, did you?"

"You never said that. You just said that your relationship wasn't the way loverboy thought it was. He thought you were a whore. You aren't. That doesn't

mean you weren't Jeremy's lover, though. How was I to
know? Besides," added Chance, looking at her lips
with hungry green eyes, "any man young enough to still
be breathing would want to make love to you."

"It wasn't like that with Jeremy," she said in a flat
voice.

"I believe you," said Chance, shifting his weight
suddenly, pulling her down onto the blanket with him.
"But I would have wanted you no matter how old I
was."

Chance's hands moved over Reba, fitting her to his
body, telling her how much he wanted her now. She
struggled to sit up again, wanting to tell him how it had
been between her and Jeremy.

"Don't fight me," Chance said against her hair. "I
just want to hold you while you tell me about the man
you loved."

Slowly the stiffness left Reba's body. "I became
Jeremy's interpreter and secretary and chauffeur. I
lived with him," she said quietly, "just like his cook and
maid and butler." She braced her arms on Chance's
chest and looked at his face. There was no doubt or
disbelief, simply interest and a hunger for her that
made his eyes very green. "Jeremy had a good import-
export business but little cash. He spent it all on his
collection. His wife had left him long ago and his son
was dead. Jeremy's only 'family' was a brainless pile of
meat called Todd Sinclair."

Reba paused for breath. Chance smiled, showing a
white gleam of teeth below his thick moustache. Beneath the heavy silk of her hair, his fingers kneaded her
scalp, sending chills of pleasure down her spine.

"Go on," he murmured.

"There's not much more to tell. Jeremy's collection
fascinated me. I began asking questions, thousands of
them. He answered every one. After five years I'd

learned enough to start my own business. Jeremy launched me as proudly as though I were his own daughter, introducing me to people who love the rare things of the earth. Sometimes I think he enjoyed my success more than I did."

Reba closed her eyes, feeling again the disbelief and the despair that had overtaken her when she realized how ill Jeremy was. "Six weeks ago, he had a stroke. I stayed in the hospital with him. I felt so *useless*. He had done so much for me, taught me, loved me, helped me to respect myself for what I was rather than for what other people wanted me to be. He gave me so much . . . and all I could do was hold his hand and watch him die. Sometimes," Reba added, her voice so tight it was harsh, "sometimes I want to scream thinking about it."

"It will get better," he said, stroking her hair.

"Will it?" she asked, watching Chance with dark eyes. "Will I finally forget?"

"You never forget watching someone you love die," he said quietly. "You learn to live around it, though. You learn not to let death rule your life. But you never forget."

"Quite a pair, aren't we?" Reba said in a husky voice. "You have nothing left of your childhood but bad memories and a lust for prospecting. And I"—she laughed bitterly—"I have bad memories and fifty percent of a worthless tourmaline mine. It can't be coincidence that we met."

Tension ripped through Chance like lightning, making every muscle of his body hard. "What do you mean by that crack?" he demanded.

"Nothing," she said, staring at him, surprise clear in her voice. "God must have a sense of humor. That's all."

She didn't understand the cold intensity of his look or his fingers so painfully tight around her arms. Slowly his grip softened. She rubbed her arms. "What's wrong?" she asked, wondering at the pain and anger and other emotions she sensed seething beneath his rigid calm.

"Nothing." Chance swore softly, violently. "I'm a fool to lie here with you, asking you questions and getting sad answers, making you feel bad when you feel so good in my arms. Let me hold you, *chaton*," he whispered. "When I kiss you I believe that anything is possible."

His need was irresistible to Reba. She forgot his frightening reaction when she had mentioned owning half of a worthless mine. She forgot the ache of her arms where his fingers had gripped her flesh. She gave herself to him without thought or reservation, holding and being held until she forgot everything but his heartbeat and his deep voice murmuring words in a strange, liquid language. His hands slid over her silk clothes, molding her to him until she was a supple column of warmth from his mouth down to the hard muscles of his thighs.

He rolled over swiftly, his body covering her in one long caress. Instinctively Reba's hands moved from his arms to his shoulders and then down the long muscles of his back, kneading his hard flesh with a sensuality that had been buried beneath layers of civilized restraint until Chance held her, teaching her how sweet wildness could be. His tongue was hot and hard as he took her mouth in a kiss that didn't end until she twisted against him, crying wordlessly, gripped by a hunger as wild as his.

Slowly Chance lifted his mouth, only to return again and again with tiny, biting kisses until Reba made a small sound in her throat. He lifted his head until he could see her soft lips and feel her breath rushing out in a long sigh. When he kissed the pulse beating in her throat, she tilted her head back and arched against him.

Chance spoke softly, strange, rhythmic syllables that were another kind of caress. His lips moved down to the smooth flesh revealed by the open neck of her blouse. The tip of his tongue touched the swell of her breast and his hand brushed over her nipple. She made a small sound and stared up at him with dazed cinnamon eyes.

"When you touch me . . . I don't know myself. Chance . . . ?"

"I'm a fool," he whispered, "a bloody fool." And then his mouth covered hers again, filling her with his heat and hunger.

Only later, too late, would she remember his words about being a fool. Then she would laugh bitterly, knowing that there had been only one bloody fool on the beach that day, and it hadn't been him.

Chapter 4

REBA SAT AT HER DESK IN THE OBJET D'ART, STARING AT the Tiger God when she should have been staring at invoices and appraisals. Light rippled hypnotically over the sculpture, creating subtle bands of gold and shimmering brown, smooth and infinitely sensuous. The sculpture captured the essence of male power and grace. And beneath it all, beneath the satin polish and sophisticated modeling, there was a wildness that called to her in a language as old as need and love.

She closed her eyes but still felt the Tiger God's radiant presence. In her mind the sculpture changed, eyes silver-green now, midnight hair and moustache, resilient muscles sliding beneath her touch, gentle hands making her ache with a need that was so new to her she had no way to control it. With her eyes closed she could feel Chance's body covering hers again, the world shrinking until there was nothing in it but him and her and the distant cry of gulls.

She hadn't known what it was to want a man. Not like that, tenderness and fierce heat, needing to please and consume him in the same instant, emotions tearing through her until she could only tremble beneath him, unable even to think. She had forgotten where she was, who she was, forgotten everything but the taste and feel of him.

When he had ended the kiss by rolling aside until he no longer touched her, she had been bewildered, lost. Then she had remembered where she was and didn't know whether to laugh or cry. She and Chance had been necking on a public beach like a pair of teenagers. As though he were reading her thoughts, his hand had closed around hers gently. The faint tremor that went through him when his skin touched hers told Reba that his restraint didn't come easily. The realization had comforted her. She wasn't alone in the dizzying new world he had opened to her.

She hadn't wanted to go back to the Objet d'Art. He hadn't wanted to take her. Nor had she seen him that night. She had had clients coming in to view a portion of Jeremy's collection. As the clients had flown in from Egypt just for the appointment, she could hardly refuse to see them. But she had wanted to. They had stayed until two A.M., too late for her to call Chance at his hotel. But she had wanted to. Since she had opened the shop at nine there had been wall-to-wall collectors, guards and nervous insurance agents. There hadn't been any time or privacy to call Chance.

By four o'clock it had become obvious to Reba that the Objet d'Art was too small to contain the interest Jeremy's collection had aroused. She had neither the time nor the energy to oversee an endless stream of collectors, or to answer their endless questions, endlessly repeated.

She had cleared out the last client at four and spent the next hour making arrangements to show Jeremy's collection in a few weeks at San Diego's Hotel del Coronado. There would be a day of viewing the collection, then dinner, an evening auction and a midnight ball. Jeremy would have approved. He had loved combining champagne sophistication with the primal competitiveness of collectors bent on owning the same rare objet.

Smiling softly, Reba ran her fingertips over the Tiger God. Even with her eyes closed she could visualize the powerful lines of the sculpture. It wasn't an idealized or incredible figure of a man, a Hercules chiseled out of stone. It was simply very male, with solid shoulders and narrow hips, well-muscled arms and powerful legs, masculine ease and assurance in every line. The face was strong rather than handsome, compelling rather than perfect.

If the Tiger God could talk, she wondered, would he have a deep voice with a suggestion of a drawl?

"May I?" drawled a deep voice.

Reba's eyes flew open and she made a startled sound. Chance Walker was standing in front of her, his hand held out to the statue. Wordlessly, she gave him the Tiger God. He turned the statue over slowly, admiring the fine specimen of tiger's-eye and the artistry of the figure itself. His brown fingers moved over the stone's satin surface, delicately following the lines of stone and sculpture.

"Extraordinary," he said quietly, giving the statue back to Reba. "I've never seen a finer specimen. Not a fracture, not a displacement, not a single flaw. A mineral worthy of the artist who worked it."

"It was part of Jeremy's collection," Reba said as she set the statue in its niche behind her desk. She gave the tiger's-eye a final stroke before she turned back to Chance.

"I'm glad he's only stone," Chance said.

"What do you mean?"

"If the sculpture were alive, he'd be hard to take out in the desert and lose." Chance looked at the tiger's-eye sculpture, smiling slightly. "He'd be a mean one to tangle with. He'd be fair, though. No ambush. He wouldn't have to. He's strong and he knows it. He'd go hunting the devil himself with that solid gold bow." Chance looked back at Reba. "Will this be for sale?"

She shook her head. "The will gave me two choices from Jeremy's collection. The Tiger God is mine."

"Tiger God," Chance said softly. "It suits him. You named him, didn't you?"

"Yes."

Delicately, Chance's fingertips traced from Reba's eyebrow to her chin. "Never thought I'd be jealous of a damned stone," he said, his voice almost harsh.

"Don't be," she said softly, caught by the changing density of silver and green in his eyes. "I chose the statue and the name after Death Valley."

She felt the change in him as he understood what she was saying. His eyes closed and his fingers tightened on the curve of her chin. When he looked at her again, she forgot to breathe. His eyes focused on her with an intensity that was almost tangible.

"*Chaton,*" he said, bending to kiss her. "We have to talk. There's something I have to—"

Tim walked into the office, talking as he came. "Boss, old man Mercer says— Oops. Sorry. Your door was open." He turned to go.

Chance muttered a pungent word before he smiled sardonically and stepped aside. Reba silently seconded Chance's muttering before she turned to Tim.

"It's all right," she said, her tone denying her polite words. Reba heard her voice and threw up her hands. "It's all right even though it isn't."

Tim smiled. "Umm, yeah, I get what you mean." He

held out his hand. Nestled in his palm was a tiny, shocking pink Chinese tear bottle. "Mercer thinks our price is too high."

Chance looked at the crystal bottle, then at Reba.

"Go ahead," she said.

He plucked the bottle off Tim's palm. After testing that the bottle's tiny stopper was securely in place, Chance adjusted the high-intensity light on Reba's desk so that the beam was behind the crystal bottle. A fine network of fractures glittered through, scattering and refracting light until the bottle glowed with a hot pink radiance that was characteristic of the mineral from which it had been carved.

"Pala tourmaline," Chance said, turning the bottle slowly, letting the beam illuminate each curve of the objet. "Beautiful specimen. Single piece of mineral. Just enough fracturing to ensure its legitimacy, not enough to endanger the integrity of the bottle itself. The color is superb. There's no other rubellite—pink tourmaline—in the world to equal that found in north San Diego County. Absolutely unique."

Chance picked up a thick magnifying glass from Reba's desk and resumed his informal appraisal of the brilliant crystal bottle in his palm.

"I don't know enough about Chinese carving techniques to date the bottle exactly. Latter part of the nineteenth century, most likely. The Empress Dowager of China had an obsession for Pala's tourmaline. The entire output of Pala's mines went to her. She had a world monopoly on pink tourmaline. When she died in 1908, the market for Pala tourmaline collapsed."

Chance bent and examined the carving on the bottle. "Nicely done," he continued. "Original stopper, sharp edges on the carved design, symmetrical and elegant, not shopworn. Whoever owned this tear bottle took care of it. The others I've seen were all dulled by handling, chipped or repaired in some way. This is the clearest pink I've seen, too."

Silently, Reba held out the appraisal sheet she had finished on the pink tourmaline tear bottle the day before. He scanned the sheet quickly.

"A fair price," said Chance. He smiled lazily as he handed the bottle back to Tim. "If your client doesn't want it, I know a collector in Australia who's almost as obsessed with pink as the Dowager was. Red Day will meet your price and thank you for the chance."

Tim grinned. "You've made my day. Mercer is a wealthy, loud-mouthed pain in the butt." Tim left, pointedly shutting the door behind him.

"My wonderful mine," Reba said, her tone inviting Chance to share the joke on herself, "isn't far from the mine that gave us this specimen. Same geography. Same geology. Not enough gem-quality pink tourmaline to fill a baby's fist. All the Farrall women ever got out of the China Queen was hard work and danger for their men, and just enough crystals to give each succeeding generation tourmaline fever."

Chance's expression changed subtly. His features sharpened, emphasizing the masculine angles of his face and the blunt strength of his chin. "Did you ever get tourmaline fever?" he asked with a light s that belied the tension of his body.

"Sure. I didn't do anything about it, though. I haven't been to the mine since Mother tried to open it when I was a kid. She'd saved enough money to pay for shoring up the entrance of the mine. The money ran out before she found anything more than a few crystals so badly fractured that they came apart in her hand. Junk."

"What about you? Have you tried shoring up the China Queen?"

"I thought about it," Reba admitted. "The dreams I

had . . . mounds of tourmaline glittering, piles of never-melting ice crystals in shades of pink and green." She laughed quietly at herself. "The reality was a bit less spectacular. As soon as I finished paying for my divorce and reclaiming my maiden name, I had someone estimate the cost of making the China Queen safe to work in. More than a hundred thousand dollars, and that was only if no blasting was ever done. To make the mine safe for blasting would cost two or three times as much."

She shrugged. "I couldn't find a bank that would lend a thousand dollars to me, much less a hundred times that much. Not that I blame the banks. What sane person would hand over that much money to a starry-eyed young woman with a half-interest in a mine that never produced more than a few hundred dollars worth of Pala tourmaline?"

"Then sell the Queen," said Chance.

Reba looked up, caught by the intensity of his voice. "It would be like selling a dream. Whatever money I got wouldn't be worth what I lost." She smiled crookedly. "I know it's silly but that's how I feel about the China Queen."

"Even though you haven't seen the mine since you were a kid?"

"Yes." Reba hesitated, choosing words carefully, trying to make Chance understand why a useless mine was more important to her than it should be. "It's all I have left of my childhood. I have no family, not really. I don't even know my father's name. Mother and I have gone very different ways. I never saw my grandparents; they threw Mother out before I was born. My mother's twin sister lives in Australia, somewhere in the Outback. I've never seen her. She and mother never write. Not even a postcard at Christmas. There's a girl my age, my aunt's daughter. Sylvie. That's it so far as I know. My family."

Reba's smile slipped. She looked at her hands. "That and half of an abandoned mine is my heritage. I may never find a single pink crystal in the China Queen, but half of her belongs to me. One hundred acres outright, plus mineral rights to several square miles." She looked away from her tightly laced fingers. "It's beautiful country," she said softly. "Broken and wild, hot in the summer and green velvet in the winter. Someday I'll build a house there. Until then it's enough just to know the land is there, waiting for me. Homecoming."

Reba looked up and saw Chance's eyes narrow as he studied her. His expression was a mixture of anger and sadness and frustration. "You'll never sell it."

"No." Then, quickly, "It's not as crazy as it sounds, Chance. The taxes on the mine are almost nothing. And . . . and I can camp there whenever I want."

"Do you?" he demanded.

"Camp there? No," she admitted. "I drove out to the mine turnoff once after my divorce. The mine road looked awful. I was afraid to try it alone. I suppose it would have been all right." She thought about it for a moment. "Yes, I'm sure it would be fine. I'll do it, soon."

"Not alone," he said harshly. "It's dangerous."

"How do you know?"

Chance hesitated. "You'd be tempted to go into the mine. Besides, any area that isolated will always be dangerous for a woman alone. But with a man who knows rough country . . ." He smiled suddenly, transforming his face. "Want to go camping?"

Reba's eyes lit with sudden excitement. With Chance along she wouldn't be jumping at every sound, every shadow, afraid even to sit in the sun and close her eyes.

The thought of sharing the emptiness and silence of the rugged land with him was intoxicating. She smiled up at her Tiger God like a child on Christmas morning.

"Yes," she breathed. "Take me camping."

"For a smile like that, *chaton,* I'd take you anywhere on earth."

His lips were as warm and gentle as sunlight. She sighed his name, letting her hands slide up his arms and neck as his tongue teased the corners of her smile. She savored the silky-rough textures of his hair between her fingers, his male scent and taste filling her senses. She felt the sudden tension of his body as she shared the kiss, her tongue shy and warm against his.

The phone rang. They ignored it.

The intercom buzzed.

"Damn!" flared Reba. "What is this, a conspiracy? All I want is—" She stopped abruptly. What she wanted was more than an uninterrupted kiss. What she needed was more complex and enduring than a simple easing of the hunger that burned in her whenever Chance looked at her, touched her, held her.

Her hand slammed open the intercom switch. "What is it?" she demanded.

"Your five o'clock appointment has been waiting for fifteen minutes," said Tim.

"Mrs. McCarey?" asked Reba, thinking quickly.

"Yes."

"Give me a minute," she said, switching off. She looked at Chance. "Mrs. McCarey flew in from Tahiti when she found out I had made my two choices from the collection. She's eighty, one of Jeremy's oldest friends."

"Will she be here long?"

"Hours. And she's not my last appointment."

Chance swore in a language Reba was glad she couldn't understand. It didn't sound nearly so musical when he was angry. "I'll pick you up here at noon tomorrow. Be ready to go camping."

Reba mentally rearranged her schedule. "I don't know how I'll do it, but I'll be here with golden bells on."

"Just bells?" he murmured, his voice very deep. "I'd like to see that."

Suddenly she realized how easily he could have misunderstood when she had agreed to go camping with him. "I'll go camping, but I'm not promising to . . ." Her voice faded.

"Make love with me?" Chance asked. His eyes searched hers, found confusion and shadows. His expression changed. "You're as innocent as you seem, aren't you?" he said softly. "What were you married to, a bloody ice cube?"

She stiffened. There was no pleasure for her in remembering her marriage.

"Just understand," Chance continued softly, relentlessly, "that I'm not innocent. *I want you.* I'll do everything I can to make you want me in the same way. But I'll never force you, *chaton,*" he said, touching her lips with his fingertip. "You'll need hiking boots and rough clothes. Do you have any?"

"No," she admitted.

"I'll take care of it," he promised, kissing her with a gentle restraint that reassured her.

With reassurance came a shiver of heat and hunger that she associated with being touched by him. He was hard and gentle and very male. Each time he caressed her he taught her about her own body, her own needs, awakening something strong and wild deep inside her, something that reached hungrily toward him.

The buzzer rang. Several times.

"Is Tim always so bloody punctual?" rasped Chance when he finally lifted his mouth from hers. Then, before she could answer, he spun and left the room in three catlike strides. "Noon," he said without looking back. "Ready or not."

At noon, Reba sat behind her desk listening to the interminable reminiscences of a man who couldn't believe that other people were less fascinated by his memories than he was. She looked at her watch frequently, hoping that the man would take a hint. It was like hinting to a boulder that it should get up and do a jig.

Chance walked in precisely at noon. "Ready?" he asked, ignoring the man sitting across from Reba's desk.

She looked at Chance's desert shirt and jeans, his hiking boots laced to his knees, the battered western hat losing its battle to control the thick, curling pelt of his hair. She wanted nothing more than to be able to stand up and walk out of the room with him.

"Not quite," she said, nodding toward the man who was waiting impatiently to finish a mumbling recital of his fiftieth birthday party.

"What time is it?" said Chance to the man.

Reba's client looked at a thick silver watch encrusted with Arizona turquoise. "Twelve and seventeen seconds."

"Right," said Chance. He walked around the desk, lifted Reba out of her chair and said to the startled client, "I told Reba I'd pick her up at noon. I'm a man of my word."

Chance strode out of the office with Reba laughing in his arms. Tim gave them a startled look, flashed the thumbs-up sign and opened the front door.

"Have a nice trip," said Tim, bowing like a doorman at a Spanish hotel. Then, to Reba, "I'll take care of the old boor," he whispered. "Don't hurry back."

Reba expected to be put down once they left the Objet d'Art behind. Chance never paused when he reached the sidewalk. People stared at them for a moment, then smiled and looked around for the cameras and production crew. For every odd thing that happened on Rodeo Drive, the immediate explanation was that someone was shooting on location.

"You can put me down now," said Reba, laughter still rippling in her voice.

Chance kept walking.

Impulsively she took off his hat and ruffled his hair. "Did you see the look on Mr. J. T. Lavington-Smythe's face? Wonderful! God, I've wanted to do something like that for years. He always takes up twice the time allotted to him. Every time I have to listen to him, I wonder if boredom isn't one of the tortures of the damned."

"Remind me to ask the devil the next time I'm in Venezuela."

"Does he live there?"

"When he's not mining diamonds in Brazil."

Reba watched Chance's profile for a moment, enjoying its uncompromisingly masculine lines. "There's only one thing wrong with being carried this way."

"Afraid of heights?" he suggested, smiling.

"No," she said, touching his mouth lightly with her fingertips. "I can't thank you properly for rescuing me."

She was shifted in his arms so suddenly that she didn't have time to do more than gasp. His lips covered hers in a hard kiss that showed how much of himself he had held in restraint beneath his smile. After the first instant of surprise, she returned his kiss with the hunger that hadn't slept since he had awakened it in the silence and shadows of Death Valley.

"We're stopping traffic," Chance murmured as he

nipped delicately at her ear, enjoying the shiver of her response.

"They're just waiting for the director to yell 'Cut!' and demand a retake," she said a bit breathlessly.

"I'd hate to disappoint them," he said, taking her lips again, exploring her mouth with slow movements of his tongue. After a time he lifted his head and smiled into her flushed face. "I never knew being an actor was so much fun."

Shaking her head, she looked at him with a mixture of humor and seriousness. "What am I going to do with you? You're definitely not . . . not . . . ."

"Housebroken?" he suggested with a rakish smile.

Reba shook her head again, laughing softly.

"Don't worry," he assured her, setting off for a nearby parking lot, "you won't notice it as much when we're camping."

Chance set Reba down next to a Toyota Land Cruiser. The dusty blue vehicle had a winch on the front, spare gas and water cans bolted to the back and camping gear behind the front seat. A tough, flexible net held the cargo firmly in place.

"You're sure you wouldn't rather take my car?" asked Reba, looking doubtfully at the Toyota's spartan interior and unforgiving suspension. "It would be more comfortable."

"On the freeway, yes," said Chance, unlocking the door for her. "On the mine road your car would be a disaster. Rocks, ruts, washouts and slides."

"How do you know?" she said, exasperated by his casual dismissal of her car.

Chance froze for a split instant, then smoothly continued handing Reba into the car. "Logic. Abandoned mine, abandoned road. If you like, though, you can follow me down in your BMW. I'll be able to pull you out of any trouble you can drive that low-slung car into."

"No thanks," Reba said, shuddering as she thought of the damage that could be done to her car by rocks tearing through the undercarriage. "I'll take your word for it. You're the rough-country expert."

Chance took her chin in his hand, holding her still for a moment. "Remember that. If I tell you to do something, don't argue. Just do it. There isn't always time to explain."

His eyes were pale green, intent, measuring her reaction to his words. He waited without impatience, knowing that she was not accustomed to taking orders.

"You know something that I don't," she said finally.

Chance's eyes narrowed until they were almost closed. The fingers on her chin tightened painfully, then relaxed. "What do you mean?" he asked in a flat voice.

"There's something that you aren't telling me. You're so sure that the mine or something about it is dangerous."

Chance was very still for a long moment. "Abandoned mines are always dangerous."

Reba said nothing, waiting for him to continue, waiting as he had waited. He shut her door, walked around the Toyota and climbed into the driver's seat.

"I never go into things blind," Chance said after a moment. "I've been to the China Queen. The road is bloody awful but I expected that. What I didn't expect was to find groups of men moving through the back country. A few hours spent in the local bars listening to gossip told me why. A lot of marijuana is either grown or shipped through the back country. The men doing it aren't happy to be seen.

"Then," continued Chance, "there are the illegal

aliens up from Mexico. They're working the fields and
avocado groves, when there's work. When there isn't,
they go into the rough country and camp because they
don't have much money and they're afraid to be seen by
anyone. They're young and bored. They spend a lot of
time drinking, and when they fight they use knives.
Some of the local residents have taken to carrying guns
whenever they go out to their groves." Chance gave
Reba a long look. "You really didn't know any of this,
did you?"

Wordlessly, she shook her head.

"A lot of the world is like that," he said. "If it
doesn't happen in a city, it just doesn't happen so far as
most people are concerned. Well, we're going out of
the city, Reba. If you still want to."

"Is it dangerous? I mean, really dangerous?"

Chance smiled slightly. "No, just unpredictable
enough to be interesting. I wouldn't take you into a
situation I thought was really dangerous. It won't be as
safe and civilized as taking a walk down Rodeo Drive,
though."

"Ha! I'll match you drug dealer for drug dealer, Mr.
Walker."

He laughed. "City wise and country foolish, is that
it?"

"Definitely. I gave up believing in the tooth fairy
long ago," she added, smiling and quite serious. "I
trust your judgment, Chance. If you think it's safe, I'll
go."

"There's no such thing as one hundred percent safe,
not even locked in your own home."

"Are you saying that you don't want me to go?" she
asked.

"No. I'm saying that the chance of having a smash-up
on these madhouse freeways is always there, but you
drive on them anyway."

Reba frowned. "Of course. You do everything you can to reduce the risks, then you just keep going. There's not much else you can do. Besides, the odds of something going wrong just aren't that high."

"It's the same way in rough country. You need experience to assess the odds, though."

"That's where you come in."

"Right."

"And?"

"I'd rather camp in rough country than drive on a freeway at rush hour," said Chance wryly.

"Then let's go camping."

The two-lane highway wound beyond Fallbrook's elegant country club homes and remodeled turn-of-the-century cottages. Golf courses and horse corrals gave way to steep granite hills covered with thick chaparral. Wild grass heavy with seeds swayed in the April wind. In a few more weeks the land would be a tawny brown, cured by the hot southern California sun. Then would come a time of stillness and heat reflecting off granite hillsides, a time when only chaparral survived, whispering its brittle secrets into the searing afternoons.

But this day was sweet and warm, the green-and-granite springtime that was unique to the Pala country. Avocado trees grew on either side of the road, groves cut into the rocky hillsides with terraces so narrow and steep it seemed impossible that anything but weeds could grow there. Yet avocado trees loved the stony adversity of the land. In harvest season, the weight of the deep green fruit bent branches to the ground.

Chance's eyes ceaselessly measured the land, noting small movements and changing shadows. He pointed them out to Reba: the hawks poised hungrily on a fencepost or riding the wind; the ground squirrels darting across open ground, then freezing to conceal

themselves from predators that depended on movement to reveal their prey; vultures high up, floating on
transparent winds, waiting for time and circumstance to
furnish a meal; and a doe with two fawns, watching
quietly from the cover of chaparral at the side of the
road.

Reba's pleasure in the trip diminished considerably
as soon as Chance turned off the highway onto the dirt
road that went to the mine. The hills were steeper and
higher here, blending imperceptibly into true mountains. The road itself was little more than parallel goat
tracks winding and doubling back, struggling over
granite ridges and then plunging into canyons thick
with boulders and brush. Washouts, rocks, holes and
landslides were the rule rather than the exception. If it
hadn't been for occasional glimpses of ruts twisting
over the land ahead of them, Reba would have sworn
that there was no way for a vehicle to get through.

And even with the ruts as proof, she had her doubts.

Chance drove the appalling nonroad with the same
ease and confidence she had displayed on the crowded
freeway. After a time, Reba unclenched her hands and
relaxed, trusting his skill as he had trusted hers. She
found she enjoyed watching him, his concentration and
quick reflexes, the strength of muscles moving smoothly
beneath his tanned skin as he held the laboring Toyota
on the rough track.

"There's a tricky patch around the bend," said
Chance without looking up from the road. "Want to
walk it?"

"Are you going to?"

His lips curved beneath his moustache. "Some
bloody fool has to drive."

"If you're a bloody fool, I'm a candy-striped snake,"
she said tartly. "I'll ride, thanks. I'm in no hurry to
break in the shoes you bought for me."

She looked down at the boots Chance had given her. At his urging, she had changed into her camping outfit when they stopped for lunch. Privately, she thought the boots looked dreadful. Clunky, graceless and dirt brown. They were supple, however, and they gripped the ground securely. The jeans he had bought her weren't of the designer variety but they fit very well. The blouse followed the line of her body as though made exclusively for her. It was a soft cotton knit, the same dark blue as her jeans, with countless tiny buttons and loops fastening in a line down her left breast to her waist. The label of a very expensive house was sewn discreetly into the high collar.

When she had come back to the table wearing her camp clothes, Chance had given her a look of approval that made her feel very female. She had mentioned that, while gorgeous, her blouse could hardly be classified as rough clothing. He had simply smiled and pointed out that the blouse was dark enough not to show dirt and washable in the bargain. What more could anyone ask of rough clothes? Besides, he added, she could always hide the blouse under the windbreaker he had bought for her.

The Toyota lurched and swung to the side. Reba looked up from her boots, jolted out of her reverie. When she saw where the vehicle was—and where Chance was going to take it—she clenched her teeth against a scream. There was no road, nothing but a chaos of dirt and rock spilling down the steep mountainside to the black ravine far below.

Bucking, roaring, wheels spinning and spewing loose dirt before biting down to bedrock, the Toyota clawed its way over the landslide. The vehicle hung perilously onto the shifting surface of the land. At times they slanted so steeply on the downhill side that Reba was sure they were only seconds away from flipping over.

Each time the Toyota seemed to be losing its battle against going end over end, Reba's nails dug deeper into her palms. Each fishtailing skid and swooping recovery made her teeth clench until the tendons in her neck ached.

At some point she realized that while the Toyota's movements were unpredictable and frightening to her, they weren't to Chance. He knew where the wheels were likely to skid on loose rock. He knew just how steep an angle the vehicle could hold without turning turtle. He knew how to keep the power steady and how to ease back smoothly, when to coax and when to command. He reminded Reba of a diamond cutter she had seen in Holland; each movement quick, clean, no hesitations, no jerky motions, total concentration and incredible skill combined.

Even so, Reba was glad to get to the other side. She sighed and sensed Chance looking at her.

"Want to get out next time?" he asked.

"Are there many more like that?"

"One or two."

She grimaced. "It will almost be worth it."

"Worth what?"

"Being scared to death just so I can appreciate you. You're one hell of a good driver, Mr. Walker."

"You're one hell of a good passenger. Frankly, I was expecting you to scream."

"I was afraid it would distract you," she admitted.

"Smart as well as beautiful," Chance said approvingly. He took her hands and kissed the red marks her nails had left on her palms. "I should have made you wear the gloves I got for you."

"Gloves? It's not cold."

"Leather is tougher than fingernails," he said, turning his attention back to the road. "So is rock. You'll need gloves in the China Queen, unless you want hands as ugly as mine."

"Your hands aren't ugly," protested Reba, remembering how gentle his hands were when they touched her. "They're like all of you, strong and sensitive and hard. But not ugly. Never that."

The Toyota stopped suddenly. Chance unfastened his seatbelt, leaned over and kissed Reba until she was breathless. Before she could recover he had fastened himself back in and was concentrating again on the brutal road. She took a deep breath and prepared herself for the "one or two" rough patches ahead.

Chance helped to distract her by talking about the geology of the area. He told her about continental plates sliding past one another with ponderous grace and world-shaking results, the crust wrinkling, magma welling up and hardening into granitic masses beneath the land, earthquakes and mountains rising, molten rock shifting beneath the surface of the earth like an immense dragon stirring in its sleep.

It was still happening today, tiny adjustments of the earth's crust that could only be felt by man's most sensitive machines. Hundreds of temblors animated the land, subliminal twitches of the incandescent dragon sleeping deep beneath the surface. And every so often the dragon rolled over, shaking the land with casual strength and devastating results.

Chance drove the Toyota over a patch of decomposed granite, rock whose chemical "glue" had come unstuck through exposure to sun and wind and rain. The rock was pale orange and crumbled easily, making it as slippery as mud to drive over.

"I could learn to hate granite," said Reba as Chance took the Toyota through a downhill curve in a controlled skid.

"What about pegmatite?"

"What's that?"

He gave her a sideways smile. "Oh, it's kind of like granite. It comes in dikes and intrusions—veins, to the prospector. There's another thing about pegmatite," he added. "Without it, there's no tourmaline."

"I'm beginning to love pegmatite."

"Thought you would."

"Where is it?"

"Where's what?"

"The pegmatite."

"We're probably driving over masses of the stuff right now."

Reba looked out the window at the countryside dropping away steeply. "Looks like dirt to me."

"Underneath the dirt."

"But where?"

Chance laughed. "If I knew that, I'd stake out a claim myself. All I know is that the Pala area of San Diego County"—he waved a hand to indicate the surrounding land—"is riddled with pegmatite, and that in some of those crumbling dikes and sills are crystals of rubellite—tourmaline to you—that have an absolutely unique color. There is nothing like Pala's pink tourmaline anywhere else on earth."

"You know a lot about it," she said, remembering his accurate assessment of the Chinese tear bottle. "Its history, geology, value. Everything."

For an instant Chance looked as hard as the land. Then he said casually, "Pala's tourmaline is world famous. Any gem gouger worth the name knows about it."

Before Reba could say anything else, the Toyota came around the shoulder of a hill. Ahead of them lay the rough turnaround someone had bulldozed out at the road's end just in front of the mine. The China Queen's entrance was little more than a ragged hole at the base of a steep ridge. But it wasn't the mine that caught Reba's attention, it was the battered pickup truck parked in the turnaround.

Someone was already inside the China Queen.

Chapter 5

CHANCE SENT THE TOYOTA INTO A SKIDDING TURN THAT didn't end until they were facing back the way they had come. He set the brake but kept the engine on. With one hand he yanked free the cargo net that had kept everything in place while the vehicle jolted over the rough terrain. He opened a large, heavy tool chest and pulled out a pump shotgun. The barrel was long enough to be legal but too short for hunting game. Chance handled the weapon as easily as he had handled the Toyota. He flipped off the shotgun's safety and pumped a shell into the firing chamber. The sound was metallic, chilling.

"You know how to use this, don't you?" he asked calmly, holding out the shotgun to her.

Reba shook her head, drawing back. "No."

"*Damn*. City wise and country innocent." He checked the China Queen's entrance quickly in the rearview mirror. There was no one in sight around the mine. "If I'm not back in fifteen minutes—or if you see something coming out of the mine that you don't like—drive as far as you can and then hike out to the highway. There's a small ranch about a mile east of the mine turnoff. You can call Tim from there."

"Can't we just call the sheriff?"

"The sheriff doesn't own the China Queen."

Chance was out of the Toyota before Reba could argue. He took the shotgun with him. The pickup was only a few steps from the Toyota's rear bumper, and the mine entrance only a few feet beyond the truck. Chance reached through the truck's open window, pulled out the keys that had been left in the ignition and stuffed them in his pocket. If Reba had to drive out, no one would be able to follow her but Chance.

She checked her watch, then checked it again. It hadn't stopped, it just was keeping time in slow motion while her heart raced.

She looked in the rearview mirror. Chance had vanished into the black mouth of the China Queen. The Toyota vibrated slightly beneath her feet, idling easily. She unfastened her seatbelt and moved over to the driver's seat. She glanced at her watch again. One minute and thirty-seven seconds. With a small sound of impatience and protest, she watched the second hand creep around toward the two-minute mark. She could have sworn that the hand was moving backwards. At this rate she'd be toothless and grey before fifteen minutes were up.

She didn't think of what might be happening in the mine. If she thought about it, she'd come unstuck and that wouldn't do any good at all. It was rather like being on the balance beam. If you thought about the worst that could happen, it did. So you thought about it *before* you got on the beam. Once on the beam you thought only about the instant you were balanced in and the next instant to come. To think any further than that was an invitation to disaster.

A series of long, deep breaths helped slow her pulse

to a more reasonable rate. Her body responded by falling into the poised readiness that immediately preceded her workouts. There were no uneven bars waiting to test her this time, no "horse," no balance beam, but the ingrained discipline of gymnastics asserted itself, calming her.

Five minutes.

Reba watched the mine entrance in the rearview mirror, forcing herself not to think of anything but the seconds ticking away in her head, time sliced into small, unmoving segments.

Eight minutes.

Nothing moved at the China Queen's entrance. The hole looked very black against the jumble of granite boulders that were strewn halfway across the steep ridge. The thought occurred to her that it might be interesting to climb the boulders, jumping from one to the other like a child playing hopscotch. . . .

Where was Chance? Was he hurt?

Reba refused to follow that line of thought. She took another slow breath and looked at her watch. Ten minutes, fifty-three seconds.

Eleven.

As she looked up from her watch she saw a dusty four-wheel-drive van with oversized off-road tires crawl around the shoulder of the mountain, coming right for her. The van skidded to a stop just a few feet from the Toyota's front bumper, blocking off the narrow road. She slammed her fist on the Toyota's horn three times, hard and fast, hoping Chance would hear and understand that the odds had just changed. Then she yanked the key out of the ignition and ran for the boulder pile, ignoring the two men piling out of the van, yelling at her to stop.

The first boulder was nearly four feet high. She gained the top of it in a single clean leap, as though mounting a balance beam. There was an instant's pause while her trained eye assessed distances and angles, then she leaped again, changing direction as she moved, as quick and sure as a cat. Before the men following her reached the bottom of the boulders, she was thirty yards up the hill and increasing her lead with every clean movement of her body.

A few instants after she dropped out of sight into a hole between boulders, she heard the alien thunder of a shotgun, the chilling sound of another shell being pumped into place and Chance's voice.

"That's the only warning you get," he said, his tone flat, final. "You two in the rocks. Get over here. *Now.*"

Reba eased closer to the ring of huge rocks that concealed her from the men below. By peering through a narrow opening between two boulders, she had a clear view down to the mine entrance below. She expected to see Chance and the two men who had chased her. What she saw was Chance and five men. The three closest to Chance had their hands behind their necks, fingers interlaced. One of the men was bleeding from a cut lip. Another looked as though he had been shoved head first into a gravel pile. The third one limped.

The two men who had run after Reba were slowly covering the fifteen feet that separated them from their friends, forcing Chance to divide his attention among the five men. The men from the mine looked at each other and silently shifted their positions, spreading out. Suddenly the man who was limping turned and dove to the ground, flailing wildly with his arms and legs, trying to knock Chance's feet out from under him. At the same instant, the other two men from the mine jumped Chance.

Chance kicked the man on the ground with stunning force, taking him out of the fight between one second and the next. The shotgun barrel flashed in the sun as Chance slammed the weapon into the second attacker. The man folded over and fell limply, all fight gone. Chance pivoted and lashed out in a high karate kick that sent the third attacker flying backwards into the dirt, unconscious before he hit the ground. Instantly Chance spun to face the remaining two men, shotgun poised, ready.

Chance's speed was as shocking as his deadly skill. The two men who had chased Reba froze in place. Chance took a quick look, saw the empty Toyota and glided toward the two men with a predatory grace that was as chilling as his voice.

"Where is she?" asked Chance, watching both men equally.

"Who?" said one of the men.

Chance flattened him with a casual open-handed blow. As the man sprawled onto his back, Chance put the shotgun's cold muzzle against the man's throat.

"Where is my woman?" asked Chance quietly, his finger taking up slack on the trigger as he spoke.

"Chrissake!" choked the man. "Last time I saw her she was halfway to Mexico! Might as well try to run down a damned deer!"

Chance stepped back and swung the shotgun to cover both men again. "Reba!" he shouted, never looking away from the men. "Can you hear me?"

"Yes," answered Reba from her hiding place deep within the rocks.

"Are you hurt?"

"No," she said, trying to be as calm as Chance was. Even so, her voice sounded like it belonged to someone else, tight and harsh. "I'm fine. They never got close to me."

Some of the deadly tension went out of Chance. "Stay where you are until I tell you to come down."

The man Chance had hit with the shotgun groaned and started to get to his feet.

Chance looked over at him. "Stay there."

The man rolled onto his side and hunched over, his diaphragm still knotted by the blow from Chance's shotgun barrel.

"On your face, legs spread," said Chance curtly to the only man who was still standing. Quickly Chance went over the two men from the van, searching for weapons. He found a rusty pocket knife, a wad of money and a roll of nickels. He stuffed it all back into the men's pockets. "Don't move."

The pickup was only a few feet away. Chance opened the cab door, slid in and checked for weapons without looking away from the five men stretched out on the ground. He found a sawed-off shotgun under the front seat and a pistol in the glove compartment. The van yielded another shotgun and the keys to the ignition. Chance put the extra weapons in the Toyota and walked back to the two men who had chased Reba.

"Get up."

The men scrambled to their feet.

"Throw that trash in the back of the truck," said Chance, gesturing with his thumb toward the three men.

When they were finished, Chance threw the Jeep keys at one of the men. "Get in the Jeep and sit."

The man got in the Jeep and sat.

Chance fired the van keys toward the remaining man. "Come back any time you feel lucky," drawled Chance.

The man tried to meet Chance's eyes, then gave up and scrambled for the van.

Chance watched as the van backed around the curve and up the slope away from the mine. The Jeep inched around the Toyota, following the van. When Chance could no longer hear either engine, he put the shotgun's safety on, went to the base of the boulders and called to Reba.

"You can come down now."

Reba leaned against the boulders that had concealed her. "I can't," she said, her voice trembling so much that the words were almost impossible to understand.

"What?" Chance swore and came up the boulders with the speed and power of a big cat. "Where are you!"

"Here," she said, trying to steady herself on a rough granite boulder.

Chance couldn't see Reba until he stood on top of the ragged ring of boulders that surrounded her. He dropped down beside her, his face grim, his expression haunted. "I should have killed those bastards," he said harshly, grabbing her as her knees gave way, "but you said you weren't hurt—"

"I'm not," she said, laughing brokenly. "Just scared!"

His arms closed around her, supporting her. He held her and murmured words of comfort against her hair.

"I'm sorry," she said, after a moment, her voice breaking. "I feel like such a fool."

"You warned me, grabbed the keys and ran to the best cover around," he said, rubbing his fingers through her hair, seeking the warm scalp beneath. "There's nothing foolish about that."

"But I'm shaking so hard I can't even stand up!"

"Enough adrenaline will do that to you every time," said Chance, tilting her chin up and smiling gently at her. "You didn't let down until the crisis was past. That's all that matters, *chaton.*"

"You're so damned c-calm," Reba said, trying to take a steady breath.

"I've had more practice at this sort of thing."

She remembered his speed and deadly skill, three men down in a few seconds and Chance standing, shotgun ready, waiting for the other two men to move. With a deep sigh she stopped fighting her reaction and leaned against Chance. His arms cradled her in a strong, supportive hug. Even when he felt the last of her trembling fade he didn't release her, simply stood with his eyes closed and his face buried in the honey fragrance of her hair.

"I'm all right now," she said finally, stirring in his arms as her strength returned.

"Sure?" he said against her ear.

She shivered, but not from fear. His moustache was like a silk brush on her sensitive skin. "Yes."

"You're still shaking." Chance looked down into her wide, cinnamon eyes. "Do you want me to take you back to the city?"

"Will—will those men be back?"

"It's possible, but not bloody likely. I'm more trouble to them than the China Queen is worth."

"Were they digging for tourmaline?"

"No. They were using the mine as a stash."

Reba blinked. "Drugs?"

"Acapulco Gold," he said dryly. "High-class grass."

"In the Queen?" asked Reba, her voice rising. "Then they'll be back!"

"Doubt it. Someone poured gasoline on their Gold and burned it to hell and gone."

"Who?"

He hesitated. "They didn't say." Before she could ask any other questions, Chance kissed her, savoring her lips as though they were a rare wine. "Do you want to go back?" he asked in a husky voice.

"I want to see the Queen," said Reba, telling half the truth. The other half was as simple and powerful as the man holding her. She didn't want to leave him.

Chance looked up at the sky. Thick gold light slanted down. "No Queen tonight. As soon as the last of the adrenaline wears off, you'll be dead on your feet for a while. I want to have camp set up by then." After a last, quick kiss, he released her. He picked up the shotgun, ejected the shell from the firing chamber and reset the safety. "Here," he said, handing her the shotgun.

She made a sound of protest.

"Looks like it's back to the city after all," he said quietly.

Reba took a deep breath and accepted the shotgun with obvious reluctance. The weapon was unreasonably heavy, despite the fact that it balanced easily in her hands.

"Keep the barrel pointed at the ground," Chance said, then turned and sprang up to the top of the nearest boulder. He smiled down at the woman standing inside the small, ragged circle surrounded by boulders like a cinnamon diamond set among baroque pearls. "*Chaton*," he said softly. "Have I told you how beautiful you are?"

Her breath caught as she smiled up at him, knowing she wasn't beautiful but fiercely glad he thought she was.

"Hand me the shotgun," he said, watching her with eyes that were more green than silver, a smile transforming the hard lines of his face.

She stood on tiptoe and handed him the gun, careful to keep the barrel pointed away from both of them.

"You did that like a pro," he said approvingly. He propped the gun in a crevice. "Hold onto my wrists," he said, clamping his hands around her wrists as an example. "Walk up the rock as I lift. Ready?"

"Yes."

Chance took Reba's weight with an ease that startled her. She barely had time to take two flying steps up the face of the rock before she was held securely in his arms again. He looked over her head at the boulder field falling broken and jumbled all the way down to the China Queen's black mouth.

"How the hell did you get up here so fast?" he asked, measuring the height of the boulders at the base of the hill.

"One step at a time," she said wryly.

"Some steps. Those are big rocks, in case you hadn't noticed."

"Oh, I did," she assured him. "But most of them aren't much higher than my balance beam at home."

"Balance beam?"

"As in gymnastics," she said helpfully.

Chance raised one black eyebrow. "No wonder you feel so good," he said, running his hands over Reba's arms and back with a sensual approval that made her breath stop. He laughed softly. "I'd like to see you on the balance beam some day. In fact, there's a lot of ways I'd like to see you."

"I don't think I'll ask for a list," she said, smiling slightly.

"Afraid of being shocked?" he asked, half teasing and more than a little serious. Before she could answer he picked up the shotgun, leaped lightly onto another boulder and turned, waiting for her to follow.

Reba's legs were still a bit wobbly, but it was only a short jump. As she landed, Chance braced her with his free hand.

"Okay?" he asked, sensing her uncertainty.

"I'd rather have wings."

"One set of wings coming right up. Wait here."

Chance went down the rocks with a lithe power that

Reba envied. He propped the shotgun against a boulder and came back to where Reba waited. He guided her back down, choosing the easiest route, never letting go of her and yet somehow managing not to get in her way. She found that her legs got stronger as she worked her way down the boulder heap.

"Last one," said Chance.

He landed lightly on the ground and turned to hold out his arms to Reba. He swung her off the top of the boulder, then drew her slowly to his chest. She saw his smiling lips come closer, his shoulders dark and powerful against the sky, and then his warmth surrounded her, filling her world. Her hands slid up his arms until she could bury her fingers in his thick black hair.

"You're not afraid anymore?" he asked, kissing her cheek and eyes and forehead, quick touches that made her fingers tighten in his hair.

"No," she whispered. "Not when you hold me."

He chuckled softly, a sound more like a rough-edged purr than laughter. "Then I'll just have to keep holding you, won't I?"

Reba's arms tightened momentarily. She smiled up at him almost shyly. In the aftermath of fear she was unsure of herself, wholly vulnerable, totally responsive to his least touch. She felt sixteen again, her heart racing when her secret boyfriend walked her to English class and handed over her books with a smile.

"If you look at me like that much longer," said Chance in a husky voice, "I'm going to take advantage of your unraveled nerves and make love to you."

Reba looked away from his silver-green eyes. "I— Chance, I didn't promise that—"

He kissed her forehead and released her. "I know. You brought a prospector to see your mine, not a lover to warm your silky little body." He smiled crookedly. "Don't worry. I won't chase you into the rocks, even though you'd very much enjoy being caught by me. We both would."

She stared at him, fascinated by the sensual promise burning in his eyes. She wanted to explore that promise, yet she was afraid. It was that simple, and that unnerving. He was a man who came and went through people's lives, never staying long. A man who prospected the wild places of the world alone. If she gave herself to him he would break her heart. Her mind knew that, but her emotions reached out to him with a hunger that frightened her. She was vulnerable, and he was the Tiger God, carved in stone, invulnerable.

Silently she watched as he unloaded the Toyota and set up camp with an economy of motion that made her feel as though she had three left feet. She was amazed at what Chance accomplished in a short time. Within minutes, camp was all but complete. Firewood was stacked neatly, a metal grill was balanced across the circle of rocks that contained the fire, and the fire itself was dancing cheerfully beneath the grate. Supplies had been brought out of the Toyota and put near the fire. Sleeping bags were stacked to one side, waiting to be unrolled.

"It's not going to rain," said Chance, coming up behind her so silently that she gasped, "but I'll set up a pup tent for you if you like."

"Are you using one?"

He smiled slightly and shook his head. "More trouble than they're worth, unless the weather is bad."

"No tent for me," she said, looking up at the cloudless sky.

The sun had gone behind the rugged hills. Shadows flowed out of the land, creating a false twilight that would last until the sun fell silently into the distant sea, taking color and light, leaving shades of darkness behind.

Chance appeared at Reba's side again, holding the shotgun. He unloaded the magazine, checked the chamber to make sure it was empty, then closed the gun and handed it to her. After a brief hesitation, she took it. Under his calm directions she put the safety on and off, worked the pump that would load shells into the firing chamber, opened and closed the gun to check that the chamber was empty and squeezed the trigger.

"Don't try to hold it at your shoulder when you shoot," Chance said, showing her how to brace the shotgun alongside her hip. "With a barrel this short, accuracy isn't possible. Self-defense is, though. If you use this, be close to your target. Hold the gun along your hip and squeeze the trigger. Good."

He made her go through the motions until she became more comfortable with the shotgun. Then he loaded the magazine again, set the safety and propped the gun against a carton of food. "If you grab the shotgun and you're not sure whether there's a round in place, just work the pump. It's better to waste a shell and be sure than pull the trigger and have nothing happen. Sometimes you don't get a second chance."

Chance turned away and resumed laying out supplies for dinner. He set out plates on a ground cloth. Next to them he put sturdy cups, forks and knives so sharp that their cutting edges glittered.

"Can I do something?" Reba asked finally, watching him choose a place for their sleeping bags.

"Smile at me," he said, looking up from the rocks and twigs he was clearing out of the way before he put down a thick sleeping pad for her.

"That's not much," she protested, smiling.

"It is to me."

He looked up at her, a quick flash of silver-green in a dark, unsmiling face. She realized that he meant it, that a simple smile from her made a difference to him. She went to him as though pulled by an invisible leash, knelt by him as he worked, touched his cheek.

"We're so different," she whispered. "I think that's why I'm . . . afraid." She sighed and felt better just having admitted her fear.

"We can be in Los Angeles before midnight," he said in a neutral voice.

"That's not what I meant."

Chance looked up from his work. His eyes roamed hungrily over her honey hair and skin, her lips as pink as Pala tourmaline. "What did you mean?"

"Us. You treated the whole thing this afternoon so casually, like having a fender-bender on the freeway. Maybe a little dangerous but no cause for particular excitement."

Chance waited but she said nothing more. "That's not all that's bothering you, is it?" he said quietly.

Reba searched his eyes. "You didn't need that shotgun, did you? You could have killed just as easily without it."

"Yes."

Chance stood in a single fluid motion and resumed setting up camp. She went to the fire and watched him over its flames, admiring his muscular grace and fearful of it at the same time. The difference between Chance Walker and the other men she had known was the difference between a jungle tiger and one in the L.A. zoo. Same animal, different level of experience and reflexes entirely.

She stared into the fire, trying to sort out her own tangled thoughts. It was very quiet, no sound but the muted crackle of flames and the whisper of wind in the chaparral. Suddenly she realized that the sun had truly set and she was alone.

"Chance?"

No deep drawl came back to Reba out of the gathering darkness.

She stood up and looked around quickly. There was no one in sight. She walked to the China Queen's entrance. The hole was utterly black.

"Chance?" she called.

Nothing answered, not even an echo.

Reba went back to the fire, drawn by its silent companionship and changing patterns of light. Flames leaped and danced, greeting her. Firelight ran hotly down the barrel of the shotgun. She stared at the weapon for a long time.

The silence beyond the fire was like a seamless black tide rising around her, threatening to overwhelm her. She crouched on her heels next to the fire and the shotgun. In her mind's eye she went through the motions of clicking off the safety and working the pump until the shotgun was armed. Alone in the center of darkness, she suddenly saw the shotgun as more friend than enemy.

She didn't call out for Chance again. The sound of her voice in the emptiness was more frightening to her than silence.

With an impatient motion she stood up. Sitting around brooding wasn't her style. She'd done too much of it after her divorce. She went to the ice chest and examined its contents, using a flashlight that Chance had left by the firewood. He had stocked the ice chest with enough for several meals. She selected lamb chops, tomatoes, mushrooms and lettuce. She might not be an experienced camper but she had a barbecue at home. A campfire and a grate couldn't be that different.

She found rice and potatoes in another carton, along with flour, salt, sugar and other dry goods. Soap, towels and utensils were in a third carton. She hesitated, then decided that her skills might not be up to making decent rice over an uncertain fire. Boiling potatoes, however, was another matter. She rummaged in the utensil carton, found a small pan and managed to fill it with water from the heavy five-gallon can Chance had left near the ice chest.

"Not as neat as he would have been," she muttered, looking at the water splashed on her boots and jeans, "but I'm not as strong as he is." She laughed shortly. "Understatement of the century."

She washed her hands in a basin of cool water and set to work on dinner. Soon water was boiling around chunks of potato, lettuce was washed and drained, tomatoes and mushrooms sliced. There was nothing as fancy as a salad bowl, of course. Another pan served almost as well, though. Best of all, she had found a bottle of Cabernet Sauvignon in among the pots and pans. She hadn't found a corkscrew yet but she hadn't given up, either.

She was head down in the third carton when she sensed someone behind her. Without thinking she lunged to the side, reaching for the shotgun. In the next instant she recognized Chance.

"What am I doing?" Reba said, staring at the shotgun she had grabbed.

"Just what you're supposed to," said Chance quietly. "I didn't mean to scare you," he added. "Next time I'll make more noise."

"More?" she said thinly, her voice rising. "You didn't make one damn sound." She set the shotgun aside and went back to rummaging in the carton, with hands that trembled. "Were you in the mine?"

"No. Just checking around."

"And?"

"There's a spring opposite the mine, hidden in the

chaparral. Racoon and bobcat tracks, rabbits rustling around. Deer are drifting out of cover to feed. Coyotes are moving on the ridgelines. Full moon coming on.''

Reba put her head in her hands and began to laugh. Chance watched her, one black eyebrow raised in silent query.

"I was alone in the dark and scared to death, imagining all sorts of awful things and then you come back and make it sound like a Disney movie." She shook her head, laughing at herself despite the erratic flutter of her pulse.

"I told you I'd be gone for a while."

"I didn't hear you."

"I know. What were you thinking so hard about?"

She turned and looked up at him, firelight shimmering in her cinnamon eyes. "A lot of things," she whispered.

Chance waited but all she said was, "I hope you like boiled potatoes with your lamb chops. I couldn't find any salad dressing. Or a corkscrew."

He pulled a folding knife out of his pocket, opened the corkscrew arm and lifted the Cabernet Sauvignon out of the utensil carton. A few quick twists, a hard pull and the cork popped softly.

"Hope you don't mind drinking wine out of mugs," he said.

"I'd be happy to drink it any way I can get it. Somehow I hadn't expected to find a lovely Cabernet on the menu."

"I'm not entirely uncivilized."

Something in Chance's voice made Reba look up quickly. "That's not what I meant."

"Isn't it?" he asked, setting the open bottle on the ground cloth. He looked down into her wide eyes. An indefinable sadness settled around his mouth, but the emotion didn't soften the harsh lines and shadows of his face. "Bringing you here was a mistake. I thought if you saw me out here I wouldn't seem like such a barbarian to you. I thought you would be less afraid of me. And then those damned dopers had to show me for what I was—not your kind of man at all." Chance laughed abruptly, then swore with a soft violence that made Reba want to cry out in protest. "Never mind," he said, reaching out to touch her and then letting his hand fall aside before he felt the silky warmth of her skin. "I'll take you back to your city after dinner."

"Did you get used to Lightning Ridge in an afternoon?" she asked, her throat tight with emotions she fought to control.

"No," he said softly.

"Then why do you expect me to?"

"I don't."

"But you're going to take me back anyway."

Chance stared beyond the fire into the dense blackness of the hillside. Silver light shimmered along the ridge, hinting of moonrise to come. "I don't really give a damn if other people look at me as though I were a wild animal. But to have you afraid of me . . ." He watched her with eyes that had seen too much of violence, not enough of love. "My God, I'd cut off my hands rather than harm you."

Blindly, Reba came to her feet and into his arms. "I'm frightened, but not of you, not in the way you mean. Yes, you're hard and quick and—and deadly. But you're not a wild animal. You could have killed those men this afternoon. You didn't. You're strong enough *not* to kill. And you're so gentle with me. Afraid of you?" she asked with an uncertain smile. "Chance, I've never felt so good as when you hold me."

"And I've never felt so good as when I hold you," he whispered, lifting her high in his arms. He murmured her name over and over against her lips, her throat, her eyes. "You're a miracle to me, *chaton*. You make me alive again."

She buried her face in his hard neck, wanting to comfort him and herself, to heal the raw scars life had left on both of them. She held him with all her strength, glorying in the feeling of his arms holding her. It was a long time before either of them moved or spoke. When he heard her long sigh, he set her gently on her feet, releasing her from his arms with a reluctance that said more than words.

"You're going to be tired soon," he said.

Reba started to protest, then realized that he was right. With relaxation had come a weariness that was unlike anything she had ever felt. It was as though strength were running out of her like sand through an hourglass.

"Adrenaline will make you leap tall boulders in a single bound," he said, smiling down at her, "but you pay for it later."

"Just so there is a 'later,' " she said, stifling a yawn.

"That's always the bottom line. Survival. How do you like your lamb chops? Well done?"

She blinked, then couldn't help smiling. "Rare, I'm afraid. Very rare. I'm not as civilized as I look. Just inexperienced."

Chance gave Reba a sideways glance. A quick smile flashed beneath his moustache. *"Touché,* I think."

Reba sat cross-legged on the ground cloth, watching Chance finish preparing dinner. He did it as he did everything else, cleanly, no wasted motions. She was fascinated by his masculine grace and by the fact that he lifted the heavy can of water with as little fuss as he lifted the pan of potatoes.

"I couldn't find any salad dressing," she said.

"I'll tell you where it is," he said, "if you'll pour me a mug of that wine."

The marvelous fragrance of the Cabernet Sauvignon drifted up as she poured the wine. She was tempted to find out if the wine tasted as good as it smelled.

"Go ahead and sneak a sip," Chance said, not looking up from the lamb chops.

"Do you really have eyes in the back of your head?" she demanded, startled and exasperated.

"Come over here and find out."

Reba walked over, crouched next to Chance and handed him the mug of wine. As he sipped the wine, she took his hat, tossed it next to the dinner plates and ran her fingers over every bit of his scalp.

"No extra eyes?" he said, laughing silently, looking at her.

"Not a one. There goes that theory."

He sipped the wine again, smiling. "Do you like the Cabernet?"

"You caught me before I could taste it," she admitted.

Chance took a quick sip, set down the mug and reached for her. He held her gently behind her neck, rubbing his lips over hers. "Taste," he said, his voice husky.

A shiver went through Reba as she saw the sensual sheen of wine over his sculpted lips. Tentatively she traced the line of his mouth with the tip of her tongue. His lips parted, inviting her to explore further. As the taste of wine spread through her, she touched him more deeply, lured by the velvet warmth of his mouth. Her hands came up to his face, caressing his cheeks, then sliding deep into his hair as the kiss passed from exploration into passion. She felt him change, felt hunger tighten his body, felt the unwavering gentleness of his fingers stroking her neck. The combination of his hunger and his steel restraint was more heady than the drops of wine she had stolen from his mouth.

Fat sputtered and smoked in the fire, warning of lamb chops cooking. Slowly, Reba lifted her lips. For an instant Chance's hand tightened on her neck. Then he let her go.

"Well," he said quietly, "do we keep the bottle or tell the waiter to send it back?"

"Keep it," she whispered. "It's a fine Cabernet," she added, running her fingertip over his mouth, "robust yet restrained, complex, with a delicate finish that's unexpected in such a full-bodied wine."

He said her name softly, kissed her as gently as moonlight glimmering down the ridge. Lamb fat crackled in the flames, followed by a visible leap of fire. With a soft curse Chance looked away from Reba's mouth. Deftly he turned over the chops.

"There's a plastic bottle in the ice chest," he said.

Reba went to the ice chest and pulled out a small yellow squeeze bottle. "This one?"

"It's the only one in there. Salad dressing," he added without looking up.

"Says mustard on the outside."

"It's like a Venezuelan diamond," said Chance, shifting the chops on the grate. "You can't tell what's inside until you take off the cover."

Reba unscrewed the cover, sniffed and said, "Salad dressing." She took a drop from the inside of the cap. "Mmmm, lemon and dill." She replaced the cover and looked at the firelight and shadows shifting over Chance's face. "What did you mean about the Venezuelan diamonds?"

"You don't find them like African or Australian diamonds. Some Venezuelan diamonds are covered in a greenish coating. Most of the ones which are coated like that are inferior. But some of them"—his hand paused and he stared beyond the flames—"some of them are clean and bright inside, shining like a lifetime of dreams condensed into a single crystal."

Chance slid the chops onto one of the metal plates he had warmed by the fire. "It's not surprising that men will do anything to find and keep such a treasure, even kill. Especially in South America. In the open-pit gold mines and at the *bombas*—diamond strikes—men swarm over the land and each other like maggots. Human life is cheaper than a handful of water there— and it rains every day."

Chapter 6

CHANCE HANDED REBA A PLATE OF LAMB CHOPS AND boiled potatoes. "Do you mind if we share the salad bowl?" he asked.

She shook her head, more interested in listening to him than in eating. She sensed that he didn't talk about his past very often. He sat next to her and began to eat. She was about to ask a question when he resumed talking quietly.

"We found enough to stay alive at the *bombas*, but never more than that. Dad and Luck didn't care. Glory did. She wanted more out of life than a dirty campsite on the wrong side of nowhere. I was too young to know how Mother felt about it. She went with Dad until it killed her. I guess that's the only answer that matters."

Chance sipped wine in silence for a moment. "I didn't like South America much. Not then. Not now. I haven't been back to Venezuela since Luck died. Australia's Outback is different. Good country. Hard. Bloody unforgiving, sometimes. But clean and fine and wild. You can measure yourself against a land like that.

Some men do, and come up short. Others find they're bigger than they thought."

Reba ate quietly, listening, watching the shifting shadows of fire and night across Chance's face, hungry to know the places and circumstances that had helped to shape the man who sat next to her.

"The basin and range country of the U.S. is like the Outback," continued Chance. "More land than people, more possibilities than rules." He smiled slightly to himself. "No black opals, though. I'd like to take you to Lightning Ridge. It's easier now than it was twenty years ago. Then it took twenty-six hours by train from Sydney. All you saw was an occasional village, herds of kangaroos, flocks of emus and flat red desert land. The tracks stopped about ninety kilometers short of Lightning Ridge. For the rest of the way you either hitched a ride on the mail truck or found a friendly rancher heading out to his station."

Chance was quiet for a moment, remembering. "Glory had her hands full on that first trip out of the jungle with me. She was up to it, though. That's one good woman. She did what had to be done and never whined."

Silently, he stared into the darkness beyond the fire. After a time he looked at the entrance to the China Queen, invisible beneath the seamless black of night. "At least you don't have to haul water in to the Queen. And I won't have to be lowered by a rickety winch into a shaft barely wider than my body. At Lightning Ridge you spend your time clawing and crawling like moles through the earth, sniffing out dark treasures. Moles . . . except that we were always armed, always awake, because the men who weren't, died."

"It sounds as bad as the jungle," said Reba.

"No. In the jungle, a 'partner' was a man who hadn't

turned on you yet. Two 'partners' would go into the jungle and find a handful of diamonds. One man would come back, saying his partner had drowned or been killed by a snake or eaten by cannibals or piranhas." Chance shrugged. "Any of those things could have happened. Funny how they only happened *after* a find, though. In the Outback, gougers only kill ratters, not partners."

"Ratters?"

"The men who sneak into someone else's claim when honest gougers are asleep. If a gouger catches a ratter, he usually belts him around a bit and puts him on the next train to Sydney. But sometimes the gouger just fills in the shaft—ratter, opals and all."

Reba's fork clattered against her plate. Chance looked at her over the rim of his mug, took a sip and set aside both the mug and his plate.

"The gougers risk their lives every day going down into the earth in narrow, unshored tunnels. There are no surface signs that say, 'Dig here. Opal below.' Anywhere is as good as anywhere else. You're either lucky or you aren't. Your tunnel either caves in or it doesn't. Thinking about it won't help, so you believe the gouger's myth that cave-ins only happen between midnight and one A.M. and you stay out of the shafts for that hour.

"The rest of the time you swing your pick in an area half again as wide as your shoulders, you eat dirt and hold your breath, listening for a gritty sound. When you hear that, you know you've found a 'nobby,' a nodule that may or may not be opal bearing. You scrape dirt away from the nobby with your fingernail or a small knife. And you do it slowly, gently, even if your hands are shaking with excitement. When the dirt is gone you nip off a corner of the rock with pliers. If your light picks up a flash of color, you keep the nobby. You won't know what you have until later, when you put it on the cleaning table. Most of the time it's nothing. Once in a lifetime it's a chunk of black fire as big as your fist."

He looked at her out of narrowed silvery eyes. "That's when the ratters come. And that's when someone can die."

Reba stared at Chance, trying to understand a life so different from hers. "It's so alien," she said finally, "the danger and the death. . . ."

"Is it?" he asked quietly.

"What do you mean?"

"Take danger. What kind of courage or foolishness does it take to roar down a concrete raceway six abreast, tons of hurtling metal and explosive fuel separated by less than a meter of air and whatever small skill or luck the drivers around you have. When it comes right down to it, you've probably seen almost as much violence on the road as I've seen in the diamond strikes. It's all in what you're used to."

With an easy motion Chance stood. "Finish your dinner. I'm going to check the area once more. I'll call out before I come into camp."

Before Reba could say anything, Chance merged with the darkness. She listened for sounds of his leaving. She heard only her own heartbeat. He had gone as silently as a breath. Slowly she finished eating, barely tasting the food, too full of his words to concentrate on anything else. She set aside her plate and sipped the Cabernet, remembering how sweet it had tasted from his lips.

Water steamed gently above the pan that Chance had set on the grate after he had cooked the chops. Reba cleaned up the remnants of dinner quickly, washing and putting away the utensils that they had used. When she was finished, she poured a little more wine in her mug and sat next to the fire.

Gradually Reba realized that she wasn't uneasy even though she was alone in the camp. She knew that Chance was out there beyond the light, moving silently, checking that no one else was near. The thought was reassuring. If there were danger, Chance would find it and deal with it. She was as safe here as she was behind the locked doors of her own home. Safer, probably.

She stretched luxuriantly, feeling more at peace than she had in a long time. She wondered how it would feel to move like a shadow through the night, to be a part of the silence and moonrise and black mountains reaching toward the stars.

"Reba?"

The voice was soft, deep, very near. She turned toward it, smiling. Chance walked out of the night into the twisting golden glow of the campfire.

"Are you too tired for a short walk?" he asked.

"I was just wondering what it's like out there."

"Quiet. Dark. Peaceful." He unrolled a sleeping bag and draped it over his shoulder. "Cool, too. The wind is moving. Bring your jacket."

Reba put on the windbreaker that Chance had bought her. "Ready."

"Not quite." He put his hands on her shoulders and turned her away from the fire. "Don't look at the flames for a bit. Let your eyes adjust to the moonlight."

"Is that why you never look directly into the fire?" she asked.

"Yes. It makes you blind."

"But it's beautiful."

"So is night."

Reba closed her eyes, enjoying the warmth of Chance's hands on her shoulders, the sense of his presence so close to her, his breath stirring wisps of her hair. She relaxed, letting her senses expand into the night.

"Can you see the boulder ahead of you on the ridge?" asked Chance after a long silence.

She opened her eyes and was surprised at how much she could see. "Yes."

"Imagine a clock in front of you. What do you see where the three would be?"

"A clump of chaparral."

"How do you know it isn't a ridge?"

"It's too light. Not the color, the feeling. The ridges feel dense."

His hands squeezed her shoulders approvingly. "You'll do fine without a flashlight."

Chance put the flashlight in a loop hanging from his belt and picked up the shotgun. He made as little fuss over the weapon as he did over the flashlight. Both were simply useful things to carry in rough country at night. When he held out his hand to Reba, she took it without hesitation.

He led her across the clearing in front of the mine and around a clump of chaparral. To her disgust, she wasn't nearly as quiet as he was. On the other hand, she didn't sound like a one-woman wrecking crew. After the first hundred yards she caught the rhythm of his walk, the careful yet firm strides that soundlessly tested the ground underfoot before trusting it with his full weight. She imitated him as best she could, walking with the same poised control she would have used on a balance beam. Immediately she found she made less noise and much faster progress.

Chance noticed the change as quickly as she did. He put her palm against his lips and whispered, "You were made for more than city streets."

She followed him up a small rise, threading between boulders that condensed out of darkness and moonlight

like immense baroque pearls. The top of the rise was
rounded, bare of chaparral. The ground became less
stony, almost soft, and the springtime smell of grass
lifted into the night.

"Look to your left," said Chance softly.

Reba turned and stood transfixed. Serrated, sable,
endless, ridge after ridge fell away in shades of black to
a distant, invisible sea. The outlines of the ridges were
clean and bold against a multitude of brilliant stars.
Chaparral made ebony lace designs against the brighter
moonlight. A vague shimmer of mist curled along some
of the valleys. Moonlight and shadows, grass a lighter
shade of black, chaparral glistening like obsidian, boulders a ghostly grey, the moon itself a silver radiance
that was almost overwhelming.

"I never knew night came in so many colors,"
whispered Reba.

"Glory used to say that only a mine and a miner's
heart are truly black," said Chance, pulling Reba down
onto the ebony sleeping bag he had spread on the grass
like another shade of night.

She shivered.

"Chilly?" he asked.

She didn't answer. "You're a miner—does Glory
think that of you?"

Chance removed the flashlight and belt knife. He lay
on his side, his chin propped on his fist. He stared out at
the rugged, black-and-silver land. "No," he said finally, softly. "Do you?"

"No," said Reba, kneeling next to Chance, watching
his face rather than the moonlight-washed land.

"Are you sure?"

"I'm here," she said simply.

"Why does that seem so close," he whispered, "and
so damn far away?" His hand went around behind her
head, pulling her closer to him. "Just a kiss," he said

huskily. "Don't be frightened, *chaton*. I won't even hold you unless you want me to."

Reba felt the tremor that went through Chance when her lips touched his. His hand lifted from her neck, slid the comb out of her hair and then released her. A shimmering fall of hair spilled over him. He whispered a phrase in the strange, liquid language she had heard him use before.

"What does that mean?" she murmured against his lips.

"There's no translation," he said, curling his fingers through her hair. "The shimmer of water at dawn . . . the flash of an opal in a miner's light . . . the kind of beauty that makes me want to shout and laugh and cry. You."

"Chance," she whispered, then was unable to say more.

She kissed the corners of his mouth, felt the sable smoothness of his moustache with her sensitive lips, kneaded her fingers into his thick hair. With a sigh she returned to his mouth, parting her own lips, silently asking him to do the same. His mouth opened to her. She kissed him slowly, savoring each change of texture, each moment of increasing intimacy.

Her hands slid from his hair down to his shoulders, his arms, the hard muscles of his torso. Slowly, she lowered herself until she was lying close to him, holding him and kissing him, her body resting along his. The longer she kissed him the more she wanted to share her pleasure the only way she knew how—by touching him.

Chance made a sound deep in his throat and shifted, bringing his body even closer to hers. His hands were clenched in the ends of her hair. Reba sensed how much he wanted to hold her, to run his hands over her, to know her body as intimately as he knew the night. But despite the hunger seething in him, when she lifted her head he immediately opened his hands and let her hair slide away between his sensitive fingers.

His restraint reassured her as nothing else could have. She lowered her head again, letting the tip of her tongue touch his lips. "Hold me," she whispered.

Slowly his arms closed around her, hard and strong and warm. A quiver of pleasure went through her. He felt it. His arms tightened, then released her before she could feel trapped. But she hadn't felt trapped. She had felt wanted. The difference was both simple and overwhelming. Her body softened, flowing over him.

"*Chaton*," he whispered hoarsely, "do you know what you're doing to me?"

Reba shivered as Chance's hand went down her spine, drawing her closer to his male heat.

"Don't be afraid," he murmured.

"I'm not. It's just . . ."

"Just what?" he asked after a moment, kissing her forehead.

"I just realized I've never made love with a man, not really. I mean, I was married and I'm not a virgin, but my husband is the only man who's touched me. And he"—she hesitated, staring into Chance's silvery eyes so close to hers, so intent—"he never wanted me the way you do. He never made me want him at all. But you"—she brushed her mouth over Chance's lips, glorying in the instant response she felt go through him—"you make me want you so much that I'm helpless."

"That doesn't frighten you?" he asked softly, kissing her eyelids, the corners of her mouth, the pulse beating strongly in her neck.

"Not any more. I just don't know what to do. I want to please you but I don't know how."

"Let me love you," Chance said, his voice husky. He nuzzled the sensitive edges of her ear, nibbled delicately on her earlobe, her lower lip. "I'll be very gentle, as though it were your first time. And in some ways it will be. There's so much woman buried in you that you don't even know about."

Reba's answer was a sigh through parted lips, a subtle change in her body against his, a soft movement that said more clearly than words that she had already given herself to him in her mind. She felt the response that shuddered through him in the instant before he controlled it. She found nothing to fear in his deep hunger for her, and much to enjoy. With the shadow of a smile, she touched the moonlight and warmth caught in his moustache.

"Love me," she murmured, asking for more than his touch or his hunger or his strength.

"I will," he said, answering only part of her words, his hands moving strongly over her. "Nothing could stop me now . . . except you. You'll always be able to stop me, *chaton*," he whispered against the hollow of her throat. "All you have to do is say no. I'll hear you, no matter how much I want you."

Chance shifted position slowly, giving her time to protest as he rolled over until she was partially beneath him, moonlight pouring over her face. His hands found the warmth beneath the cool softness of her hair. He whispered her name as her lips parted for him. Gently, powerfully, his kiss consumed her, slow movements of his tongue foreshadowing the more intimate claiming to come.

Reba felt her body change, felt unfamiliar fire shimmer through nerve endings she didn't know she had. With a small sound she softened beneath him, calling to him wordlessly in a language older than civilization. He responded by kissing her even more deeply, his body hard with passion and restraint, his hands gentle as they slid through the moon-bright softness of her hair.

Slowly he unzipped her windbreaker and stroked her from throat to waist with knowing hands. She closed her eyes and smiled, enjoying his touch as she had never enjoyed any man's.

"When I saw this blouse," Chance murmured against her lips, her shoulder, the soft skin of her neck, "I had to buy it for you." His fingers undid the first of the many buttons that went from the neckline over her left breast and down along the length of the blouse. "Tiny buttons shaped like gems. I couldn't wait to see you wearing this. And when I saw you, I couldn't wait to undress you. Now"—his laugh was short, almost harsh—"my fingers are shaking so much that I can hardly undo the buttons."

The idea of being able to affect his strength to that degree made Reba's breath stop. Chance loomed above her, his eyes pure silver, radiant with moonlight. She saw a man who was rough, hard, dangerous, aroused . . . and so gentle with her that she had never felt safer, more cherished, more exquisitely alive.

"It's all right," she said, turning to kiss his hand. "Whatever you want is all right. I trust you, Chance. Teach me how to love you."

The breath came out of him in an explosive rush. "My God," he said hoarsely, "you already know how to love better than I ever will." His lips came down over hers as he kissed her with a deep hunger that sent fire through her. "But I'll teach you about pleasure, *chaton*. I promise you that."

His hand moved over the buttons, fingers deft, no longer trembling. The dark blouse parted in an ever widening triangle, revealing the warmth beneath. In the moonlight her skin had the purity and sheen of a pearl. His hands had already told him that she wore nothing beneath the soft fabric, but even so, he wasn't prepared for her beauty.

Reba sensed his sudden stillness. "What's wrong?" she asked, her eyes searching his face.

"Nothing," Chance breathed, brushing his moustache over the tip of her breast, feeling it swell in response. "You're perfect, firm and silky, changing as I touch you. Yes, my woman, change for me."

She started to speak, to tell him that she felt perfect when he touched her, but his mouth had gently closed over her breast. Sensations radiated through her. She shivered until she felt the velvet roughness of his tongue on her nipple, and then she moaned and her fingers tightened in his thick hair. She didn't feel the sudden coolness of night as her blouse opened fully. She felt only his touch, the heat of his mouth pulling gently on her breast, teeth delicately tormenting her.

When Chance lifted his head, Reba made a small sound of protest, wanting more. He laughed softly and teased her with the hard tip of his tongue, then caught her in his mouth again with a strength that made her arch against him in an instinctive response to the fire spreading through her. His hand found her other breast, caressed it. He brushed the nipple slowly, coaxing it into hardness. Then he caught the tip of her breast between his fingers and rolled it deftly, enjoying the shudders that went through her body.

His mouth roamed between her breasts, licking and biting gently, teasing her until she twisted against him. And then he increased his tender assault, caressing her breasts while he claimed her mouth in a kiss that was as deep as it was powerful. When she arched against him again, his body shifted until he was lying between her legs. He moved once, letting her feel his arousal. When he lifted his head to look down at her, she wore a smile as old as woman.

"Thank God," he said, covering her with tiny, swift kisses. "Some women like being petted but are put off by a man's need. I didn't think you were like that, but it would have explained why you haven't slept with a man since your divorce."

Surprise showed for a moment on Reba's face. She slid her hands over his back again, enjoying the resilience and strength of him. "I didn't want the men who wanted me. But you—I want you, Chance. Being wanted by you is the most exciting thing I've ever felt."

"Is it?" he asked softly, watching her eyes.

"Yes," she whispered. "Yes."

She unbuttoned the top button of his shirt, then the second and the third and the rest until he rolled aside and pulled off the shirt with a supple twist of his body. His tanned skin gleamed beneath the midnight hair curling across his chest. Moonlight flowed over ridges and swells of muscle, leaving highlights and shadows that she lovingly traced with her fingertips. When her nails scraped lightly through the mat of hair and over his nipples, a tremor of desire ripped through him.

"You like that," she said, her pleasure in the discovery showing in her voice. "Do you like this, too?"

She ran her tongue over his dark male nipple, caught it lightly between her teeth, tugged, caressing him as he had caressed her. The heightened desire that coursed through him was as clear to her as the pattern of moonlight on his skin. She laughed softly and continued her exploration of him until he moved swiftly, pinning her beneath him again.

"The second time you can tease me," said Chance, his teeth white beneath his sable moustache, the tip of his tongue glistening as he bent to caress her, "but not this time. There's too much I want to show you the first time. You make me very hungry, Reba," he whispered against her breasts, "so hungry I don't want to wait."

His hands devoured her, removing her clothes, savoring the feminine curves and silky firmness of her body. When she was naked in the moonlight, he looked at her with molten silver eyes. For long moments he didn't touch her, fighting to control the hunger hammering in his blood.

"Chance?" she whispered.

"It's all right," he answered in a husky voice. "I didn't know I could want a woman like this. But I know now."

He took off his own clothes with swift motions and lay down beside her. When he touched her, it was lightly, a breath of a caress that went from her temples to her toes. The delicacy of his fingers made her burn for more. She arched beneath his hands, asking silently. He answered with a deep kiss that consumed every bit of her mouth. His hand moved from her breast down her body to the springy thickness of her hair. He savored the satin curve of hip and thigh, teased her until she sighed and shifted her body, inviting a more intimate touch.

His hand slid down, seeking the warm darkness between her thighs. When he felt her liquid softness and heat, he knew beyond any doubt that she wanted him. He touched her slowly, learning the intimate textures of her desire, stroking her until she cried out and her warmth flowed over him. A fine sweat misted his skin as he felt the deepest rhythms of her pleasure. Taut with desire and restraint, his body gleamed above her like polished stone in the moonlight.

She opened her eyes, dazed by the sensations that shivered through her. "Tiger God," she whispered wonderingly, her hands sliding down his hard male body, touching him.

He made a hoarse sound and covered her, all of her, holding her hair like hot silk between his fingers, Tiger God burning bright inside her, pleasure expanding with every movement of his body until she cried out and came apart in his arms. He let go of his steel restraint, sharing her ecstasy as release shuddered through him.

Then he held her until they could breathe evenly once more. He kissed her lightly, repeatedly, as though memorizing her face with his lips. Her breath sighed out, pleasure and contentment in a single soft sound. Arms around her, lifting her, he rolled onto his side without disturbing the intimacy of their embrace.

"If I'd known what was going to happen," said Chance, nuzzling her ear, "I'd have brought one of the sleeping pads. I'd hate to bruise your lovely body on the hard ground."

"I hadn't noticed," said Reba, burrowing into his warmth, holding him close.

He smiled and teased her ear with the tip of his tongue. "Let me know when you begin to get cold."

"What are you going to do then?" she asked lazily, smoothing his chest hair with her palm.

"Put your clothes back on you."

"I think I'd rather be cold," she said, smiling, enjoying the confidence that came from being certain that she had satisfied him as fully as he had satisfied her. It was a new feeling to her, peaceful and yet almost bold.

Silent laughter vibrated in his chest. "I'll let you put my clothes back on me," he offered.

Reba made a face at him. "You feel better without your clothes."

"So do you," he said, moving against her with an intimate knowledge that made her breath catch all over again. "You feel better than anything I've ever touched. *Chaton.*"

She gave herself to his embrace with unconcealed pleasure. Her lips opened beneath his, meeting his tongue with sweet changing pressures of her own that she had learned from him. When the kiss finally ended she curled against his shoulder, drawing warmth from him. For a time they lay quietly, motionless but for his hand stroking the long curves of her body.

The wind moved in the chaparral on the slope of the hill. Grass bent and trembled in the moonlight.

"You're cold," said Chance, feeling her flesh roughen beneath the cool wind.

Reba said nothing, not wanting to move out of his arms, to dress, to wake from the dream of him filling her senses until she felt nothing but a pleasure so great she could only cry out and hold onto him.

With a lingering kiss, Chance separated himself from her and gathered up her clothes. "No," he said when she reached for the jeans. "Let me."

The wine lace of her underwear looked black in the moonlight. He smoothed the lace over her, kissed her navel lingeringly, then slowly pulled her jeans into place and fastened them. As he picked up the blouse, its tiny faceted buttons glittered and winked. He eased the soft fabric over her arms and shoulders. Beginning at the bottom, he fastened each button.

When he reached the point where he would have to cover her breasts, he stopped. He cherished each breast with his mouth, murmured another liquid, alien phrase and buttoned the rest of her blouse with obvious reluctance.

"Warmer?" Chance asked softly, stroking her cheek with the back of his fingers.

"Yes," said Reba, her voice trembling slightly, "but I'm not sure it's the clothes."

His smile was a flash of white against the dark planes of his face. He stepped away from her to gather up his own clothes. She moved quickly, scooping up everything in sight. She knelt in front of him, her arms crossed possessively over his clothes. He looked at her quizzically.

"I thought you were going to let me dress you," she said.

"It's more fun to undress me," he drawled.

"I'll remember that," she promised demurely.

The first piece of clothing Reba pulled out of the tangle in her arms was Chance's shirt. She set the rest aside and stood. She pulled first one sleeve and then the other over his arms. Standing very close, she rubbed her hands over his chest beneath the folds of cloth, enjoying the masculine textures of hair and muscle and rippling strength. Finally she buttoned the shirt, standing on tiptoe to kiss him as she fastened the last button. His arms closed around her, holding her tightly.

When his arms loosened she slipped from him to kneel at his feet. She reached for the rest of his clothes, hesitated, then let the cloth fall from her fingers.

"Not yet," she whispered, running her hand along the strong column of his leg.

Chance's muscles shifted and flexed beneath her touch, moving smoothly under skin that had been burned dark in the deserts and jungles of the world. Reba cupped her hands around his muscular calf, enjoying the feel of his strength. With a shadowy smile, she closed her eyes and moved her hands from his ankle up to the powerful muscles of his thigh. As though pulled by a magnet, she put her cheek against the outside of his thigh. Underneath the hair-roughened surface, his leg was hard and warm.

The wind stirred again, blowing her hair across his bare legs, wrapping silky strands around his hips, caressing him like cool flames. She smoothed her cheek against his thigh as her fingers shaped the contours of his leg, oblivious to everything but the unique male textures of her Tiger God.

Suddenly Reba found herself pulled to her feet, held

immobile in hard hands. "What's wrong?" she said. "Don't you like—"

The question died in her throat as she saw Chance's hot silver eyes. His mouth came down over hers with a force and demand that would have frightened her an hour ago, but now it sent streamers of fire through her. She buried her hands in his thick hair and kissed him with a hunger that she had learned from him. His hands swept over her, peeling away the clothes that he had so carefully put on her just moments before.

With fingers that shook, she unfastened the few buttons on his shirt. Her breasts touched the tantalizing roughness of the hair curling across his chest. His hands moved powerfully down her back, cupping her hips, lifting her until she fitted over him. The intimate contact sent heat racing through her. She made a small sound in the back of her throat, pleasure and demand and surrender at once.

Moonlight spun as Chance lowered Reba to the ground and buried himself in her softness. He found the wildness deep inside her, called to it, demanded it and then drank her cries of fulfillment, giving himself to her as wildly as she had given herself to him.

When Chance could breathe evenly again, he caught Reba's face between his hands, holding her motionless, looking at her as though he had never seen her before. With infinite care he bent over her lips, his kisses as delicate as moonlight. The liquid words he murmured had no translation and needed none. They were part of the night and his warmth and his arms cradling her. She stirred slowly, echoes of ecstasy shimmering through her.

"I love you," she murmured, framing his face with her hands.

His answer was another kiss, a tightening of his arms

around her. "I don't know enough about love to use the word," he said. "I only know there has never been another woman for me like you."

Reba traced the sensual line of his mouth with her fingertip and fought the ache in her throat. She closed her eyes, hoping he wouldn't see the tears caught at the base of her lashes. When she could trust her voice, she said quietly, "So I'm the best so far. Well, that's something."

"Chaton—"

"It doesn't matter," said Reba, covering his lips with her fingers, silencing whatever words he had been going to offer in place of the only ones she wanted to hear. "I'm a big girl, Chance. I don't need empty words from you. We please each other greatly. That's enough," she said, brushing his lips with her own.

His hands clenched in her hair as though he sensed her retreating from him. He kissed her with a hunger that had nothing to do with passion. She smoothed his hair away from his forehead, unconsciously comforting him as though it had been he rather than she who had been hurt.

"Reba," he said, his voice roughened by emotion, "we have to talk."

"Don't worry," she said calmly. "Now that I understand, I won't embarrass you again by talking about love."

"That's not what I—"

"I'm cold, Chance. I think it's time we went back to camp."

He looked down at her, frustration tightening his lips into a thin line. He was holding her naked in his arms, yet she had never been further away from him. For a second he was tempted to keep her there, to make love to her until she came apart in his arms again. The temptation showed in every line of his face, in the sudden tension of his powerful body.

"You're very special to me," he said, searching her eyes for the emotion that had blazed there so recently. He kissed her lips gently but sensed no softening. "Damn it, Reba, you're a hell of a lot more to me than a good lay!"

"And a hell of a lot less than a good love," she said, smiling crookedly. "It's all right, Chance. I've had a lot of practice at not being loved. I'll settle for being enjoyed. But not this instant, okay? There's such a thing as recovery time."

He knew that she didn't mean recovery time from lovemaking; he also knew that if he pointed that out, she would retreat even further from him. With a last kiss, he moved away from her. When she held out her hand for the clothes he had gathered up, he hesitated before giving them to her, plainly telling her that he would rather dress her himself.

Reba pulled on her clothes quickly, fumbling over the buttons that had given Chance so much pleasure. She sat down and began lacing up her hiking boots, struggling with the unfamiliar fastenings. He was already dressed, standing silhouetted against the moon, flashlight in one hand and shotgun in the other, waiting for her.

A twig snapped loudly in the chaparral just down the ridge. As Chance spun toward the sound, he braced the shotgun against his hip and pumped a shell into the firing chamber. A cone of dazzling white blazed out from the flashlight. Caught in the unexpected brilliance, a young buck froze with one foot lifted. The flashlight winked out, freeing the deer. With a single clean leap the buck vanished back into the chaparral.

Breath held, Reba listened to the retreating sounds.

The image of Chance was burned into her mind. His speed, his skill, the flashlight held on top of the shotgun's barrel to ensure that whatever came within the cone of light would literally be under his gun. Yet he had not pulled the trigger. She doubted that she would have been as discriminating under similar pressure. The sudden sound out of the darkness had sent her pulse into overdrive as she imagined being surrounded by dope smugglers bent on vengeance. Even now, her hands were shaking.

Chance knelt in front of Reba and laced up her boots. When he was finished, he pulled her to her feet and held her close. She hesitated, then put her arms around him, returning his hug. Whatever Chance was or wasn't, whatever he said or didn't say, he was gentle with her. It was enough.

It had to be.

Chapter 7

REBA SAT UP, HER HEART POUNDING WILDLY. ALL around her was night, not even a pale shimmer of moon to outline the ridgelines. A billion stars blazed coldly overhead, emphasizing rather than lighting the darkness. She shivered, wondering what had awakened her.

"Go back to sleep, *chaton*," said a deep voice from beside her. "There's nothing to worry about. It was just a twitch of the dragon's tail."

"What?" she said. Then, "Oh. An earthquake."

She sensed Chance's smile in his voice. "Yes. A few more fractures in the tourmaline buried beneath us."

With a yawn, she lay down again. He reached out, pulling her into the curve of his body. Last night he had zipped their two sleeping bags together, over her protests. Now she was glad for the intimate nest. She put her head on his shoulder, her arm across his chest, and felt very safe. She yawned again.

He laughed softly and nuzzled her hair.

"What's so funny?" she asked sleepily.

"You. Only someone from Los Angeles would be frightened by a deer and yawn at an earthquake."

"It was just a tiny shaker," she murmured sleepily.

"The deer wasn't very big, either."

Reba fell asleep before she thought of a suitable answer. She stirred restlessly during the minute aftershocks of the earthquake, but she didn't wake again until dawn.

The first thing she was aware of as she drifted slowly up from the depths of sleep was Chance's warmth, his hands moving over her, bringing a pleasure that made her body melt in liquid waves. His mouth caressed her from her temple to her navel, a sliding heat that sealed the breath in her throat. Half awake, half asleep, wholly vulnerable to his touch, she could only twist languidly, helplessly, consumed by her Tiger God.

When he finally came to her, she was crying his name, suspended in a sweet agony that only he could end. He moved slowly, powerfully, claiming her more deeply with each wave of pleasure that shook her until she came apart, giving herself to him without reservation. Only then did he succumb to her softness and heat, the siren call of ecstasy deep within her.

For a long time afterward, Chance simply held Reba, caressing her with gentle lips and hands. She lay without speaking, holding onto his solid warmth, slowly becoming aware of her own identity again. She knew she had been taken without warning, without even the smallest opportunity to say no. He hadn't given her a chance, but in the aftermath of sharing such extraordinary pleasure, she couldn't be angry with him.

"Forgive me," he whispered against her cheek. "I had to know if I had driven you away last night. I had to know that from the core of you, not from whatever civilized expectations have been pasted on you by people who don't know better or don't care. Now I know. No matter what is said or isn't said, you want me as deeply as I want you."

Reba wondered if love could be one of the "civilized expectations" Chance was referring to. She didn't ask, however. She had promised him she wouldn't speak of love again. It was a promise she would keep as long as she could. The day she broke it would be the day she would walk away from him and never look back no matter what it cost her.

"Reba?" he asked, holding her face between his hands, looking at the cinnamon brilliance of her eyes. "Are you still angry about last night, *chaton?*"

"No," she said, kissing Chance before he could see the sadness beneath her honesty. "How could I be? You give me . . . beauty."

With a hoarse sound he held her painfully close. She returned the fierce hug without protest. This morning she knew the simple, devastating truth: She would rather be wanted by Chance Walker than loved by any other man.

"Just for that," he said after a long moment, loosening his arms reluctantly, "you get breakfast in bed."

"I didn't see the bell for room service."

"No bell. Magic."

"I believe it."

"You do?"

"Sure," she said, laughter just beneath her words. "I went to bed wearing clothes and woke up wearing you. What other explanation could there be but magic?"

Chance smiled like a tiger. "I'll explain it to you sometime, in intimate detail. Very intimate."

He unzipped the sleeping bag and stood beside her, as naked as the mountains and as unconcerned. The thick gold light of dawn poured over him like honey, flowing over his skin, underlining the power of his body with velvet shadows.

"I was wrong," she said softly.

He turned toward her with the grace of fire, his eyes transparent green, watching her.

"You're more beautiful than the Tiger God."

For an instant he changed, emotion rippling through him. When he spoke, his voice was husky. "Close your eyes, my woman, or the only breakfast you get will be me."

Slowly, dark lashes swept down, concealing Reba's radiant cinnamon eyes. She drifted into a half-sleep until she heard the sound of a hatchet splitting wood. She opened her eyes and saw Chance. He was a few feet away, dressed in jeans, a black flannel shirt and a leather jacket that had seen much use in rough country. His back was turned to her as he worked. She admired the easy skill that reduced stovewood to kindling. He looked over his shoulder suddenly, sensing her attention.

"Coffee in a few minutes," he said. "How do you feel about steak and eggs?"

"Predatory," she said, stretching like a cat and then hurriedly bringing her arms back inside the sleeping bag. "Brrr! I've heard of hotels conserving energy, but this is ridiculous." With a disgruntled sound she pulled the sleeping bag all the way up to her eyes.

"I'll speak to the management about it," Chance promised, smiling to himself.

"Do that. And while you're at it, ask the laundry service what happened to my clothes."

"Try my side of the sleeping bag."

Reba groped around and found her clothes. She held them in the light and looked at them. "Your clothes are clean," she said accusingly. "Mine aren't."

"I had to walk to the Toyota."

She smiled winningly. "I knew you'd understand."

Laughing, Chance went to the Toyota and pulled out

a change of clothes for Reba. He handed them to her and waited. He wasn't disappointed. As soon as the cold clothes touched her, she yelped.

"Warm them up in the sleeping bag while I shave," he said, smothering a smile.

Muttering to herself, Reba did just that. When she could touch the clothes without shivering, she pulled them on. The second pair of jeans he had bought for her fit as well as the first pair had. The shirt was a bit more practical than the many-buttoned blouse had been. Long-sleeved, flannel, in shades of orange and russet, the shirt warmed her immediately. She rubbed her cheek approvingly over the soft material.

The fire crackled, sending heat and a pale silvery smoke into the dawn. When Chance finished shaving, he looked over in time to see Reba smoothing her cheek against the soft shirt he had bought for her. Smiling, he walked over to her.

"Warm enough now?"

She nodded. "There's just one thing," she said, pushing her heavy hair away from her face.

"Yes?"

"I can't figure out where the maid put my brush when she cleaned the room."

"This brush?" asked Chance, pulling a beautiful ivory hairbrush out of his jacket pocket.

"How did you guess?" she said dryly.

"The amber inlay matched this," he said, pulling an ivory-and-amber comb out of another pocket.

"I was wondering what happened to that. Have you noticed that my combs have a habit of sticking to your fingers?"

Chance examined his hands with interest. "Now that you mention it, I am getting quite a collection of your combs." He knelt behind her. "I'll make it up to you."

Reba smiled as his hands caressed her hair. "There goes breakfast."

Chance lifted her hair and gave a lingering kiss to the nape of her neck. His moustache brushed softly over her skin, sending shivers visibly through her. With a soft curse, he let her hair sift out of his hands and began brushing the honey-colored waves. She made a sound of pure sensual pleasure and closed her eyes. He brushed her hair until it was a gleaming mass swirling down the center of her back. Even when the last tangle was smoothed, he continued brushing with firm, gentle strokes, enjoying the shimmer and feel of her hair.

"You can steal every comb I have," sighed Reba. "In fact, I insist on it."

The rough-edged purr of Chance's laugh tingled over her. He gathered her hair in his hands and began braiding it in a single long braid down her back. "No hair piled high for you today, my woman. Shorter is better down in the China Queen." He finished braiding quickly, secured his work with a rawhide thong and admired her hair. "I missed my calling. I should have been a lady's maid."

Reba nearly choked on her laughter at the thought of Chance Walker as a dainty dresser of wealthy women. He let her laugh for a moment before he pulled gently on her braid until she fell backwards against him. He kissed her until all thought of laughter fled. Then he tucked her firmly into the sleeping bag and went back to preparing breakfast.

The smell of steak broiling made Reba realize how hungry she was.

"How do you like your eggs?" asked Chance.

"Cooked the fastest way you know," she answered, listening to her stomach growl.

"Hungry?" he asked, laughter rippling beneath the question.

"Starving," she admitted. "Must be the night air and all."

"Especially the 'and all.'"

"Such modesty," she said tartly.

Chance looked at Reba with eyes that reflected fire. "Such honesty," he said quietly. "I'll never lie to you, even as a joke. Just as you haven't lied to me."

Reba started to say that she wasn't telling him the full truth, either, and hadn't been since the subject of love was closed between them. But to say anything would be to open the subject, to break her promise to him and herself. So she smiled and spoke about something else entirely.

"When do we go into the China Queen?"

Chance's head came up sharply, eyes narrowed, his face as hard as the mountains. He searched Reba's expression ruthlessly, looking for something beneath her smile. Her smile faded. Silently she wondered why he responded almost savagely whenever she raised the subject of the mine.

"What's wrong?" she asked.

"I was wondering why lies and the China Queen are connected in your mind," he said bluntly.

She hesitated, off balance. "They aren't," she said, confusion and honesty clear in her voice. "Are they connected in yours?"

Chance turned the steaks, squinting against the sizzle and spatter of fat falling into the flames. "Two eggs or three?" he asked, reaching toward the ice chest.

"Two," she said quietly, realizing that he wasn't going to answer her question. No lies, no evasions, just silence.

In a few minutes Chance brought Reba's plate to her, then returned for his own and sat next to her.

"Some day," he said evenly, "I'll answer your question. But not now. In some ways you know me better than anyone alive, and in others you don't know me at all. You would misunderstand whatever I said now." He took her hand and pressed his lips to her palm in a quick, fierce kiss. "How do you like your coffee? Cream or sugar? Both?"

"Black as a miner's heart."

Chance's eyes narrowed for an instant, then he smiled unwillingly. "Black it is." He released her hand and went back to the fire, returning with two steaming mugs of black coffee. "Careful," he said softly as she reached for a mug. "It's as hot and strong as a certain woman's love."

Reba's hand jerked, then steadied. "Sounds undrinkable," she said lightly, taking the cup and setting it aside. "I'll let it cool."

"Some things never cool," said Chance, tilting her head with his finger until she was forced to meet his eyes. "The sun. The core of the earth. You. Me. Give us time, *chaton.*"

She looked into his silver-green eyes and said the only thing she could: "Yes."

They finished breakfast and cleaned up the camp in a silence that was as natural as the sunlight streaming down the rugged granite slopes above the China Queen. When the last utensil had been put away, the last ember buried and the food locked in the Toyota beyond the reach of small animals, Chance turned toward Reba.

"Ready for the China Queen?"

Excitement made her eyes brilliant. "I thought you'd never ask."

He smiled and explained how to use the equipment he had gathered, particularly the miner's lamp.

"The battery pack goes on your belt. This switch turns it on. There are three positions on the switch.

We'll use the low illumination most of the time. Once you start using your lamp, don't look directly at me when we talk. That way we won't blind each other."

In addition to the helmets with built-in lamps, Chance had laid out the shotgun in a leather carrying sheath, two flashlights, two pick-hammers, two canteens, a pick, a shovel, two hunting knives with sheaths and a small leather rucksack. He slipped one flashlight, one hammer and one knife in place on a wide leather belt rather like a carpenter's. He put the belt around Reba's hips, saw that it was too loose and shook his head.

"You're too strong to have such a slender body," he said, pulling the hunting knife out of its sheath and making another hole for the buckle's tongue. He pulled the belt around her again. It fit well this time, riding securely on her hips. "It will feel awkward at first but you'll get used to it."

"Are we going to be separated?" she asked, looking at the duplication of equipment on her belt and his.

"Do you wear a seatbelt because you expect to have an accident?" he asked dryly.

"I see your point. What's in that?" she asked, gesturing to the single rucksack.

"Food."

"We don't need two of that?"

"You can go for weeks without food. Water is another matter. So is light. Men have gone crazy in the dark long before they died of thirst."

Reba moved uneasily. "Not a pleasant thought," she said finally.

"Neither is a crash at one hundred kilometers per hour."

"*Touché,*" she sighed.

"Still want to go into the Queen?"

"Yes."

Chance caught Reba's face between his hands. "There's just one other thing."

She waited, searching his silver-green eyes. "What?"

"Once we're inside the Queen, if I say stop, you stop. If I say jump, you jump. If I say don't dig, you don't dig. If I say quiet, you're quiet. All right?"

She measured his intensity, knowing that he wasn't requiring that kind of obedience from her on a whim. "All right," she said quietly.

His kiss was both gentle and hard at the same time. "I'd rather you didn't go into the China Queen at all," he admitted in a husky voice. "Mines can be as unpredictable as drunk drivers. I don't want anything to happen to you."

"I won't be wrapped in cotton and kept in a safe, boring place," she said evenly. "I had enough of that when I was a child. I'll obey you when we're in the mine, Chance, but I'll obey because I *am* an adult, not a child."

"How well I know," he murmured. "Very much a woman. My woman." His thumbs slowly caressed Reba's cheekbones, then he sighed and released her. He shrugged into the shotgun sheath, carrying it across his back like a quiver of arrows. He swung the rucksack into place over the flat sheath, fastened on his own belt and said, "Let's go before I decide there is something I'd rather explore than a cranky old mine."

"Cranky?" she asked, falling into step beside him.

"That's her best mood," said Chance flatly. He looked down at Reba, saw curiosity lighting her cinnamon eyes. "Mines are like ships," he explained. "They have personalities."

"And, like ships, mines are feminine?"

"Yes," he said, smiling crookedly, "because most miners are masculine."

"And you see the China Queen as cranky?"

"A regular bitch," he said in a matter-of-fact tone. "She's been ignored for a long time and she doesn't like it."

"An understandable reaction," said Reba wryly.

Chance grunted and said nothing. He led the way into the Queen's black mouth, switched on his lamp and waited for Reba to switch on hers. The illumination from their helmets looked like pale yellow broth in the brilliant cataract of white light pouring through the mine's opening.

"Once we get further inside," said Chance, walking easily over the dirt and rock floor, "it may seem like the mountain is riding just above your shoulders, waiting to fall and crush you. If the feeling doesn't pass, tell me. It's nothing to be ashamed of. Being underground simply takes some people that way."

"Claustrophobia."

"Call it what you like. Just tell me if it gets to you. I'd a hell of a lot rather turn back early than carry you out of the mine sweating and screaming."

"You've had to do that?" Reba asked, her mouth suddenly dry.

"A time or three. Never twice with the same person, though. Once they lose faith with the earth they don't come back."

"There's more to prospecting than picks and shovels, isn't there?"

"Too bloody right," Chance said flatly.

The last remnant of daylight faded unobtrusively behind them. In the sable darkness the helmet lights seemed like solid cones of white brilliance sweeping the tunnel. Light reflected from Chance's face, revealing the hard lines of his cheek and jaw. His eyes glinted silver-white. The walls of the tunnel absorbed light, giving back only a subliminal wash of illumination.

Though Reba said nothing, she was disappointed. She had expected something more spectacular, some sparkle or glitter that would hint at the wealth of beauty that could be hidden beneath the earth.

The tunnel divided. The right-hand fork was wider than the left, and the walls were composed of lighter rock.

"Pegmatite vein," said Chance, sweeping his light over the wall. Flakes of mica and minute quartz crystals mixed with other reflective minerals winked back at him, creating a glittering tapestry that excelled the brilliance of a starry night.

"Oh . . ." sighed Reba.

"More like what you expected?" asked Chance, taking her hand.

"Yes. It's beautiful."

"Most mines are ugly, little more than holes gouged out of unwilling ground. Tourmaline mines are one of the few diggings that live up to our childhood fantasies of sparkling rocks heaped up in a dragon's black lair."

"Or the Seven Dwarfs' diamond mine."

Chance laughed briefly. "If there's anything uglier than an underground African diamond mine, I haven't found it. Gold mines are a close second."

"But quartz crystals are beautiful," objected Reba.

"Bloody little gold is found in 'jewelry' rock," he said. "I've seen one rich pocket of gem-quality quartz crystals laced with sunbursts of gold. It was stunning, almost overwhelming—and the whole pocket would have fit in your kitchen sink. Most gold is refined by ounces out of tons of dark rock." Chance's headlamp swept the glittering tunnel walls. "But here," he said softly, "everything is bright."

He brushed the wall lightly with the pointed side of his hammer. A small shower of material glittered to the floor. "Glad I'm not planning on dynamiting anything," he said. "The vibrations would tear this place apart."

Reba looked at the wall and said nothing, listening to the whisper of rock particles sifting down. She sensed Chance studying her, weighing her reaction to being beneath earth that was more fragile than it appeared.

"I'm all right," she said quietly. "It's just hard to believe that anything bigger than my fingernail could come out of that mishmash of minerals."

"Pala tourmaline is a miracle," he agreed. "Have you seen samples of tourmaline in matrix from the Empress mine?"

"Once. In a museum. Pink crystals as long as my hand, set in a matrix of opaque quartz crystals. You could see the fracture lines in the tourmaline, hundreds of lines, yet the larger crystal structure remained intact. The idea of finding something that beautiful in the China Queen has haunted me ever since," she admitted softly, playing her headlamp over the pale, rough tunnel walls.

"A lot of the Empress' tourmaline in matrix didn't stay together," said Chance. "That's why the ones that did are literally priceless. There is nothing to equal them in any mine in any place on earth."

Reba listened to the excitement surging just beneath his calm voice and realized that being in the China Queen must be a dream come true for a man like Chance—to be in the one spot on earth where a unique treasure might be found. What wouldn't a man do for that? Certainly it would take more than the risk of crumbling tunnel walls to deter him.

"Reba?"

She turned toward him with a start, then looked away quickly, realizing that she had flashed her headlamp directly in his face.

"You all right?" he asked.

"Just thinking," she said.

"About tunnel walls?"

"No. About you. In some ways, being here must be the culmination of a lifetime of dreams for you."

Chance moved his head slightly, illuminating her face in the backwash of his harsh white helmet lamp. He looked at her for a long time without saying anything. Then he turned away and played his helmet light over the pale tunnel walls. "Yes. It is. I'm sure there's tourmaline here, Reba. It's been waiting for millions of years to be found. *And I will find it.*"

The quiet intensity of his vow held her motionless for a moment. "It's too dangerous, Chance," she said finally. "Even for a man of your experience. No one will lend me enough money to make the China Queen safe to work in as long as I can only offer fifty percent of an abandoned mine as collateral. I doubt if even one hundred percent would be enough."

"There will be a way," he said, moving slowly down the tunnel's steepening decline, examining the wall as he went. "When you want something badly enough there's always a way."

Reba watched Chance's helmet lamp slowly withdrawing down the tunnel and tried not to cry out in protest. She was beginning to understand what Chance had meant when he'd said that prospecting got in the blood worse than malaria. He was barely aware of her now. She might as well be alone in the mine. Slowly she played her light over the part of the tunnel she had left behind. The walls glittered, then opened into darkness that eventually led back to sunlight.

When Reba looked forward again, Chance was little more than a small cone of brightness moving down and away from her into a darkness unlike anything she had ever known before. She doubted that he'd notice if she turned and walked out of the China Queen, leaving him alone. And perhaps she should do just that. What right did she have to hitch a ride on his dream, distracting him with her foolish questions and clumsiness underground and . . . jealousy.

Because she was jealous of the China Queen, its hold on Chance, the incredible depth of emotion called out of him by the mine's timeless night and glittering promises.

"Reba?"

The voice was gentle, reassuring, as warm as the hands stroking down her arms to her fingertips, catching and holding her.

"It's time to go back to camp, *chaton*." Chance lifted her into his arms. "It's all right," he murmured soothingly, starting back the way they had come. "Close your eyes. When you open them there will be nothing around you but sunlight."

Reba's arms went around his neck. "It's not that," she said. "I'm not afraid of the mine. Not in the way you mean."

"Then what are you afraid of?" he asked softly. "And don't tell me that you weren't afraid. I saw your face."

"I was watching you." She hesitated. "I'm glad you didn't know who I was in Death Valley," she whispered in a rush. "If you had, I'd never be sure whether you wanted me or my mine."

"Don't say that." Chance's voice was savage, his arms bruising. *"Don't even think it!"* He glared at her with feral silver eyes. The light from his helmet was like a blow, making her flinch away. "Do you hear me? *Do you?"*

"Yes," Reba said, eyes closed, unable to bear either the white light or his eyes.

She heard two distinct clicks, then forgot everything as his lips came down over hers in a bruising kiss. She was too startled to respond. With a hoarse sound he forced her mouth open, taking her sweet warmth. For an instant she stiffened, overwhelmed by the primitive power of his kiss, then she softened beneath his invasion, responding to the raw need in him, a need that transcended simple male hunger.

As Chance sensed her response, he groaned softly. His mouth gentled, savoring rather than demanding, sharing rather than dominating. Without lifting his lips he shifted her weight, letting her slide down his body. He held her in a cage of strength and warmth, molding her to each breath he took, each tremor of need that whispered seductively through him.

Reba's head tilted back over the hard muscles of his arm as her body became a warm outline of his. Clinging to Chance, she gave him the response he so urgently sought, telling him with her touch that she was his.

After a long, long time he lifted his mouth.

"Chance," she said shakily, eyes still closed, "I didn't—"

"No," he said, taking her lips once more, devouring them tenderly, fiercely. "I don't want to hear about it again. *Ever.*"

Reba opened her eyes, only to see impenetrable darkness all around her. She had never experienced such a total absence of light. If she hadn't been holding Chance she wouldn't have known he was there.

The darkness was a living thing with weight and texture and a presence that overwhelmed everything it touched . . . and it touched everything, a soundless primal tide of black lapping over her, dissolving her. With a sense of icy certainty, Reba knew why men went mad before they died of thirst.

"Chance, what happened to our light?" she asked carefully, her voice strained, rising.

"Close your eyes," he murmured, then put his

calloused hand over her eyes to make sure that she
obeyed.

She heard two clicks.

"Open your eyes," he said, tilting her face to the side
with his hand.

She looked. Two white cones of light illuminated the
mine again. She sighed and leaned against him.

"Sorry," Chance said, smoothing his moustache
over Reba's cheek. "I thought you knew I'd turned
out the lights. I didn't want to blind you." His
lips felt the racing pulse on her neck. "Are you all
right?"

"Yes," she said, feeling foolish now that the lights
were on again. "I'd just never seen, or *not* seen,
anything like that. Even the blackest night has a star or
two."

"The first time is always a shock," said Chance,
taking Reba's hand and leading her back down into the
China Queen. "Three days after my mother died, Dad
took me down in a mine and turned out the lights on
me. No warning, just darkness like the end of everything. I screamed my bloody head off. Luck grabbed
me and hugged me until I stopped screaming. Then he
cussed Dad hot enough to burn my ears. It was the only
time I ever heard Luck angry with Dad.

"I worshipped Luck after that. No matter how he
teased me when I got older, I thought he walked on
water. I always wanted to repay him. But when the
time came, I was digging and he was drinking with a
diamond miner. Luck died before he even knew his
brother was coming to help."

Reba's fingers tightened within Chance's hand. She
wanted to say she was sorry, but the words sounded
banal even in her mind. And the only other words she
could offer—*I love you*—weren't wanted.

"Don't look so sad," he murmured, tracing her lips

with a fingertip. "It was twenty years ago. A long time."

"It still hurts, doesn't it?" she asked quietly.

"Yes."

"Then it's as though it just happened. And it will keep on happening."

"It doesn't hurt as much as it used to. It doesn't happen as often." Chance lifted Reba's hand, kissed the fragrance of her skin. He made a startled sound as he remembered something. "Where are your gloves?"

"I took them off to scratch my head. The helmet itches."

He chuckled. "Remember them when we dig."

"I'm glad you mentioned that."

"Gloves?"

"Digging. When and where?"

"Patience is a virtue."

"Tell it to your mirror," she retorted.

"We have to go through a few more twists and turns and tunnel choices. Your ancestors had bad luck guessing where the pegmatite would go next. Part of their trouble came with the territory. Earthquakes are notorious for snatching away promising veins and hiding them with the devil's own cunning."

"What was the rest of my ancestors' trouble?"

"Ignorance," said Chance bluntly. "From the looks of these tunnels, there wasn't a real miner in the lot. Well, maybe one. A long time ago."

"Great-grandfather Mitchell," said Reba promptly. "Or was it great-great-grandfather? Anyway, family legend has it that he was a hard-rock miner from South Africa. He was the one who bought what became the China Queen, plus the mineral rights to the surrounding land. He didn't have long to mine the Queen, though."

"Cave-in?" asked Chance.

Reba took a quick breath at the casual way Chance mentioned dying in a mine. "No. Cholera."

Chance grunted. "He was a miner, all right. Bad earth, bad water, bad men and bad luck."

"I don't know about the men, but—"

"Quiet!"

Reba froze, caught more by the pressure of Chance's hand than by his command. She held her breath. From somewhere in the darkness came the tiny sounds of grit sifting down. After a few moments Chance's grip on her fingers eased.

"Feel that?" he asked softly.

"What?"

"The dragon's tail twitching," he murmured. "Very subtle. More a vibration in the air than anything else."

Reba shuddered. "I didn't feel anything." Privately, she was glad she hadn't. The idea of an earthquake inside a mine was much more disturbing to her than it had been when she was on the surface, curled in Chance's arms. "Is it safe?"

She sensed more than saw his shrug. "How safe is safe?" he asked. "The quake wasn't nearly hard enough to bring down the mine, if that's what you mean. There's no guarantee about the next one, though. Want to go back up?"

"I want the earthquakes to go away," Reba said firmly.

"Sorry," Chance said, his voice wry. "I can make the lights come on but keeping the rest of it together is beyond me."

"You don't seem worried."

He hesitated. "I'm always worried when I'm down in a mine I don't know. When I was here before, I took only a very fast tour of the Queen, just enough to reassure me that she wasn't a bloody great trap waiting to be sprung. There are several tunnels where I won't take you. There's only one where I won't go myself."

"Where's that?"

"The left branch where we first came in. Partway down the tunnel there's a slab of rock hanging from the ceiling. It's been there since the tunnel was dug, but I wouldn't bet a grain of sand on that slab being up there tomorrow. On the other hand, the rock may still be hanging when the rest of the tunnels are no bigger than a worm's gullet. Mines aren't a sure thing, Reba. You simply ante up and play the hand you're dealt the best way you know how."

"Sounds like the freeway during the first rains of the season," she said. "That's when the oil that has seeped into the cracks over the dry months is forced out by the rain. The oil floats up to the surface of the road. Slippery time in the City of the Angels."

"Do you stay off the freeway?" Chance asked curiously.

"No"—dryly—"just off the brakes. Gently, gently, as the saying goes."

Light flashed startlingly as Chance bent and gave Reba a quick kiss. "You'll be a bloody good miner. That's the way to treat a mine, too. Gently, gently, until you've taken its measure. Then you can swing your pick as hard as you like."

The pale walls of the tunnel became dark between one step and the next. Reba paused, swinging her light over the nearer wall. "What happened?"

"Discontinuity," Chance said, tugging irresistibly at her hand. "A long time ago, this was the surface. The pegmatite was eroded away. Later this layer of dirt was deposited on top, then compressed as more stuff was deposited on top of it. Earthquakes shifted it all around, too, tilting some layers, breaking others, and burying the rest."

"Nothing valuable in the dirt?" she hazarded.

"Not unless you want to raise crops."

"No thanks. I kill plants faster than the average defoliant. It's so bad that the nurserymen in the area all know me. The last time I went in the man gave me a pet rock and told me not to come back."

Chance's deep laughter echoed through the tunnel, returning doubled. "Definitely a miner," he said, rubbing his moustache over her knuckles. "Definitely my woman," he added softly. "Watch your head. Your family never bothered to dig this one out. Just as well. It's crumbly stuff here."

Reba waited while Chance ducked into an unappealing little side hole in the larger tunnel. As he went in he gouged two lines on the right-hand side of the smaller opening. She looked up the tunnel and saw other small holes leading off in other directions. She wondered where they led, and why Chance had chosen the opening he had just disappeared into.

"Coming?" Chance's voice floated back into the main tunnel.

"Right behind you," sighed Reba.

She ducked and walked bent over for what seemed like a long time but probably wasn't more than a hundred steps. The floor was ragged, catching at the sides of her feet with unpredictable ruts, legacy of dead miners' wheelbarrows. Gradually the composition of the tunnel changed, became lighter, dirt mixed with minerals, as though a pegmatite vein had burst and blended with more ordinary earth. Finally, mineral masses predominated.

"You can stand up now."

Chance's voice was some distance off to the right. Reba stood and turned, keeping her head tilted down so as not to blind him accidentally.

"Oh . . . !" Slowly Reba turned in a full circle,

trying to measure the dimensions of the unexpected room. In the end she gave up, unable to estimate distances in the tricky light. Bigger than her living room, surely. Two times? Three? Five? It was impossible to tell without pacing off the area, because rough pillars of earth supported the ceiling at random intervals, breaking her cone of light into brightness and deep wedges of shadow.

From every point, minerals glinted back at her, even from the most dense shadows. The far wall was almost white.

"Granite," said Chance, seeing the direction of her light. "Hard rock and no reward. This is as deep as the Queen goes, at least in this direction."

"All this and no tourmaline," she sighed. "My poor ancestors, scratching at a mountain, looking for shiny little mites that never existed."

"There could be tourmaline under your feet, above your head, in the pillars, in the walls."

Reba turned, moving her light just enough so that Chance's expression was visible to her. "You mean that, don't you?"

"Of course. You're surrounded by pegmatite," he said, his voice deep, rich with certainty and excitement. "You'll never be closer to tourmaline until you hold it in your hand."

Her head tilted back as she scanned the ceiling. Light flashed back from a pocket of white overhead.

"Don't move," said Chance suddenly. Then, in a reassuring voice, "Everything's all right. Just don't move."

Reba froze. Chance's light swept over the ceiling until the two cones of illumination joined.

"Okay, you can move. I just didn't want to lose the white witch you discovered."

"Try that again," she said flatly. "In English, please."

Chance's teeth reflected the shine of helmet light. "See that pocket of lepidolite near the column, all white and shiny, mica flakes as big as your smile?"

She stared along the beam of her light. "I see it."

"Then you're closer to tourmaline than you've ever been."

Reba's light jerked, then steadied. "What do you mean?"

"Tourmaline matrix," he said calmly; but currents of eagerness seethed just beneath his control. "I wonder why I didn't see it the last time I was here. . . . Hold your light steady."

Chance waited until he was sure that Reba wouldn't move before he swept his own light in a pattern across the ceiling, then down to the floor just beneath the pocket of lepidolite. He laughed softly as he realized that the recent tremors in the earth had caused part of the ceiling to slough away, revealing the white witch beneath.

"Thank you, dragon," Chance murmured, walking over and kneeling swiftly.

His light raked over the small mound that had fallen from the ceiling. With quick, sure movements he probed the crumbling matrix. He unhooked the canteen, poured a bit of water into his palm and smiled.

"Come here, *chaton*."

Reba walked over quickly. Her light outlined his powerful shoulders as he sat on his heels, holding something hidden in his hand. "What is it?"

His hand opened. On his palm glittered shards of shocking pink crystal. Nested among them was one tiny, perfect needle of tourmaline.

Chapter 8

REBA MADE A SOUND OF DISBELIEF AS SHE LOOKED AT THE fuchsia glitter in Chance's palm. He saw the pleasure and the wonder shining in her eyes. He looked at the tourmaline fragments in his hand, seeing them as she did . . . pieces of dreams condensed into molten pink, hot promises shimmering and whispering in the cold wash of a miner's light. He smiled and plucked the shattered crystals from their white bed of crushed matrix. Tiny flakes of mica stuck to his fingertips, making them almost as silver as his eyes.

"Hold out your hand," he said softly.

He poured the crystal fragments into her soft palm, reserving the perfect needle of tourmaline. She sighed and shifted her hand, making light melt and run over the piled shards of pink. After a few moments she looked up and saw him watching her.

"I know, I know," said Reba, laughing at herself. "These aren't worth two cents at a garage sale, but to me they're . . ." Her voice faded.

"Signposts on the road to Oz," Chance finished for her, smiling gently.

"Yes," she sighed, watching the play of light over shattered tourmaline. "If only we'd gotten here sooner."

"Before the dragon rolled over and crushed them?" Reba's lips curved. "How did you guess?"

His fingertip touched her nose, leaving a shiny residue of mica. "If it makes you feel any better, coming down here last night wouldn't have helped. We're several million years too late for these poor beauties. But not for this one," Chance added, holding out the slender, flawless needle of tourmaline between his thumb and forefinger.

The crystal was an inch long, a sixth of an inch wide, and naturally faceted into a many-sided shaft. Though too small to have the shocking pink color of the larger crystal fragments, the shaft of tourmaline clearly showed the tricolor progression along its length that was unique to Pala's tourmaline. It was as though the crystal were a cylinder lifted out of a watermelon. Nine-tenths of the tourmaline's length was a pale, clear pink. Then there was a thin band of transparent white, like the rind of a fruit. A blunt cap of clear green marked the terminal phase of the crystal, recalling a watermelon's dark skin.

Hesitantly, Reba touched the crystal with her fingernail, afraid that the mineral would vanish like a dream at the first touch of reality. "It's real," she breathed. "Oh, Chance, it's real!"

"Very real," he agreed, "but not half so beautiful as your smile." His lips moved slowly over hers as he placed the crystal in her palm. "Welcome to Oz."

She laughed softly, her breath a sweet warmth on his lips. "Thank you." Then, with an eagerness she couldn't conceal, "Can we dig some more?"

Chance smiled ruefully. "Spoken like a true gouger. Yes, we can dig. But first . . ."

Reba, who had been turning toward the pale fall of lapidolite on the floor, looked back. "First?"

Instead of answering, he pulled her against his body, wrapping her in his strength and warmth. She closed her eyes and let him flow over her, opening her lips to him with a surrender and invitation that had become as natural to her in his arms as her own accelerated heartbeat. The sweet, firm movement of his tongue over hers sent sensations shimmering through her like light pouring through crystal. When he lifted his head she had forgotten all about the tiny fragments and single perfect tourmaline held inside her closed hand.

"Thank you," sighed Chance against her lips.

"My pleasure," she assured him, laughter and longing making her voice smoky.

"Not the kiss"—he smiled—"although it was well worth the thanks."

"Then what?" she asked, smoothing her lips over his moustache, enjoying the rough silk of its texture on her sensitive skin.

"You," he said simply. "Seeing the China Queen through your eyes is like being young again, everything new and shining, hope and laughter."

He kissed her slowly, moving his hands over her as though he wanted to memorize everything about her and the moment that she melted against him and they discovered again how perfectly they fit together. After a long time he reluctantly lifted his head.

"If we don't stop," said Chance huskily, "the only thing you'll find in this mine is me."

Reba smiled. One hand moved down hi. .st, tracing the muscles beneath the black flannel shirt. She paused at his belt before letting her hand drift lower. She heard his breath catch and thicken in the instant before he pulled her wandering hand to his mouth. He bit the pad of flesh at the base of her thumb with a restrained ferocity that made her shiver.

"The Queen's floor is too rough for your satin body," he said regretfully, "no matter who's on top when we make love."

Her eyes shimmered with desire and laughter and love. "It would be worth a few scrapes here and there."

Chance's eyes changed as he reached for her. He gave her a hungry, penetrating kiss that filled her senses with his taste. His arms crushed her but she didn't protest, wanting to be even closer to him, wanting to feel him inside her, a part of her. With a hoarse, male sound he held her at arm's length.

"I don't trust myself to be gentle enough with you," he said roughly, his eyes devouring her. "If I get you down on the floor I won't want to let you up. Once, twice, three times. It wouldn't matter. All I'd have to do is look at you and I'd want you all over again. You're a fire in me, *chaton*."

Reba's fingers trembled as she touched Chance's lips, feeling her own body burn with need of him. With a reluctance that she couldn't conceal, she stepped back out of his arms.

"Tourmaline," she said in a determined, shaky voice. "That's why we're here, right?"

His laugh was almost harsh. "I never thought I'd have to be reminded why I was down in the China Queen." He drew a deep breath. "Tourmaline it is," he said firmly.

But his eyes followed the lithe curves of her body as she knelt next to the small mound of lepidolite. The rock had sloughed from the ceiling near one of the thick pillars that had been left when the rest of the room was excavated.

When Reba began sifting through the crushed and

broken minerals, Chance knelt beside her. Together
they uncovered a few more shards of bright pink. They
found a half-inch-wide shaft of pink tourmaline still
embedded in a chunk of lepidolite. The tourmaline was
a mere fragment of what it had been before the dragon
twitched and shrugged and rolled the earth like a cloak
over its massive shoulders. Even in the specimen's
diminished state, the contrast of hot pink tourmaline
and cool silver-white lepidolite was quite arresting.

"A few million years sooner," sighed Reba, when
her fingers found the bottom of the white pile and
scraped over the hard floor of the mine.

Chance smiled slightly and put the fragments of
tourmaline crystals they had gathered into a small
pouch on his belt. He would have left the worthless,
glittering pieces behind entirely but he knew that Reba
would object. He wasn't sure he blamed her. Even to
his skeptical eye they looked special, a reflection of her
joy.

Chance pulled Reba to her feet and led her a short
distance away. "Stay here," he said, getting a pair of
transparent goggles out of the rucksack. He pulled
them over his eyes and went back to the patch of white
on the ceiling. Using the sharp end of his hammer, he
probed the lepidolite. The ceiling was barely an inch
above his head. Soon his face and shoulders were
covered with shiny white grit and shimmering particles
of mica.

Reba shifted impatiently, training her light on the
pocket of rock where Chance was working. "Do you
have another pair of goggles?" she asked finally.

Chance wiped his mouth on his sleeve before answering. As he turned toward her, bits of mica and crystal
glittered in his moustache. "Yes. And no, you can't use
them. All the stuff I've found so far is small, but there's
no law that says it will stay that way. Lepidolite is

nothing but a fancy name for hunks of minerals of all sizes that crystallized out of a particular kind of magma. The only thing keeping the different minerals together is proximity and habit. I'd hate to loosen a few kilos of rock and have it come down around your tasty little ears."

She swallowed. "If it's that dangerous, why are you doing it?"

"It's not that dangerous for me," he explained with a wry smile. "I just calculate the risks differently when it's your head on the block."

Before Reba could think of an answer, Chance went back to probing the lens-shaped pocket, pausing occasionally to lower a double handful of coarse minerals to the floor. Soon he had covered the short distance to the top of the nearby column. The lens of bright white continued into the column. Chance didn't. He took off his goggles, spat grit from his mouth and turned toward Reba.

"You going to help me look for tourmaline or are you planning to stick me with all the work?" he asked innocently.

"Chance Walker, you are the most maddening—" began Reba, but whatever else she said was lost in his laughter.

With a smothered word or two, she knelt and began sifting through the loose stuff he had piled up. He worked beside her, still chuckling from time to time. She ignored him until their hands met inside the pile of shiny white. His fingers entwined in hers. He lifted her hand, kissed it quickly.

"Even grit tastes good on you," he said, his voice deep and his eyes very silver.

She shook her head, sending light swinging crazily. With a quick motion she brought his hard hand to her lips. The tip of her tongue flicked out, tasting him. Mica glittered on her tongue for an instant before it disappeared behind her smile. "You're right," she said. "On you, anything tastes good."

"You're tempting me," he said, leaning forward to kiss her. When he lifted his head, particles of mica shone above her lips where his moustache had brushed. "My woman," he murmured, "shimmering wherever I touch you."

Her lips parted and softened, shining. With a soft curse he went back to searching for tourmaline. They found many fragments and a few cylindrical segments that had been shafts of tourmaline as long and thick as Chance's finger before the earth had twisted, fracturing and finally shattering the tourmaline's crystal integrity.

"Well," sighed Reba, looking up at the patch of white shining at the top of the pillar, "back to digging in the ceiling."

Chance followed the line of her light. "No."

"Why not?"

"Let me tell you a story about digging in pillars," he said, "or shaving, as we called it on Lightning Ridge. No piece of earth is exactly the same composition through and through. The Queen, for instance, is like a haphazardly layered fruitcake filled with different-sized goodies. The cake is what holds it all together, but in some places the cake is thinner than in others. Those columns may be no more than pockets of lepidolite held together by a veneer of chemically bonded dirt."

Reba looked uneasily at the pillars rising throughout the underground room.

"On the other hand," said Chance, smiling, "the columns may be as solid as the granite at the far end of the mine. I could shave a few and find out if you like."

"Er, no thanks," she muttered, moving her head so that a nearby pillar was bathed in light. Now that she knew what to look for, she could see the differences. They may be standing in a pegmatite dike, but pegmatite was another name for a mixed mineral pudding.

"Smart woman," he said. "The Arabs weren't that bright."

She turned. "What do you mean?"

"They took some of their oil money and bought mining rights to the world's only known tsavorite mine. It was a bargain. The African government that owned it was bankrupt."

Reba frowned. "I read something about that. . . ."

"Did you read to the end?" Chance asked dryly.

"No."

"It's simple, really. Most human greed is. The Arabs decided that rather than pay to develop more of the mine, they'd just have the miners shave all those fat pillars. It worked, too. There were as many green garnets in those columns as there had been anywhere else in the mine . . . until the roof came down. Then there was only death. The stupid bastards who owned the mine weren't the ones to be buried alive, of course."

"I think," said Reba, swallowing dryly, "that the China Queen's columns look just fine the way they are. No shave. No haircut. Not even a bath."

"Wise decision." Chance's headlamp slowly picked out each pillar in the room. "Only five," he said. "That's not a hell of a lot, given the restlessness of Pala's dragon, not to mention the faults, the discontinuities and the general chemical mishmash that passes for rock around here." His light revealed the worried expression on her face. "I've worked in worse mines," he said. "But now that I've had a better look at this mine, you won't come into the Queen with me again."

"I'm not that frightened."

"No more poking about for you until I've seen the reports your geologist wrote when you wanted to know what shape the mine was in," said Chance as though Reba hadn't spoken. "Maybe not even then. In fact"—his headlamp swept the room once more—"I think it's time I took you back for lunch and a nap in the sun."

"I thought we were going to eat lunch down here."

"Not this time."

"What about you? Are you going to give up on the Queen?"

He smiled. "I'll prowl around a bit while you sleep."

"If it's safe enough for you, it's safe enough for me," she said, her voice even, stubbornness in the set of her jaw.

"I've already explained about that," Chance said easily, drawing Reba to her feet. "My standards are different for your safety." When she would have argued he kissed her into silence. "Don't you want to go back to the hill where the grass is as soft as the wind?" he murmured, moving his tongue over her lips with each word. "But nothing is as soft as you, *chaton*. . . . My God, how I want you." With a deep sound he pulled her close, possessing her mouth as he hungered to possess her body.

"You win," she said breathlessly when he finally lifted his head. "Let's go find that hilltop."

Chance bent and pulled the rucksack into place. After a last look around to make sure he hadn't left anything, he gathered both pick and shovel in his left hand, held out his right hand to her and smiled. "I'm going to enjoy loving you in the sunlight," he said softly, "all of you, sweet and hot and soft around me."

A delicious languor shimmered through Reba. She wanted to stretch and rub over her man like a honey-haired cat, purring the demands of love. "Chance," she said in a low voice, "it's such a long walk to sunlight. . . ."

Before he could answer, the floor shifted minutely. A tiny shower of dirt came down. Vibrations shivered through the air, rock strata groaning in octaves too low for humans to hear. The ceiling stretched and tilted subtly, shifting rocks that had sagged beneath a skin of dirt since the room had been dug more than a half-century ago.

Chance's body hit Reba in a flying tackle that sent both of them rolling toward the hard white granite wall at the end of the mine. Behind them the ceiling sighed and shuddered in the moment of release. With a ragged roar, a cataract of rocks poured down, burying the place where Reba and Chance had just been standing.

Chance covered her body with his own, protecting her the only way he could from the cave-in. Dirt and rock dust billowed outwards from the fall, covering them in a choking mass. When the last of the rocks had fallen and it was quiet again, Chance shifted his weight. Rocks the size of his fist rolled off his back and clunked to the mine floor.

"Reba," he said urgently, "are you hurt?" His hands ran over her trembling body, searching for injury.

"A little bruised," she said, her voice shaking, "and a lot scared. What happened?"

"One little shaker too many."

"Like the straw that broke the camel's back?" she said, lifting her head and giving him a tremulous smile.

"Yeah. Only we had the bad luck to be riding the bloody beast when it happened."

"You're hurt!" said Reba, seeing rivulets of blood bright against Chance's dark cheek.

"Just a bit of flying rock," he said, dismissing it.

The cone of light from Chance's helmet moved over

Reba, checking for cuts. Her clothes—and his body—had protected her from the worst of it. Her shirt was torn and she had some scrapes and bruises, but she was more scared than hurt. Reassured, he sat up and began looking for the tools he had thrown toward the granite wall when the cave-in occurred. They were nearby, buried but for a bright wedge of steel pick poking up out of the fringes of the rubble. He pulled out the pick and shovel and set them beside her.

"Stay put," he said. "If the ceiling starts to go again, hug the granite wall. It's the safest part of the mine."

Reba watched as Chance carefully walked along the edges of the cave-in. At first she thought it was the grit filling the air that made the room look so small. Then she realized that the cave-in had filled half the room. Cold fear crawled over her skin as she leaned forward, staring across the room, trying to pick out the small tunnel where they had entered.

There was no tunnel, simply a mound of dirt and rock that went from floor to ceiling without interruption. The entrance tunnel had been sealed beneath tons of earth. She and Chance were trapped in the China Queen.

Buried alive.

Panic went through Reba, shaking her until her teeth clattered. With a strangled noise she forced her fist into her mouth, biting down until no sound could escape. Pain cut through her panic, wrenching her out of mindless fear. She forced air into her fear-paralyzed lungs, forced herself to breathe deeply and evenly despite the thick air, forced herself to think instead of react.

After a few minutes the worst of her panic passed, leaving her sweating and shaken but in control of herself again. Watching Chance had helped. His strength, his stillness, his calm prowling along the perimeter of disaster all reassured her. If anything could be done, Chance would do it. And whatever happened, she wasn't alone. He was there, strength and light moving through the darkness toward her.

Chance knelt easily in front of her, his head tilted to the side so that he could look at her expression without blinding her with his helmet light. He took her hand, saw the livid marks left by her teeth, the extreme paleness of her skin, the fine tremors that shivered through her every few breaths. Very gently, he put his mouth to her palm.

"It could be worse, *chaton*," he said. "Neither one of us is injured. The oxygen should last as long as our water. But the tunnel entrance is gone." When there was no reaction from Reba, he squeezed her hand. "You knew that already, didn't you?"

"Yes." Her voice cracked. She swallowed dryly and tried again. "Yes, I saw."

"There are at least six meters of loose rock and dirt between us and the tunnel, and no guarantee that the tunnel itself isn't gone. The cave-in started at that end of the room."

Reba waited, holding his strong hand with both of hers.

"If I have to, I'll tunnel through that mess," Chance continued calmly. "It would be a real bastard, though. I don't have any way to shore up the sides. And it's loose now, really loose. It will come apart at the first sneeze."

Reba nodded slightly, sending light dipping across the face of the cave-in.

"I think we'd have a better chance if I tunnel through that side," Chance continued, turning his head until his light shone on the wall to her left, which ended in a pale thrust of granite. "There should be another tunnel not more than a few meters away, one of the narrow ones your family dug trying to locate the pegmatite again."

She hesitated, searching his dirt-streaked face. He met her eyes, but there was something hidden beneath his calmness. "Is there something you aren't telling me?"

Chance frowned and held her palm against his cheek. "There's no guarantee that the tunnel I'm looking for parallels this room at this level," he admitted. "Digging for it is a gamble."

"But it's less of a gamble than digging in that?" she asked, gesturing toward the cave-in.

"Yes."

"Do what you think is best," she said simply.

"Chaton," he whispered. "I never should have brought you into this bloody hole."

"With or without you, I would have come to the China Queen eventually. If it's possible to get out of this, you're the man who can do it. Alone, I'd be . . ." Reba threw her arms around Chance suddenly, hung onto him with surprising strength, then let go. "I'm glad I'm with you," she said, touching his hard mouth with fingertips that trembled. "Whatever happens, I'd rather be with you than anywhere else."

Chance closed his eyes, unable to conceal the emotion that gripped him. When his eyes opened again they were very silver, very bright. Without a word he stood and began pacing off the distance from the cave-in to the wall where he hoped to dig through and find a tunnel leading up to the sun.

"When I came to the Queen before," he said, prowling the wall that came into the granite at a right angle, "I could tell that she'd been dug by amateurs. All those tunnels leading off the main one are pretty much parallel to each other in three dimensions. A real gouger would have dug up, down and sideways looking for the displaced vein. At the time I thought those parallel tunnels were amusing. Now, I'm damned grateful your family didn't know the first thing about tracking a drift."

Reba didn't answer, knowing he didn't expect her to, that he was talking to reassure her with the sound of his voice. She kept her helmet light trained in front of him when she could, helping him to judge the composition of the wall.

He paced the wall and edges of the cave-in several times, measuring angles and distances with an experienced eye. From time to time he stood very still, eyes closed, as though reviewing or creating a map in his mind. Finally he chose a place just a few feet out from where the granite and earth walls angled together.

Before Chance began digging, he came to Reba and knelt in front of her. He smiled slowly, his teeth very white against the dirt-streaked tan of his face.

"One kiss for luck."

She felt his lips warm and sweet, his arms as hard as the granite wall, heard beautiful liquid words she couldn't understand and then he was gone from her arms. The harsh, gritty sound of a pick gouging into mixed earth and rock came back to her. She eased down the granite wall until she found a position where she could add the light from her helmet to his, making it easier for him to see as he worked.

For a long time the only sounds were those of metal and rock and steel. A mound of earth formed at Chance's feet. He ignored it, swinging the pick rhythmically, tirelessly, more like a machine than a man. Sweat turned his dust-covered shirt into a wet blackness that clung to his flesh. He peeled off the rucksack, shotgun sheath and shirt with hardly a break in rhythm. Rubble piled around his feet.

Reba pulled her gloves out of her back pocket, put them on and picked up the shovel. "If I stand on your left, I can shovel some of this junk out of your way."

Chance's lamp swiveled suddenly, picking out Reba's shape in the darkness. Her determination was clear in every movement of her body. He hesitated, then said only, "Shovel it as far away as you can, otherwise we'll just move it again." His teeth flashed in a thin line. "You'd be surprised how much dirt there is in a few cubic meters."

For the first few minutes Reba struggled with the heavy, unfamiliar tool. The last time she'd used anything remotely like a shovel, it had been in a kindergarten sandbox. On the other hand, gymnastics built coordination as well as stamina. Before long she had established a rhythm that allowed her to handle the shovel with a minimum of wasted effort. She hadn't a quarter of Chance's muscle but she had a gymnast's appreciation of leverage that allowed her to get the most out of the strength she did have.

Even so, it wasn't long before her muscles began to ache from the unusual exercise. She ignored it, knowing from her past gymnastics experience that physical discomfort didn't mean the end of the world. When her muscles began to tremble and cramp and refuse to work, then she would rest. Until that point she would work as hard as she could.

By the time Reba looked at her watch, her shoulder muscles had settled into a steady burning that she knew would eventually lead to cramps. She was surprised to discover that more than an hour had passed since the cave-in. She leaned on her shovel as she wiped her face on the sleeve of her flannel shirt. For a moment she was tempted to shed her shirt as Chance already had done. In the end, she settled for rolling up the sleeves, unbuttoning all but two buttons and tying the shirttails in a knot just under her breasts.

"Drink some water."

Chance's voice startled Reba. She looked up. He hadn't stopped swinging the pick. He hadn't paused at all except to heave aside stones that were too heavy for her to shovel out of the way.

"What about you?" she asked, watching the rippling power of his body as he buried the point of the pick deep in the wall. Sweat tangled in his hair, threw back glints of light like crystal drops, gleamed and followed the line of muscles down his body. He was extraordinary in his movements, his presence, his determination and grace, as elemental and male as the Tiger God.

"In a bit," said Chance. "I know my limits."

Silently, Reba wondered if he had any. Even though he was kneeling in order to reach into the crawl space he was digging, Chance seemed to tower above her, filling the room with his tireless strength. She pulled the canteen off her belt and drank sparingly, knowing the dangers of filling her stomach with water and then going back to hard work. She replaced the canteen, stretched burning muscles and picked up the shovel again.

After the second hour she stopped looking at her watch. Time was measured shovelful by shovelful, seconds punctuated by the ring of steel on stone, minutes by the grating fall of rubble out of Chance's narrow tunnel, hours by the fatigue pooling like a grey sandy tide in her body. She became an automaton, seeing only the rubble that had to be moved, hearing only her own breath, aware of nothing beyond the flat cone of her helmet light.

Suddenly, strong hands gripped Reba's shoulders, rubbing out knots and cramps that had become as much a part of her as the blisters forming beneath her gloves. Chance's breath moved coolly across her hot cheek.

"I've been in a lot of mines with a lot of men," he said quietly as he stood behind her, soothing her knotted shoulders with his hands. "I couldn't ask for a better partner than you. Where did you learn to be so brave?"

Reba took a ragged breath and leaned against him. "I'm screaming inside," she admitted.

His hands hesitated. His helmet rubbed against hers as he kissed her shoulder. "So am I." With a gentle squeeze he released her. "Rest. There isn't enough room anymore for both of us to work. If you get cold, use my shirt."

"Cold?" she said in disbelief.

"Lean against that granite wall for a few minutes and tell me how hot you are." Chance turned away, then paused. "If it wouldn't bother you too much, you might turn out your light while you sit. But if you'd rather keep it on, do."

Reba hesitated, then reached for the battery pack on the back of her belt. Chance wouldn't have asked unless he thought it necessary. Her light clicked off.

Black closed around her.

"You don't have to, *chaton*," he said softly.

"I know."

Chance touched her face and murmured something in the fluid, unknown language she had heard no one but him use. Though she didn't understand the words, she was comforted.

When his light vanished into the crawl space, sending

back little more than a pale shadow of brilliance, Reba put her head on her knees and closed her eyes. At least that way she didn't expect to be able to see anything. She took several long breaths, coaxing her body into relaxation, knowing that there was nothing else she could do at the moment. Chance needed the shovel now, because the tunnel he was digging was too small to swing a pick in.

After a few minutes she turned on her light, got up and positioned herself so that she could see into the tunnel where Chance was working. He had all but disappeared into the opening, lying on his side, the eyelets of his boots gleaming in the backwash of light. She turned off her light and fastened her eyes on Chance, allowing herself to think only of his power and determination as he lay on his side and battered his way into the mountain inch by inch, using only the power of his shoulders and the shovel's steel edge.

Her own muscles quivered with weakness now that she was no longer working. She ignored the sensations, knowing that they would pass. From time to time she stretched in a series of careful exercises, flexing sore muscles, hoping to keep herself from getting too stiff. Chance had been right. It was cold sitting on the China Queen's unforgiving floor.

A hoarse shout brought Reba to her feet. She stumbled toward the tunnel, fumbling for the switch on her belt. She went down on her hands and knees beside him, straining into the small space.

"Chance! Are you all right?"

"Getting better by the second," he said. "I broke through into some kind of tunnel."

Relief washed over Reba in a wave of weakness, making her glad she was already on her hands and knees. She waited, barely breathing, while Chance enlarged the opening.

Within a few minutes it was clear how close they had come to missing the new tunnel entirely. The floor of Chance's tunnel intersected the ceiling of the other tunnel at an acute angle. If Chance's tunnel had been dug a few inches higher or to the right, he never would have intersected the second tunnel at all.

Reba looked at the opening, visualized the three-dimensional geometries involved and shuddered. She hadn't realized just how much of a gamble digging the tunnel had been. If this had represented the least amount of risk, Chance must have known that digging through the cave-in would have been all but impossible. She was glad she hadn't known that at the time. It had been comforting to believe that if this didn't work there was a second chance waiting.

"What's wrong?" said Chance, shining his light toward her. "You should be smiling."

"I just realized how bad the odds really were."

Teeth gleamed whitely beneath a dusty black moustache. "Miracles always have bad odds, but they happen just the same." Long fingers curled under her chin. "Smile for me, my woman."

She smiled and laughed and ignored the tears sliding down her dirty cheeks onto his hand.

"It's going to be a squeeze," said Chance, measuring the flattened, lozenge-shaped opening. He stuck his head through and swept the helmet light over as much of the new tunnel as he could.

Reba sensed the sudden tension that coursed through him. She started to ask what was wrong, then kept silent. Chance pushed himself backwards until his head was out of the opening.

"Feet first will be best," he said, his voice neutral.

"I'll go in first. You hand all the equipment down to me, then come through yourself. Take off your tool belt. It will just get in the way."

Numbly, Reba retreated from the tunnel to follow his instructions. While he levered himself feet first through the tunnel and then the hole, she gathered up everything that they had left along the edges of the cave-in. She pushed the equipment in front of her as she wriggled through the narrow escape tunnel to the even smaller opening at the end.

Chance's hands appeared in the opening, startling her. She put equipment at his fingertips, watched it vanish piece by piece until it was gone. Her belt was the last thing to disappear. She began to turn around in the tunnel so that she could exit feet first. Only the flexibility of a gymnast permitted her to accomplish the reversal.

"Ready?" asked Chance, his headlight appearing in the opening just as she finished reversing her position. He made a sound of astonishment. "I'd have sworn nothing bigger than a cat could have turned around in that tunnel."

Reba rolled over onto her stomach and began wriggling backwards without answering. She felt Chance's strong hands close around her ankles, then her calves, then her thighs as he helped her move. When she was dangling half in and half out of the crawlspace, he lifted her carefully into the tunnel he had discovered. He put her on her feet, but didn't let go of her. She turned slowly, taking in her surroundings.

The new tunnel was surprisingly large, six feet high and nearly that wide. A feeling of abandonment and time overlaid everything. Each motion of her feet stirred a thin, powdery layer of dust.

"I expected something smaller," she said at last.

"So did I," he said flatly.

She turned, caught by something seething just beneath his control. "Tell me," she whispered.

"It's an abandoned tunnel."

Reba waited, not understanding.

"The tunnel is blocked at both ends," said Chance quietly. "It doesn't go anywhere at all."

Chapter 9

REBA LOOKED AT CHANCE'S EYES, NARROW SHIMMERS OF silver in the darkness of his face. "Where do we dig?" she asked simply.

His eyes closed briefly. She felt his fingertips trace the line of her lips, her cheeks, her eyes as though he were blind and had to use touch to see her. "So brave . . ." he said, kissing her with a gentleness that made tears burn behind her eyes.

He bent, brought up her tool belt and fastened it around her hips. He was wearing his shirt and tool belt again. He shrugged the shotgun and rucksack into place, wrapped his left hand around the pick and shovel and took her hand in his right. Without a word, he led her into the tunnel.

"What's behind us?" she asked.

"Two meters of tunnel and a granite wall."

"Ahead?"

"A cave-in."

Her steps faltered. "The same one?"

"An old one."

"How can you tell?"

"The only dust in the air is what we've stirred up with our feet."

The further they walked, the more ragged the tunnel became. Dirt and rocks were piled at random, as though men had simply turned over their wheelbarrows and walked out. The width of the tunnel varied from six feet to less than half that. The walls were dark, unmixed with glints of quartz or mica. The pegmatite vein had eluded her ancestors in this tunnel, only to be discovered years later and a few feet further to her right.

"Is this similar to what we crawled through to get into the big room?" she asked.

"Same stratum," he agreed. "You have a good eye. I'll make a miner out of you yet." He squeezed her hand gently.

"Why did they make the tunnel so big here and so small a few feet over?"

"Different miners," said Chance laconically. "Whoever dug this was an optimist. He was so sure of a strike he dug a tunnel big enough to drive a wagon through. He didn't know much about mining though."

"Why?"

"The bigger the hole the bigger the chance of a cave-in. Look around you. This tunnel started crumbling as soon as it was dug."

Reba realized that the piles of dirt and rock scattered through the tunnel were the result of minor cave-ins. The tunnel was slowly dissolving back into the earth.

"There was a hell of a cave-in here," said Chance.

Reba looked from side to side and saw only more dirt. "How can you tell?"

"Look up."

She tilted her head back and saw a large, ragged hole in the ceiling. The shape was roughly that of a pyramid. She shuddered and began to walk faster.

"Don't hurry," he said. "This is the safest place in the whole bloody Queen. What's going to fall already has."

The tunnel angled off to the right and ended in a ragged rubble wall. Chance let go of her hand and approached the cave-in. He studied it for a few minutes, then climbed up as far as he could and began poking hard at the top with the shovel handle. The handle went in for one-third of its length. Chance yanked it out, reversed it and began shoveling.

Reba watched the sudden flurries of dirt skate down the sides of the pile, wondering what Chance was doing. After a few minutes she realized that he was gradually disappearing into the top of the rubble pile. Suddenly he slithered out of the passage he had dug and turned his light toward her.

"Stand back."

She backed up several paces. The pick, rucksack, shotgun and his tool belt slithered down the side of the cave-in. He went back to digging. After a few minutes the only sign of his presence was a glimmer of light and the sound of dirt sliding down to the tunnel floor. She timed the intervals, retrieved his belt and tools and retreated again. Just lifting the pick had sent hot needles of protest up her arms and shoulders; she couldn't imagine how Chance had the strength or stamina to keep digging.

"Reba, can you hear me?"

Chance's voice was distorted, sounding far away and weak.

"Yes."

"I'm past the cave-in. I'm going further up the tunnel for a few minutes. Wait where you are."

She swallowed the fear and protests sticking in her throat and said evenly, "I'll wait." Then, despite herself she added, "Three minutes."

She thought she heard him laugh but couldn't be sure. She shoved up her dirty sleeve and watched the second hand crawl from mark to mark. One hundred and eleven seconds later she heard Chance coming back over the top of the cave-in toward her. She looked up, saying nothing, almost afraid to ask what he'd found.

"I don't know yet," he said, answering the question she hadn't asked. "There's another cave-in about eighty meters further along."

Silently Reba took off her tool belt and prepared to follow Chance up and over the rubble pile. When she got to the top she realized that, unlike the cave-in she had just experienced, this one hadn't filled the tunnel quite to the ceiling. There was just enough space to wriggle through, once Chance had evened out the top. She handed the equipment down to him, then slid down into his arms. He held her against his chest, wrapping her in warmth and his sharp male scent in the moment before he let her go.

The light from Chance's helmet slowly roamed over the tunnel. "This was a real bitch of a tunnel to dig."

Chance's light stopped on a few beams that had been set into the tunnel floor like fat fenceposts placed so close together that a man would have a hard time pushing between them. Other beams were laid on their sides behind the vertical row, making a wall to hold back the crumbling side of the tunnel. The beams were old, warped, dry. The wood was still dark, however, for it had never known the sun's bleaching.

The tunnel inclined at an even rate. The angle wasn't steep enough to be awkward for a man with a wheelbarrow. As Reba and Chance walked they found other crude wooden dams built to restrain the Queen's restless earth. Some of the beams had given way, releasing tongues of rubble across the tunnel floor. Other beams were slowly being overwhelmed, one handful of grit at a time. It was as though the tunnel were alive, but inhabited a different time scale entirely, one where human life was little more than a vibration passing through the earth.

One of the areas that had been shored seemed to particularly interest Chance. He studied the wall and beams for a long time, moving his light over the crumbling rock stratum of the wall so slowly that it was as though he were trying to read fine print. Reba stared, but all she could see was that the stratum was like a ragged, diagonal stripe through the earth. On either side the strata were darker, heavier, obviously more stable.

Finally Chance turned back to Reba. She waited, but he said nothing. Together they followed the tunnel as it bent off to the left, climbed steeply and terminated in a boulder-strewn heap.

"Dynamited," said Chance, looking at the angular fragments.

"How can you tell?"

He shrugged. "I've used my share of dynamite. Never like this, though."

"Like what?"

"To close down a mine."

"What do you mean?"

Chance bent down and picked up a piece of granite. Even after all the decades in darkness, the stain of formerly living lichen was clear.

"This came from the surface," he said, pointing to the lichen. "And look at the color of the granite itself. It's been weathered by sun and rain and wind." He stared at the heaped shards of rock packed together with dark earth. The sun was out there somewhere, but in which direction? And how could he shift those massive granite slabs? "So near and yet so bloody far," he said.

Chance swore for a moment with a soft violence that was all the more chilling for its restraint. After another long look, he turned and went back down the tunnel the way they had come, taking Reba with him. She walked slowly, understanding that she was turning her back on sunlight somewhere beyond that last fall of rocks.

"I'll bet he gave up on the Queen in 1908, when the Empress Dowager of China died and the market for pink tourmaline collapsed," said Chance calmly, as though the moment of his rage had never occurred. "Christ, how he must have hated this mine."

"Who?"

"The man who lit a match and blew the Queen's entrance to hell and gone."

Neither of them said anything more until Chance stopped once again in front of the part of the tunnel wall that had fascinated him before. He took off his gloves and ran his fingertips delicately over the wall just above the shoring. Reba waited quietly, too numb to question what he was doing. The thought of sunlight so close almost overwhelmed her control, so she didn't think about sunlight anymore, concentrating instead on Chance.

"I'm going to try something," he said finally, stepping back from the wall. "If it doesn't work, we'll eat and then decide whether to tackle the old entrance or the new cave-in." He slipped off the rucksack and shotgun, and laid them to one side. He propped the shovel against the wall, keeping the pick. Then he looked at her and smiled. "Another kiss for luck?" he asked, reaching for her.

Reba went into Chance's arms in a silent rush,

hungry for his warmth, for the safety that she always felt when he held her. With an inarticulate sound she clung to him, felt him curl around her body, enveloping her in his strength. She tasted the salt of his sweat and the sweetness of his mouth, felt herself tasted in turn, caressed with a gentleness and hunger that made her never want to leave his arms.

"If the luck is half as fine as the kiss," said Chance in a deep voice, holding Reba so tightly she couldn't breathe, "we're as good as out of here." His arms loosened. "Stand about three meters up the tunnel," he said, pointing her back toward the shattered granite. "If the shoring goes, I don't want you to get dirt in your boots," he added, smiling grimly.

Reba walked five steps, turned and watched. To her surprise, Chance ignored the closely spaced upright beams in favor of the beams that had been piled behind in a solid wall. He squared off to the side of the upright beams, brought the pick up and buried its point in one of the beams that had been laid on its side behind the upright rank. Though old, the wood was surprisingly strong. Instead of splitting or crumbling as Reba had expected, the beam remained intact.

Chance yanked hard on the pick handle, trying to move the beam rather than remove the pick. The thick piece of wood shuddered, shedding dirt as it jerked forward a fraction of an inch. He yanked again. The beam shifted slightly. His muscles bunched beneath black flannel, straining the cloth. As he yanked on the pick handle again, his shirt split down the back. The beam leaped forward a few inches. He shifted his grip on the pick handle and pulled hard again and again, dragging the heavy beam out of its decades-old resting place.

There were seven more beams, each one as thick and heavy as the one before. Once, when one of the beams

he had removed threatened to roll back underfoot,
Reba darted forward and tried to push the beam out of
the way. She could barely shift the wood an inch. Six
feet long, eight inches thick and as heavy as stone.

In the end, the best she could do was brace a rock
against the beam to keep it from sliding back under
Chance's feet. He didn't notice. He was locked in battle
with the stubborn shoring, his breath rasping in the
stillness of the tunnel, his eyes like hammered silver in
the occasional flash of her helmet light. Beneath the
long tears in his shirt, muscles coiled and slid and
gleamed like oiled metal.

Reba stood and stared, forgetting about time, forgetting about fear, forgetting everything but Chance. She
couldn't look away from him, fascinated by his elemental power and endurance.

As Chance went to work on the last of the lateral
beams, the tunnel wall crumbled. He leaped sideways,
sweeping Reba back with him. Together they watched
dirt seethe around the upright beams, burying them for
half their height.

"Chance," she said hoarsely, feeling the heat and
sweat of his body against hers, "all your work."

He touched her lightly with his lips. "It saved me a
lot of digging."

Chance went back to the half-destroyed shoring. His
light picked out the gap left when earth had flowed out
and through the closely spaced upright beams.

"Turn off your light," he said.

Reba clicked off her light without asking why. Delib-
erately Chance shut off his helmet light. Darkness—
seamless and absolute. He turned on his light again and
attacked the wall with the pick. In the reflected light,
his face was grim. She watched and said nothing. She
didn't turn on her light.

Dirt and rock tumbled forward. Chance brought the pick back again, sank its point into the wall as though it were the first stroke of the day rather than the thousandth. Sweat gleamed and ran down his body. That and his deep breaths were the only signs of how hard he was working. The rhythm and power of his strokes never varied.

The pick sank through dirt and rock into wood. The wood shattered. Blue-white light poured into the tunnel.

"What is it?" asked Reba, coming to stand beside him.

"Daylight," said Chance simply, laughter and triumph rippling beneath the calm word.

She stared in disbelief. "But it's so *blue*."

"It always looks blue after you've been down in a mine with artificial light." He held his hand between the upright beams, letting sunlight pool in his glove. "The most beautiful color on earth, as rich as life itself." He laughed softly and began removing his tool belt. "Think you can squeeze between these beams, *chaton?*"

Reba turned toward him, hardly daring to believe they were truly free of the China Queen's dark embrace. The silvery green of Chance's eyes convinced her. They were only that color in sunlight, when he was laughing.

She threw her tool belt between two upright beams, turned sideways and slid between the splintery wood. Chance tossed tools through, picked two beams that were a few inches further apart than the others, and forced himself between them. Reba was waiting a few feet away, standing just inside the entrance to the China Queen, her arms raised, sunlight pouring in a soundless cataract over her. As she heard Chance's footsteps, she turned toward him. Her face was rapt, her smile more beautiful than the radiance surrounding her.

"It's incredible," she breathed, "like being in the center of an immense blue-white diamond. Everything perfect, vivid, alive." She swept off her helmet and shook out her hair, laughing, her arms held out to him as though he were the sun. *"Alive!"*

Chance lifted Reba high in his arms, spinning her around, laughing with her. He looked into her eyes, cinnamon brilliance in the sunlight, her lips as pink as Pala tourmaline. She was laughing, disheveled, scratched and streaked with dirt . . . the most beautiful thing he had ever brought out of the dark earth. He bent and kissed her with endless hunger, drinking her life and beauty, feeling her melt and dissolve in his arms, sinking through his flesh into his very bones.

"Marry me," he said, his voice almost harsh, his lips pleading and demanding at the same time. "Marry me, *chaton.*"

Reba looked up, her eyes dazed, her lips trembling with the passion that Chance radiated as surely as the sun radiated light. Tiger God, burning in her arms.

"Yes," she said, because she couldn't say no. Not to him. She could refuse him nothing, least of all herself. "I don't think I could live without you."

Chance looked at her for a long moment, his eyes ablaze. Then he kissed her with a reverence that made tears stand brilliantly in her eyelashes. She felt exquisitely fragile, unbelievably beautiful, wholly consumed and protected at the same time. She wanted to tell him how much she loved him, but she could not. There were no words except the ones she had promised not to say.

And did the words really matter that much? Facing death together had collapsed ordinary time into dust and then blown the dust away, leaving behind only those things that were solid and enduring. She knew that Chance was courageous, ruthless, gentle, disciplined, harsh, passionate, powerful, dangerous and would risk his life to protect her. He had found and released the woman inside her, the wildness that only he could summon. He wanted her as she had never before been wanted. She wanted him in the same way.

She loved him, with or without the words.

"Come with me, my woman," Chance said, smiling very gently, brushing her lips with his own. He set Reba on her feet, gathered up the loose equipment and stacked it beyond the dark arch of the China Queen's entrance, keeping only the shotgun. "I'm going to show you what gougers do when they bring something precious and beautiful out of the earth."

Reba smiled up at him. " 'Whither thou goest,' " she said, her voice as warm as her smile.

Chance took off his gloves and hers, held out his hand and led Reba into the sunlight beyond the China Queen.

The early afternoon was hot and bright, filled with the desert wind that poured invisibly through mountain passes to the east, foretaste of the summer heat to come. Chance led Reba around the shoulder of the ridge to a shallow crease slanting down a rugged hillside. The ravine was deeper than it looked. Within moments they were concealed inside it. Chaparral grew to the height of small trees, casting delicate, shifting patterns of darkness and light beneath fragrant branches.

"This is the only tricky part," said Chance, leaping down a steep ledge of crumbly granite. He turned and held his arms out to Reba, lifting her down to more secure footing with a strength that still surprised her each time she felt it.

The ravine widened, becoming a gently slanting natural bowl before it narrowed once more and plunged wildly down into the deep, rugged canyon below. The bowl was quite small, hardly larger than her living room. A spring sparkled among boulders, becoming a tiny stream that threaded through the bowl in a series of curves worn out of solid stone. Between the edges of the stream and the steep sides of the ravine, grass trembled, heavy with sunlight and seeds.

"It's beautiful," sighed Reba. "How did you ever find it?"

"I smelled it."

She looked up at him in disbelief.

"This is a dry land," said Chance, smiling at her. "The scent of grass and water are like red flags marking a trail. That's how I found our hilltop. The water there is underground, though. Little more than a seep." He laughed at her amazement. "I've spent a lot of time in deserts, remember?" He kissed the tip of her nose and gently pushed her until she sat in the lush grass. "Rest here while I bring some things from camp." His fingers searched through her hair for the unique warmth of her scalp. "I'll be right back," he murmured, reluctant to leave her for even a moment.

Reba watched Chance vanish into the shaded ravine. She closed her eyes and leaned back, bracing herself on her hands, her face turned to the sun. She waited for him without impatience, feeling sunlight and heat seep into her body, letting the last of anxiety and darkness slide away.

After a few moments she realized how tired and dirty she was. The thought of a bath became almost irresistibly attractive. But the nearest bathtub was hours away. With a sigh, she put away the seductive thought of water cool and sweet on her skin, water washing away the residue of hard work and fear that clung to her. She listened to wind and the tiny stream flowing, sounds blending into serenity and peace.

Reba sensed Chance's return before she heard him. When she felt his fingers unbuttoning her shirt, she opened her eyes and smiled lazily. He was kneeling next to her, naked to the waist, his powerful muscles sliding smoothly beneath tanned skin.

"Is this what gougers do after a hard day?" she asked, laughter and desire making her voice throaty.

"It's an old and hallowed tradition," he assured her, smiling.

"What do you call it?"

"Washing off the find."

She laughed silently, watching his eyes as he unbuttoned the orange-and-russet shirt he had given to her.

"It's true," Chance said. "The first thing any gouger does is clean off whatever he's found. If it's opal," he added smoothly, "most gougers just lick off the dirt to see what's beneath."

Reba's breath stopped.

"In fact," he continued with a slow smile, "it's said that you can tell a gouger by his tongue."

"You're making this up," she said, divided between laughter and desire.

Chance smiled down at her, his eyes brilliant. His hands peeled away her grubby flannel shirt. "Every word is true," he murmured, unhooking her bra, "as true as you are beautiful." He bent and touched the pink tip of her breast with his moist tongue. "And you're very beautiful," he said in a husky voice. "As pink as the best of Pala's riches."

His sable moustache brushed over her breast, making her breath stop again. His teeth closed delicately over her nipple. He drew her into the heat and pressure of his mouth, caressing her until she shivered and called his name. Reluctantly he lifted his head.

"I promised myself I would wait," he said, his voice almost rough. "I keep my promises. Always." His hand cupped her breast gently, then slid down to unfasten her jeans.

"What promise?" she said, her voice a bit ragged.

"That I would wash every bit of that she-bitch Queen off us before I came to you again." Chance's voice was hard, his eyes the silver-green of spring shimmering beneath a potent sun. "We've been given a second life, *chaton*. We should be baptized before we begin it together."

He took off the rest of her clothes and his own before he led her to the lowest of the pools. Water brimmed and rippled over stone at the far end, making a tiny waterfall no taller than Chance and barely as wide as Reba's hand. She shivered at the first cool shock of water on her skin, then surrendered to the taste and feel of liquid flowing over her, Chance's hard and gentle hands touching every bit of her, washing her, leaving her as clean and strong as her love for him.

"My turn," she said, smiling up at him and holding out her hand for the soap he had brought from camp.

He gave her the soap and stepped beneath the tiny cascade. Water shivered over him in flashes of silver brilliance. She washed his hair first, then his face, lingering over the sensual textures of his lips and moustache. The muscles of his neck fascinated her fingertips, twisting and rippling beneath her touch, flowing into shoulders and arms powerful enough to dig her out of a deadly black trap and bring her into the pouring sunlight beyond.

She turned him gently. When she saw the long scrapes and bruises on his back, she sucked in her breath, afraid to touch him. She remembered the moment when he had knocked her off her feet and then put his body between her and the rockfall. As lightly as a breath, her fingertips settled on a bruise.

"Does that hurt?" she asked.

"Nothing hurts when you touch me."

With hands that trembled, she washed away dirt and dried blood. He turned beneath her touch with a suppleness that mocked even the idea of pain.

"I'm all right," he murmured, tipping her face up for a kiss. "Don't look so pale."

"You put yourself in danger . . . protected me. . . ."

"Of course," he said, his voice velvet and rough. "You're my woman. I'll always protect you."

She knelt before him, washing his strong legs from ankle to thigh, enjoying the dark warmth of his flesh beneath the soap and silver water. As her hands moved higher, she felt the tremor that went through him. She washed him as gently as he had washed her, feeling no self-consciousness with the intimacy, only pleasure. He was her man, hers to touch and enjoy without false modesty or inhibitions, like water and sunlight and life itself.

He bent and lifted her into his arms, kissed her with a searching need that made her want to soften and run over him like honey. He felt the change in her, felt the heat and sweetness of her flowing over him. Murmuring the strange and beautiful phrase she had heard before, he held her against his hard body until they both trembled.

Silently he carried her away from the rocks and water, to a place in the sun where he had spread the joined sleeping bags to make an iridescent black blanket. Gently he put her down, releasing her completely, touching her only with the intensity of his look.

"If I take you now I'll never let you go," Chance said, his voice almost harsh. "No matter what happens, no matter what we've said or not said, done or not done, you'll be mine in a way more elemental and enduring than any marriage vows could make you. Do you want that?"

"Will you belong to me in the same way?" asked Reba, her eyes as intense as his, searching his face for the words he would not say because he believed he knew nothing about love.

"I have no choice," he whispered.

"Neither have I," she said, holding out her arms to him. "And I don't want one. I want you, Chance. Only you."

"You'll have me," he promised, sinking down beside her. "Only me."

He drew her into his arms, held her along the muscular length of his body, savoring the softness of her. His lips met hers as though for the first time, caressing her, as warm and undemanding as sunlight falling on her skin. The tip of his tongue licked the corners of her smile, teasing her until she laughed, opening her lips for him. The rough velvet of his tongue slid over hers, coaxing her to slide over him in return. The taste and feel of him went through her like lightning. She melted against him with a tiny moan.

"Yes," he whispered, biting gently along her earlobe, her neck, her shoulder, her breasts. "Come to me."

She shivered beneath his touch, feeling her body change to meet his loving demands. Her breasts swelled, silently asking that his mouth close over them. His tongue shaped each hard nipple with excruciating thoroughness, then he sucked gently on her until she twisted slowly, moaning. His mouth roughened, giving her a lover's caress that would have hurt just moments before but now made fire burst beneath her skin. Heat pooled inside her, then spread outward in expanding rings of sensation. Her hands clenched and unclenched on his arms, her breath came raggedly, shaking her.

"Chance," she said urgently, her legs moving restlessly, seeking his hardness, "please . . ."

He laughed and slid further down her body, teasing her navel with his tongue. Strong hands rubbed over her calves and thighs, parting them as his teeth gently ravaged the soft skin beneath her navel. He rubbed his cheek against the honey roughness of her hair and shuddered in answer to her sinuous response. His moustache brushed the softness of her inner thighs, making her tremble. When his tongue probed, seeking her most sensitive flesh, she gasped.

"Chance—"

"Shhh, my woman," he murmured against her warmth, holding her hips in the gentle, irrevocable vise of his hands. "You're so soft, so beautiful. Let me know all of you."

Whatever Reba had been going to say was lost in the exquisite sensations coursing through her. The heat and overwhelming sensuality of his caress, the pleasure he so plainly took in her body, completely undid her. She gave herself to him, reserving nothing, consumed to her core by the liquid fire that he brought with each movement, each rough velvet touch. When his teeth closed with savage delicacy on her flesh she arched like a bow, clinging to him and shuddering, calling his name in broken sounds and sighs, wholly lost.

While she was still shaken by the aftershocks of a pleasure more overpowering than any she had ever known, he flowed up her body in a muscular surge. He took her swiftly, holding both of them motionless, savoring the extent of his possession. Then he moved once, hard, setting fire to her again. She cried out and sank her nails into his shoulders without knowing it,

gripped by a pleasure so intense it was almost indistin-
guishable from pain. He laughed and moved slowly,
powerfully, watching her come apart with each movement, her eyes a cinnamon blaze in a face transformed
by an ecstasy as fierce and potent as the man inside her.

He called her name once, a cry wrung from the
depths of his need. She shuddered and flowed over
him, nails raking down to his hips, asking him to ride
the liquid waves of her ecstasy. With a hoarse sound he
let go of control, sinking into her endlessly, giving
himself to her as wholly as she had given herself to him.

Chapter 10

REBA TOOK THREE STEPS ON THE NARROW BEAM, DID A back walkover, two forward walkovers and a cartwheel off the beam onto the resilient pad that covered the floor of the room. Breathing deeply, her skin misted with perspiration, she reached for a towel.

"Finished?" asked a deep voice from the doorway.

She turned suddenly, gracefully, startled as always by Chance's silence of movement. "Where did you come from?"

"The Objet d'Art. I left the press release about Jeremy's collection on the coffee table. Gina wants your okay before closing time. She was frothing about not being able to mention the wedding," he added in a neutral voice.

"I told her we'd announce it at the del Coronado when we show Jeremy's collection," said Reba. "Until then, I don't want to cope with all the curiosity and nasty cracks. I just want to enjoy you in peace."

Chance looked at Reba for a long moment, then nodded. "I see. I was beginning to wonder if you'd changed your mind about marrying me."

She ran lightly over and threw her arms around him. "You don't get away that easily," she said, smiling and very serious as she looked into his unique, silver-green eyes.

"It's not me I'm worried about." His hard, slightly rough hands caged her face. "It's you, *chaton*. Things that you see very clearly when you look at death tend to fade with safety. The further away we get from that cave-in, the longer you stay in the city, the more I'm afraid you'll decide not to marry me."

Closing her eyes, Reba put her cheek on the warm, hard flesh that beckoned through the open neck of Chance's forest-green shirt. It had been less than two days since they had come back from the China Queen, but it seemed as though she had loved Chance forever. She had no doubts. Tomorrow they would be married.

"Tomorrow is my birthday," whispered Reba against his skin. "You promised me the only gift I want. You. You won't get out of that if I have to lock you inside the Objet d'Art's walk-in safe."

Chance's laugh was little more than a vibration against her cheek. Long fingers lifted out the bone chopsticks that held her hair in a tight coil on top of her head. He rubbed her scalp while honey hair whispered and slid over his skin. The tip of his tongue found the pulse beating in her throat. He felt it quicken as his hand moved down her body, savoring the heat and firmness of her flesh beneath the fuchsia leotard she wore.

"I'm yours," he said almost roughly, "marriage or no marriage. I meant what I said before I made love to you by that spring. You belong to me with or without the vows. But I'd rather be married to you. I want my ring on your finger and my name after yours—Reba Farrall Walker. I want men to know that you're mine."

"And I want women to know that you're mine." She smiled crookedly. "I have your ring all picked out."

"Are you possessive?" he asked softly, his eyes very green as they memorized the shape of her mouth, the tip of her tongue glistening pinkly as she touched her lower lip.

Reba looked into Chance's eyes and felt the wildness stir in her, powerful currents of emotion and need only he had ever tapped. "I never was possessive before. When my husband started seducing his students I was more disgusted than angry. But if you so much as touched another woman, Chance Walker, I think I'd do something rather violent."

He smiled like a hungry tiger and kissed her until she melted against him, her softness and strength fitting perfectly along the hard length of his body. "Don't worry, my woman. Once a prospector has touched diamonds and gold dust, he'll never settle for less."

He kissed her again, gently this time. Reluctantly he loosened his arms. "If I don't stop soon, I'm going to find myself suggesting that I help you take a shower." His look and hands wandered over her, touching the hard buttons of her nipples, the provocative curve of hip, the shadowed warmth between her thighs. "The next thing you know," he said, his voice husky, "I'd be nibbling on you, tasting you from your delicious little ears to your ticklish toes."

Reba's breath shortened as she arched into his touch.

Chance closed his eyes and moved his hands back to her shoulders. "But if I did that, I'd never leave and we wouldn't be able to get married tomorrow. Why does your bloody government insist on so much paper-work?"

"It's your bloody government, too," pointed out Reba reasonably, her eyes brilliant with desire.

He sighed and stepped back. "Right. I keep telling myself that every time I want to just grab you and say to hell with all the rules." His fingertips smoothed the line of one dark honey eyebrow. He brushed his lips over hers. "Be here when I get back."

"Always."

Reba watched the door closing behind Chance and had to use all her discipline not to call his name. The fact that he'd be in her arms this evening didn't ease the ache she had now. It was more than simple desire; now that she knew what life could be with Chance sharing it, life without him was like an inferior gem—faded, bland, flat and dull.

She showered quickly, ate a midafternoon snack in place of the lunch she had forgotten and settled in the living room to read Gina's press release. As usual, Gina had said what needed to be said with a minimum of fuss and a maximum of clarity. Reba set aside the papers, reached for a phone and called the Objet d'Art.

"Gina? The press release is excellent. Send it out right away. Any calls for me, or hasn't anyone noticed I'm playing hooky?"

"Todd Sinclair dropped by. I finally told him what your two choices were from the collection. I hope you don't mind. It was the easiest way to get rid of him, short of Tim's method."

"A blackjack?" hazarded Reba.

"That's my Tim," said Gina dryly. "Not that I blame him. I could cheerfully take a blackjack to Todd myself."

"I'm glad I wasn't in the office."

"Not as glad as Todd was. He was definitely relieved that you—and Chance—were nowhere around. I do believe that your man put the fear of God in Todd Sinclair."

"Hallelujah. Maybe I've combed that toad out of my hair for the last time."

"The other calls didn't amount to much. Everyone is unhappy about having to wait until the del Coronado to see Jeremy's collection, but Tim is holding firm. No special previews, just as you wanted."

"Good. If we let in one, we'll have to let in all. I'd rather enjoy my honeymoon in peace."

"Somehow, peace and Chance Walker seem a contradiction in terms."

Reba's smile wasn't transmitted over the phone, but the throaty softness of her voice was. "Not really," she murmured, remembering how peaceful it was to fall asleep in Chance's strong arms. "He can be a very soothing man."

There was a sudden commotion on Gina's end of the line, an unknown woman's voice and then Tim's voice.

"Hold on, Reba," said Gina.

The sound of the phone changed, telling Reba that she had been put on hold whether she liked it or not. She waited with relative patience, assuming that a customer had needed Gina.

"Reba?"

It was Tim's voice. "Still here," she sighed. "What came unstuck this time?"

"Nothing. Chance's sister is here, looking for him."

"What? Glory is there?"

"So that really is her name?" asked Tim, trying to smother a laugh. He spoke in a muffled aside that Reba could overhear. "Sorry, Mrs. Day. Your name struck me as, er, unusual. And we've had a lot of news types sniffing around here lately, what with Jeremy Sinclair's collection and all."

Reba heard the phone change hands. A woman's voice spoke, her Australian accent clear. Unlike

Chance, Glory had totally lost the vocal rhythms of her birthplace, using instead the sounds of her adopted land.

"Chance?" asked Glory. "It's about bloody time I found you."

"Not quite. I'm Reba."

"Chance's woman." Satisfaction sounded in every syllable. "He won't be far away then. He's been a long time looking for you, Reba Farrall. Can I talk to him for a minute?"

"He's out cutting red tape."

"Bloody hell," muttered Glory. "Well, back to the hotel to wait for him, then."

"Chance won't be coming back to the hotel. I don't even know when he'll be coming here. Why don't you let Tim drive you over to my house? We can wait together."

"I'd like that." Glory chuckled, a slightly rasping sound that reminded Reba of Chance. "I'm curious about you, Reba. A lot of sheilas went prospecting for Chance. Not one of them found anything but hard rock and heartache."

"I'm quite ordinary," said Reba dryly.

Glory laughed and turned the phone back over to Tim, who assured Reba that he'd bring Chance's sister over right away. Reba hung up, showered and dressed. She pulled on a black cashmere sweater, plucked a few long golden hairs off her soft wool slacks and went into the kitchen to start coffee. She'd spent enough time in the throes of jet lag to know that Glory was going to be punchy after her long flight from Australia.

Besides, the weather had turned cold and cloudy again, a typical Los Angeles reversal—yesterday eighty degrees, today fifty-five. Hot coffee and cashmere felt good today, especially with a wind off the ocean rattling her windows.

She walked barefoot across the wine-colored rug, enjoying its resilience and warmth. The long, low couch was done in a subdued oriental pattern, heavy silk shot through with cream and wine and midnight blue. The colors were repeated and combined in huge pillows piled randomly about, pillows that invited lingering touches with their suede and cashmere and silk textures. Cream brocade wallpaper gleamed subtly, giving the room a feeling both of space and intimacy.

Beyond the floor-length windows, wind leaped and pounced, shaking grass and houses with equal ease. A western wind was rare in southern California, but when it came, it came with a vengeance. From her cliff-top house, Reba could see that the sea had been churned into burnished silver and exploding whitecaps from shore to horizon. There were no boats on the water. Today, the Pacific was not an ocean for small craft or dilettantes.

Reba sat and watched the wild sea until chimes rang, telling her that Glory had arrived. She went quickly to the front door and opened it. For a moment, she and Glory looked at each other with equal curiosity.

Chance's sister was perhaps fifteen years older than Reba, no taller and nearly as slender. Her short hair was black, combed back from her tanned face. Gray was sprinkled in the midnight color, turning into shining wings of silver on the sides of her face. Her mouth was wide, shaped for smiling. Her eyes were pale green, but without her brother's silver shading. Lines of laughter and sadness and strength radiated out from her eyes, giving her face a character that was both beautiful and calm.

Without thinking, Reba smiled and held out her arms, drawn to Glory as intuitively as she had been drawn to Chance. Glory's expression changed to relief and pleasure and sheer happiness.

"Thank God," said Glory, giving and receiving a hard hug. "I was afraid Chance had settled for a city sheila with no more idea of love than a handful of rock."

"And I was afraid that Chance's very special sister might be the kind who wouldn't like any woman her brother liked."

" 'Very special'?" said Glory, laughing and sinking into the comfortable couch Reba had led her to. "Honey, the only thing special about me are these damned white wings in my hair."

"There must be more than that. As far as I can tell, you're one of the few human beings on earth that Chance loves."

"Did he tell you that?" said Glory, surprised.

"Not in so many words. It's there, though, in his eyes and voice when he talks about you."

Glory sighed. "Chance doesn't use the word love. Ever."

"I know." Reba's voice was quiet, constrained. Even knowing that she was going to be Chance's wife hadn't removed the hurt of not being told she was loved. "But he shows it in other ways," she said firmly.

"It would go better on him and the world if he could talk about it," said Glory, her eyes distant, sad. "That may never be, though." Pale eyes focused on Reba. "Can you live with that?"

"I don't have any choice. I love him."

Glory sighed and closed her eyes, leaning tiredly against the back of the couch. "I know he loves you. You're the only woman he's ever wanted to marry. He's in such a bloody great rush to make you a Walker that he wouldn't even wait a week no matter how I pleaded. So I moved heaven and earth and my husband, and here I am." She yawned. "I've been up since I got Chance's call thirty-four hours ago. I hope that he's going to be one surprised gouger when he sees me here." She smiled tiredly. "It's my only wedding present to the brother I love."

"It's the only kind of present that matters," said Reba. Her smile widened into laughter. "I can't wait to see Chance surprised. He's a hard man to sneak up on."

Glory's yawn ended in a chuckle. "Don't hold your breath, honey. No one's taken Chance by surprise since he was fourteen."

"When Luck died?"

Glory's eyes opened, green and speculative. "Did he tell you about that?"

"Some of it. He told me how much it hurt—still hurts—that Luck was killed before Chance could prevent it. Although I don't know what a fourteen-year-old could be expected to do."

"Nobody expected anything, least of all what happened." Glory looked closely at Reba. "What did Chance tell you about that day?"

"That he was too late. That Luck was dead. That he found the miner who had killed Luck."

"And then?"

Reba shook her head. "He wouldn't say any more. But I think," she said, remembering the men in the mine and Chance's swift, deadly skill, "I think that if Chance had been older, the other miner would be dead."

"You're half right," said Glory, her eyes haunted. "Chance was only fourteen but he killed that miner just the same. Size never counted for much with Chance."

"My God . . ." Reba's voice died.

"If you'd seen what was left of Luck," said Glory grimly, "you wouldn't blame Chance. I stole a gun and went looking for that bloody miner myself. Chance found him first. The miner had a knife. It didn't do any good, though. Chance took it away and killed him with his bare hands." Glory shook her head. "Lord, it's been a long time since I remembered that. I used to wonder why Chance went crazy over Luck's death like that."

"It was the time in the mine," said Reba slowly, "when your father turned off all the lights and Chance screamed and Luck held him and cursed your father until he turned on the lights again."

The older woman looked carefully at Reba. "When did that happen?"

"Just after your mother died. Chance always wanted to help Luck as much as he had been helped."

"Chance never told me about that, even after Luck was dead." A thoughtful expression crossed Glory's face. "It explains a lot. Dad never had much use for Chance. Even as a child, Chance was independent. The only one he gave a damn about was Mum. Luck was different. He was Dad's child, period. But Luck loved Chance, too. Bloody odd, watching those two together. Never saw two brothers closer, or with less in common. For all his charm, I never really liked Luck. Chance was different. Tough little beggar with a smile like sunrise."

Glory yawned again, then apologized. "It's not the company, honey, just the hour. Back home, I'd be asleep."

"That's all right," said Reba. "Jet lag always hits me like a falling mountain. Do you want coffee or a nap?"

"Coffee," said Glory promptly.

Reba went to the kitchen and returned with thick mugs of steaming coffee. "Cream or sugar?"

"No thanks." Glory smiled. "That much of me is still American." She sipped the black brew and sighed. "Heaven, Reba, pure heaven. Pretty name you have. Is it short for something?"

"Rebecca."

Glory looked over the rim of her mug. "Of Sunnybrook Farm?"

"Only in my mother's fantasies," said Reba. "The real me was a considerable disappointment."

"Parents can be a bloody pain in the arse," said Glory bluntly. "You're not a Becky, either, are you?"

"Much to my ex-husband's disappointment."

Glory blinked, then laughed shortly. "You haven't had an easy time of it, have you, honey?"

"I wonder if anyone has."

Glory sighed and closed her eyes for so long that Reba thought she was asleep. "You'll do, Reba Farrall. You'll do just fine. And thank the Lord for it. If ever a man deserved a break, it's Chance."

Glory's eyes opened, clear and green despite her obvious tiredness. She looked at Reba. "You know that you're marrying a legend, don't you?"

Reba looked startled. "Er, no."

"Chance Walker, the man who knows where God buried all His treasures and where the devil keeps the hottest women. Chance has taken more money out of played-out and abandoned mines than most gougers see in fifty lifetimes. He's hit a few genuine glory holes and a lot of decent strikes. So men stand in line to stake him and women line up right behind, hoping for a piece of his action. He takes what he wants from the women. As for the men"—she shrugged—"Chance has found fantastic wealth for other men on a day-rate basis and a small percentage of the take."

Glory looked shrewdly at Reba. "Don't take me wrong. My brother is neither a fool nor a pauper. He's just a gouger through and through. Hooked on the treasure hunt. What you haven't found is like an itch that can't be scratched, driving you crazy." She shook her head. "Prospecting gets in your blood worse than malaria."

"That's what Chance said. You can survive malaria, though. In the right climate you can even control it."

Glory laughed warmly. "I'm going to enjoy having you for a sister, Reba. You've got what it takes to make a man like Chance come back for more. The ways of the Lord are indeed strange. Who would have thought that a played-out tourmaline mine would lead Chance to the one woman he could love?"

Smiling crookedly, Reba said, "So he told you about my mine?"

"He didn't have to tell me," snorted Glory. "Your aunt was so mad when Sylvie lost her half of the China Queen playing poker with Chance that everyone in the Outback heard her yelling. And if they didn't hear your aunt, they sure as bloody hell heard your cousin. Sylvie screamed like a bandsaw when she offered to earn back the mine in Chance's bed and he turned her down flat." Glory smiled thinly. "After Chance grew up he became very particular about his women. And Sylvie, well, that sheila just never was particular about her men."

Reba barely heard. She set her mug very carefully on the table, desperately trying to conceal her reaction to Glory's words.

Chance had known about the China Queen before he met Reba. The ramifications of that simple fact went through her like a shockwave, destroying her.

Glory yawned despite the coffee she had drunk. "Lord, I'm bushed. Getting too old for batting about the landscape like a crazy 'roo. Would you be upset if I just called a hack and went back to the hotel to sleep until Chance comes back?"

"You can sleep here," said Reba with automatic politeness, her thoughts still spinning around the terrible truth that Glory had so casually revealed: Chance hadn't wanted Reba for herself after all, but for the China Queen.

"Thanks, but all my gear is at the hotel," said Glory, muffling another yawn.

"I'll drive you over."

"You look like you could use a nap yourself," said Glory, "if you don't mind my saying so."

"Yes," said Reba tonelessly. "I've been a little short of sleep lately. Excuse me. I'll call a cab for you."

Later, Reba couldn't remember what she and Glory had said until the cab finally came. For a long time after Reba shut the front door behind Chance's sister, Reba stood in the middle of the living room, looking out over the wild silver-green ocean, trying not to think at all. Then she realized that she had to think, and think more carefully than she ever had before in her life.

Chance owned one-half of the China Queen. She had told Chance that she would never sell her half of the Queen. The only way Chance could get the other half was to marry her.

Ergo. He would do just that.

Even as Reba told herself that a worthless, abandoned tourmaline mine wasn't worth marrying for, she remembered what Glory had said. Chance was an expert on played-out mines. A legend. He'd spent a lifetime finding money for other people. It was his turn now.

What was it Chance had said? *No sacrifice too great if a big strike is the reward.* Besides, marriage was only a temporary thing, after all. Her husband had taught her that.

Part of Reba screamed silently that it couldn't be like that; Chance couldn't be that dishonest. The other part remembered how savage Chance had been whenever she had brought up the subject of the China Queen. Like a man with an uneasy conscience? Like a lying, cold-blooded bastard, perhaps?

Think carefully. Had Chance ever told her a lie? Had he ever said he didn't know who she was in Death Valley, or that he'd never met her cousin or that he'd never heard of the China Queen? No. He'd never said any of those things. He'd simply let her believe them. Not lies, precisely.

And a hell of a long way from the truth.

There must be an explanation. There must be something that would convince her that she hadn't been a bottomless fool to fall in love with a man so ruthless and self-assured that he needed nothing from her but half of a deadly mine. There must be something that would convince her that she was worth loving whether or not she owned a goddamned hole in the ground called the China Queen.

"Chance . . . !"

Reba didn't realize she had called his name until the anguished sound came back to her in the empty room. She shuddered and forced herself to breathe deeply despite the knives scraping over her nerves. Falling apart now would be useless. There must be an explanation. She couldn't have been that kind of fool. She was worthy of a man's love.

But if she were wrong, if she were a fool and unworthy, if there were no explanation . . .

She turned away from the window and walked quickly to the phone. Jeremy's lawyer could tell her what she needed to know. He had told her to call if she needed advice. Well, she was calling now.

When the lawyer came onto the line, she asked a terse question, listened to the answer and hung up as the lawyer began asking questions of his own. She went to her desk and began writing. When she was finished, she went to her wall safe, took out an old legal paper and put it in a large envelope with what she had written. She wrote Chance's name across the face of the envelope in an even, steady hand.

Then she went and stood by the window, watching the sea, waiting for the man who had never said he loved her.

By the time Chance returned, twilight had spread over the water, absorbing scarlet light into its endless grey embrace. Reba felt like the light, calm and untouchable, as remote as the indigo island floating on the pewter horizon. She could face anything, do anything, accept anything. There was no other choice except to break, and that she would not do.

The front door opened quietly.

"Reba?" Chance's voice was as dark and deep as the descending night. "What are you doing standing over there with the lights out?"

"Thinking of the sixteen questions I never asked."

"What? Oh, Twenty Questions."

The living room lights came on, a warm golden glow that transformed the floor-length windows into mirrors. Reba watched Chance's reflection walk toward her. Something stirred beneath her calmness, something as searing and elemental as molten rock seething beneath the earth's cold crust. She realized that if she hoped to get through the next few minutes with any kind of dignity, she couldn't allow Chance to touch her.

"Yes, Twenty Questions," she said easily. She started to look at Chance over her shoulder but even simple eye contact threatened her calm. "Coffee?" she asked, moving toward the kitchen, away from him.

Chance stopped in the center of the room, watching her with sudden alertness. "Is that one of your sixteen questions?" he asked, his voice casual, his eyes narrow and intent.

"Sure."

"I'd rather have a kiss."

"Into each life a little rain must fall," she said flippantly. "Or, in your case, coffee. Black as a miner's heart, right?"

"Reba, what's wrong?"

"No fair," she said, pouring coffee for both of them. "I have the questions and you have the answers. That's the way the game is played."

"I don't play by the rules."

"Tell me something I don't know," said Reba, trying and failing to keep the bitterness out of her voice.

She handed the cup of coffee to Chance without meeting his eyes. She turned her back and went to stand in front of the window again. His reflection was as close as she could safely come to him.

"Coincidences are such dicey things," she said, ignoring the coffee steaming between her hands as she stared at the colorless sea. "We would never have met if we hadn't happened to be in the same part of Death Valley at the same time. And good old Todd Sinclair, of course. I guess I owe him one." She waited, but Chance said nothing. "No answer?" she murmured.

"Was there a question?" Chance countered, his voice as controlled as his body.

Reba looked at Chance's reflection and saw the self-assured Tiger God, solid gold bow slung over his shoulder, ready to go hunting the devil himself. He was so much stronger than she was. He had all the answers. She had only questions. She had given him everything. He had given her . . . half-truths, evasions. How had he put it? *If you know something that gives you an advantage, you bloody well keep it tucked.*

She couldn't say he hadn't warned her.

The elemental fire in her coiled and seethed, testing the strength of the cold cage she had built around herself while she waited for Chance to come back.

"Then there's that other coincidence," said Reba, sipping at the coffee, barely noticing its scalding heat. "I own half of a worthless tourmaline mine and you're a man famous for finding treasure where other men have given up."

Chance's posture changed subtly, a ripple of feral alertness that told Reba more clearly than a shout that he understood where the questions were going. She waited, but he said nothing, explained nothing, gave her nothing to make her feel less a fool. He simply waited.

"No answers?" she said.

"I still haven't heard a question." His voice was controlled, flat.

"How's this one—you knew my cousin in Australia, didn't you?"

"Yes."

"You're half-owner of the China Queen, aren't you?"

"Yes."

"You need the other half before you can get a loan to mine it, don't you?"

Chance hesitated, then shrugged. "Yes."

"Yes," she repeated numbly, watching the seething twilight sea. She was grateful for the cold cage she had built around herself. It was all that was supporting her now. "Yes and yes and yes."

"Reba—"

"No. It's still my turn, Chance. This is one time you'll play by the rules." Her voice was as cold as the pewter sea. She turned gracefully, put her coffee mug on the low table and picked up the large envelope. Chance's name stared up at her. The even, flowing handwriting had a calming effect on her. She held out the envelope to Chance. "Happy birthday."

"It's not my birthday."

She shrugged. "It will be someday, won't it?" Then, *"Take it."*

Chance took the envelope, opened it, read the stilted legal words written in her clear hand, saw the old deed. As of this moment, he owned one hundred percent of the China Queen.

"Why are you doing this?" he asked, his face still, his eyes very green in the subdued light. "When we're married the China Queen will be *ours.*"

"We aren't getting married."

Chance's eyes narrowed. "Why not? Nothing has changed. And"—brutally—"you said you loved me. Remember? I do."

"And you never said you loved me. Remember? I do. In that, at least, you were completely honest." Reba watched him with eyes that were too dark, breath held, waiting to hear her own worst fears confirmed.

"I told you," he said softly, "that I don't know enough about love to use the word."

"I believe you," whispered Reba, despair like twilight taking color from her life. She felt her nails digging into her palms. "There's an old Chinese curse: 'May your fondest wish come true.' All my life I've wanted to be in love, truly in love." She smiled oddly. "I wished for the wrong thing, didn't I? I should have wished to be loved."

"Chaton—"

"Is that a euphemism for fool?" she asked with a brittle, aching calm. Then, quickly, "No, don't answer. You've told me all I need to know. Good luck with the

Queen, Chance," she said, turning away from his reflection, leaving the room, walking away from her Tiger God. "And may your fondest wish come true."

Chance followed Reba with long gliding steps, stalking her. She sensed his presence and spun around before he touched her.

"No," he said curtly before she could speak. "It's my turn now. Nothing has changed, Reba. Not your feelings for me or mine for you. We're getting married tomorrow."

"There's no reason to get married," she said, meeting his eyes for the first time. She flicked her fingernail against the envelope he held in his hand. "You have what you want."

"I want you."

"Do you?" she asked calmly, belying the emotion seething beneath her careful surface. "Do you really? Then get rid of that damned mine now, right now. Give it to the first person who walks down the street!"

"What in bloody hell would that change?" he demanded.

Reba's only answer was a sad, bitter laugh. "If you have to ask that question, there's no answer in any language on earth."

"You're not making any sense," Chance said savagely. "Look, I know I should have told you sooner. God knows I tried to tell you but—" He swore viciously. "To hell with it. It happened and there's no going back. Giving away the Queen won't change anything." He reached for her. *"Chaton—"*

"She doesn't live here anymore," snarled Reba, stepping away.

But Chance was too quick for her. He had always been too quick. His hand closed on her arm, pulling her close. His palm caressed her cheek.

"Give us time, my sweet woman. What I said or didn't say just doesn't matter. All that matters is this," he murmured, bending to kiss her.

"No!" she said harshly, shoving against him with all her strength. "The mine is yours but *I am not!*"

It was as though she had said nothing, done nothing. His strength was impervious to her attempts to escape. Up to now she had been calm, far too calm, determined to resolve everything in a rational, civilized manner. But when his lips touched her the rage seething beneath her control simply exploded. Kicking, twisting, clawing, as wild in her fury as she had been responsive in love, she tried to fight free of his grasp.

After the first shocked instant, Chance kicked Reba's feet out from under her and took her down to the floor, controlling her with his superior weight and strength. He let her spend herself in a futile effort to dislodge him while he held her, waiting for her rage to pass.

With a shudder, self-control finally returned to Reba. She closed her eyes and tried to breathe slowly, deeply, but even that simple action was beyond her. Chance was too heavy, too overwhelming. She was chained beneath him, feeling his breath flowing over her skin. He covered her like a supple, living blanket. She shuddered again, appalled at the warmth coursing through her, the hot shimmering response of her nerves to his body pressing down on hers.

And then she felt his heat and hardness, knew that he wanted her as wildly as she wanted him.

"I want you," he breathed against her neck, echo of her own thoughts.

She went rigid beneath him, refusing even to speak.

"I could make you want me," Chance said quietly. His moustache moved over Reba's lips and neck like an exquisitely soft brush, sending visible chills of response over her.

She said nothing.

His mouth moved down until he found her breast, caressed it. The black cashmere couldn't conceal her response, her nipple tightening eagerly beneath his touch.

"That's what I meant after we dug our way out of that she-bitch Queen and bathed each other at the spring," Chance said, his voice hard and sure. "You belong to me, Reba, and words don't have a bloody thing to do with it. Don't you know that yet?" His fingers closed gently, irrevocably on the nipple outlined beneath her soft sweater. "I could take you right now and you would scream with pleasure," he said, watching her fight against the desire consuming her. "Wouldn't you, *chaton?*"

She said nothing.

"Answer me," Chance said roughly, sliding his hand beneath her sweater with a swift, almost savage movement.

"Yes," she hissed, her voice as feral as her eyes, rage and humiliation and passion sliding hotly in her blood.

He watched her wild cinnamon eyes for a long moment, letting her know the weight and heat of his own desire before he sighed and touched her mouth gently with his fingertips. "But if I did, it would be a long time before you forgave either one of us," he said.

"It would be forever."

"I'm not marrying you for the mine," he said, his voice sad and angry at the same time. "Do you hear me, you little fool?"

She laughed wildly, bitterly, consumed by the shame and the rage ripping through her. And the desire. "You're not marrying me at all." Her voice was flat and cold, her eyes opaque. She looked through him, focusing her eyes behind him as though he were no more than a reflection in her living room window.

"You're mine whether you marry me or not," Chance said bluntly. "But you're in no mood to admit that tonight, or to be reasoned with. Not logic, not love . . . You even think you hate me, don't you?" he said, his eyes narrow, silver, as hard as his smile. "I'll be here in the morning before you open your eyes, and then we'll find out whether it's love or hate you feel. You'll wake smiling at me, my woman. I promise you.

"And," he added, moving powerfully, sensuously over her, "that will be the end of this crap about love and the China Queen!"

Chance was on his feet and out the door before Reba realized she was free. For a long time she lay on the floor, feeling the imprint of his heat and hardness and strength on her body, not knowing whether to scream or laugh or cry. So she did nothing, letting shudders of conflicting emotions shake her until she was calm again. Slowly she pulled herself to her feet, certain of only one thing. When Chance came in the morning, she could not be here. She did not want to know how she would react if she woke up in her Tiger God's arms again.

Loving him was bad enough. Hating him would destroy her.

"Where the hell are you?" demanded Tim.

Reba held the phone away from her ear and looked out over the parking lot of a small shopping mall in Oregon. "Out of state," she said succinctly.

There was a long silence. "I thought you were getting married today," said Tim finally.

"Easy come, easy go."

"Reba—"

"No." The word was flat, cold and hard, an accurate reflection of Reba's state of mind. "This is a courtesy call, Tim. No courtesy, no call."

Tim sighed explosively. "Sorry, boss. Chance has been all over me like a cat in a sandbox."

"That's why I didn't tell you where I am. And I won't."

He hesitated. "Are you all right?"

She laughed abruptly, a sound without warmth or humor. "Is there anything at the Objet d'Art that requires my immediate attention?"

"Some shipments and insurance forms need your signature."

"Forge it."

"When are you coming back?"

"I don't know."

"Are you coming back?"

"Who's asking—you or Chance?"

"Both of us," admitted Tim. "He's been my shadow since I got here this morning. Will you talk to him?"

"Does he still own the China Queen?"

There was a brief pause, then a deep voice said, *"Chaton—"*

"Do you still own the China Queen?" she interrupted coolly, ignoring the weakness that made her hands tremble so badly that she nearly dropped the phone. Just hearing his voice made her want to crawl into his arms as she had in Death Valley, crying until the ice and agony were gone. But this time he was the one who had hurt her. "No lies, no evasions. Just one word, yes or no. Do you still own the Queen?"

"Yes."

"Good-bye, Chance."

Very gently, Reba replaced the receiver in its cradle.

Chapter 11

IT WAS A FEW MINUTES BEFORE REBA'S FINGERS STOPPED shaking enough for her to look up a number in the small leather notebook she had taken from the Objet d'Art. She punched in the number with unusual care, not trusting her own reflexes.

"Jim Nichols? This is Reba Farrall. I know this is short notice, but I happen to be in Oregon unexpectedly and wondered if you would have time to show me the Eskimo kikituks you mentioned in your last letter?"

Reba wrote down directions to the house, hung up and went back to her rental car. She drove quickly, trying not to think that the last time she had visited West Coast collectors Jeremy had been with her. If she thought about that she would come undone. If she thought about Chance she would shatter like a carelessly struck stone. So she thought about her work, matching collectors with rare objets d'art from all over the world. Jim Nichols' kikituks might be just what a wealthy New Zealand collector of primitive ivories was looking for.

As Reba knocked on the front door, she felt the tingle of excitement that always came when she was going to see another collector's treasures. It wasn't simply Nichols' ivories that were intriguing. Like many collectors, he had spent a lifetime swapping with people all over the world. Trade, not cash, was the rule. As a result, collectors always had an assortment of rare and beautiful and sometimes bizarre pieces that had been taken on trade. Quite literally, Reba knew that she might find anything on earth in Jim Nichols' house.

"Mr. Nichols?" asked Reba, holding out her hand.

"Jim," corrected the man, taking her hand in a dry, large-knuckled grip. A lifetime of trapping and prospecting in the far north had left its mark on the French Canadian. The arthritis that had driven him south showed in swollen knuckles and stiff knees. "You called me Jim when Jeremy was alive."

"Jim," she agreed, trying not to show the pain of hearing Jeremy's death mentioned so casually. Even so, tears stood in her eyes for a moment.

"Don't look so down in the mouth, gal," said Jim in a voice that had known too many cigarettes, too much whiskey. "When you get as old as me and Jeremy, death looks kinda friendly."

Jim offered Reba coffee, settled her at a scarred plastic table and sat beside her with a cracked mug held in one fist. She noticed that the mug held Scotch rather than coffee.

"Best arthritis medicine in the world," he said in his scratchy voice. "Pretty slick on memories, too. Just leaves the good ones."

Reba looked at the Scotch with new interest. "Really?" she murmured. "I think I'll develop a taste for it."

"Wait a few years," he advised dryly. His wrinkled hand patted hers. "Sit tight."

Jim left the room and came back carrying a cardboard carton filled with kikituks. With the casual skill of a man who has handled precious things all his life, Jim took out the carvings and lined them up on the scarred table. As he did, he pointed out the flaws and virtues of each one.

Reba watched, hardly able to repress a shudder. Though different sizes, none of the kikituks was bigger than her palm. All of the carvings had a malevolence about them that was as much a part of them as their ivory sheen. Like long-bodied, fanged hippos, the kikituks watched her with their mouths agape.

"You know the legend behind these, don't you?" asked Jim, taking the last kikituk out of the box.

"Yes. You give a kikituk to an enemy and it eats their soul."

An image of the Queen's black mouth rose in Reba's mind, a kikituk carved out of a mountain, swallowing a man's soul.

"Don't like them much, do you?" asked Jim.

"I know a collector who will," she said tightly. "He has some African demons carved out of elephant tusk that make my blood run cold. The kikituks will be right at home."

Jim chuckled dryly. "Don't much like the little devils myself. But the carving is good and the ivory is first rate. Men are real careful about their vengeance."

Numbly, Reba bargained for the kikituks, trying to banish the horrifying picture of the China Queen from her mind. Would Chance go into the Queen alone? Would the earth shift again, sealing him forever in darkness?

With hands that shook, Reba wrote out a check and gave it to Jim, sealing the bargain for the kikituks.

"I heard you're keeping the Green Suite."

"Yes," she said, her voice raw.

"Sit tight."

Jim left, then returned with a brown paper bag in his hand. "Took this in trade a few months ago," he said, digging into the bag. "Was going to call Jeremy about it."

He held out a mineral specimen for Reba to look at. Embedded in a nondescript chunk of rock was a clear, silver-green crystal the precise color of Chance's eyes. Reba's breath came out in a rush. She looked at the incredibly colored octahedron for a long time, then closed her eyes and shook her head. It was impossible. A diamond still in its matrix was one of the rarest finds for a collector. Add to that a unique color, and you had a specimen that was literally priceless.

"Fellow told me it was a diamond in the rough," said Jim. "I can tell fake ivory at fifty feet, but diamonds?" He shrugged. "Figured Jeremy would know."

"May I?" said Reba carefully, holding out her hand.

"Sure." He dropped the specimen in her hand with heart-stopping casualness.

Reba pulled a jeweler's loupe out of her purse and went to stand in the strongest light she could find. She examined the specimen carefully. There was no trace of glue holding the crystal to the stone. The crystal's natural facets were unpolished, unmarked by man's tools. There were no visible fractures or flaws. At a guess, the diamond was just under three carats.

She returned to the table. "I'd have to perform a few tests to be positive," she said, "but it looks good to me. How much do you want for the specimen?"

"Is it for one of your collectors?"

Reba's fingers tightened possessively around the crystal that was the exact color of Chance Walker's eyes. "No. This one is for me."

Jim patted her hand gently. "Then it's a gift."

"Mr. Nichols . . . Jim . . . I can't—this is priceless!"

"That makes it a fair trade," he said simply.

"I don't understand," she whispered.

"Jeremy and me used to get together and drink a bit, back when we still had enough vinegar to tear up a town. We'd been at it for a few days once when he turned to me and started talking about dying. Told me he'd give anything he owned if somebody cried for him when he died. I never forgot it."

Jim's faded eyes peered down into Reba's face. "You cried for Jeremy when his own flesh and blood was lined up waiting to dance on his grave. That kind of love is priceless. Glass, quartz or diamond, the rock is yours."

Reba stretched out on the too-soft motel bed and rubbed her eyes wearily. She knew she should go on to another city, another collector, get on with her life. But she couldn't. The days were weeks long. The nights had no end. Her mind and emotions were a shambles. She wheeled between loneliness and rage, fury and despair. The China Queen haunted her dreams, a black kikituk leering at her, black fangs devouring Chance's soul.

She hadn't phoned Tim for five days. She knew he would be worried about her, but didn't trust herself to call. If Chance were still there, if she heard his voice again, she didn't think she'd have the strength not to go running back to see his untamed smile, to warm herself in his sun-browned arms.

Someone knocked lightly on the motel door. Reba's heart leaped in the instant before she realized that it couldn't be Chance. He had no way of knowing where she was.

"Who is it?" asked Reba, abruptly wary. She had

objets d'art packed in boxes around the room and locked in the trunk of her rental car. She was beginning to wish she'd followed Jeremy's example and traveled with bodyguards.

"It's Glory, Reba."

Reba was off the bed and at the door before she had time to think. "Is Chance with you?" she demanded breathlessly, throwing open the door, hope making her eyes brilliant.

Glory's face changed, older, clearly showing her fatigue. "I was going to ask you the same question."

"What do you mean?"

"Chance is gone," said Glory flatly. "Can I come in? I'm dead on my feet."

Reba pulled Glory inside and shut the door. Automatically, Reba poured what was left of a thermos of coffee into a plastic cup and silently handed it to Glory. The older woman finished the lukewarm liquid in a few swallows and handed back the cup.

"Thanks," sighed Glory, sinking into an ugly plastic chair. "I may live." Her eyes opened clear and green. "What the hell happened with you and Chance?" she demanded bluntly.

"He wanted the China Queen," said Reba tonelessly, appalled by the depths of disappointment washing through her. She had hoped for a few wild instants that Chance had missed her as much as she missed him. But he hadn't. He wasn't even looking for her. "I gave it to him."

"Why do I have the feeling you left out something?" asked Glory. Her eyes narrowed. "Well, honey, I'm not going to leave out anything. I woke up six days ago feeling all warm and squishy because my brother finally got lucky in love. The next thing I know Chance is in my room. He's killing mad. I've never seen him like that," she said flatly. "Never. Not even when Luck died." She closed her eyes. "Sweet God, Reba, what did you do to him?"

"Why don't you ask what he did to me?" Reba's voice was clipped, harsh, her eyes brilliant with anger and shame.

"I'm asking."

"He wanted the China Queen more than he wanted me. So I gave him what he wanted. The China Queen."

"I'm still asking."

"I gave him a choice," said Reba, "me or the Queen. Guess which he chose?"

Glory closed her eyes again. "My God . . . what did Chance do to make you hate him so?"

"I don't hate him," said Reba in a strained voice.

Glory laughed oddly. "Couldn't prove it by me." She looked narrowly at the woman standing in front of her. "The China Queen represents everything Chance thought he ever wanted out of life. And you"—Glory shrugged—"you're the woman he's been looking for all his life. So you stand there like a queen and tell him he can have one or the other but not both. You're acting like the mine is another woman. Who the hell do you think you are?"

"Nobody," Reba whispered, her voice shaking. "That's just the problem. I'm nobody. But you wouldn't understand that, would you? You have a man who wants you for what you *are,* not what you *own.* I thought that was the way Chance wanted me until you came and told me that he owned the other half of that goddamned mine!"

"Oh, no," breathed Glory, finally understanding. "It's a wonder Chance didn't kill me." She stood and put her arms around Reba. "You still love him, don't you?"

Reba nodded, unable to speak.

"Then help me find him before he does something he can't undo. I've called everyone I could think of, but no one's seen him. He hasn't called any friends, he's not in his hotel and he hasn't left any kind of trail out of Los Angeles."

"You found me," pointed out Reba. "You'll find him."

"Honey, you left a trail of checks and motel chits a blind man could follow. Chance went to ground."

A chill moved over Reba. "The China Queen." Then, quickly, "No, he wouldn't. It's too dangerous. It nearly killed us the last time."

Even as Reba denied her fears, she reached for the phone. A moment later she was talking to Tim.

"Where are you?" said Tim. "Is Chance with you?"

"No. Has he called?"

"Are you kidding? You should have seen him after you hung up on him. I've never seen anyone that . . . that . . . *wild*. Gina still gets the shakes when she thinks about it. And frankly, so do I."

"He didn't do anything, hurt anyone?" asked Reba, remembering the violence that Chance could unleash, the strength and the fierceness of the man. Yet it was fear for Chance rather than for anyone else that made her voice shake.

"It wasn't like that. He was so calm it scared hell out of me. He didn't say anything except to Gina. She was wearing that cross you gave her at Christmas. Chance stopped in front of her, touched the cross and said, 'Do you mind? I'm going to need that where I'm going.' He snapped the chain like it was cheap thread, took the cross and left."

"He's gone to the China Queen," Reba said dully.

Chance had chosen but he had not chosen her. She had given him the Queen and he had taken it without a backward look. All choices made.

Numbly she told Tim where she was and hung up.

"Well?" said Glory.

"Your brother is doubtless in his mine," said Reba. "Is it safe?"

"No," whispered Reba, "it's not safe at all."

"Then go get him out!"

Reba laughed despite the tears clinging to her dark lashes. "Just how should I manage that, Glory?" She turned on the older woman with sudden rage. "Don't you understand? He doesn't want me. *He's keeping the China Queen!*"

There was nothing Glory could say to penetrate the shell Reba pulled around herself. She and Reba flew back to Los Angeles together. Reba spoke only once, to give directions to the China Queen. She refused to consider going to the Queen with Glory. Chance had chosen and there was no more to say. Eyes closed, body rigid, Reba sat on the plane and thought about the man who wanted the unyielding earth more than he wanted her.

After a few days Reba's rage faded but the icy shell remained. Arranging for Jeremy's collection to be shown at the del Coronado had kept her mind occupied during the days. During the nights she had sorted through photos of Jeremy's collection, remembering Death Valley and the two men she loved in such different ways—and had lost just the same. Remembering was painful, but it was better than waking up screaming Chance's name, trying to warn him about a voracious black kikituk with shattered pink crystal eyes.

She hadn't seen Glory since they'd left the airplane together two weeks ago. She'd heard from Glory once, confirmation of what Reba had already guessed:

Chance was in the China Queen, digging through darkness in search of Pala's incomparable pink tourmaline. The thought of Chance alone in the endless subterranean night, vulnerable to the least twitch of the restless earth, made Reba's skin move and tighten with fear for his life.

She had hoped coming to the Hotel del Coronado would provide relief from the emotions that seethed just beneath her calm exterior. Seeing Jeremy's collection auctioned off would put *finis* to that part of her life, *finis* to grief and longing and wondering why only one kind old man had found her worthy of love. But nothing had touched her except fear for Chance, and fury. For long moments she sat without moving, nails gouging her palms as she thought of Death Valley and the China Queen and a man called Chance.

A knock on the door startled her. She blinked and looked around the room, disoriented for a moment. When she saw the spacious suite with its gold brocade wallpaper and old-fashioned furniture, she remembered where she was. Hotel del Coronado, San Diego. Jeremy's collection. The auction. It had all been a huge success. The bids had been spectacular. Everything had been sold. Disappointed bidders had come to her with their want lists, assuring her enough work to make the Objet d'Art as profitable as Jeremy's collection had been.

The knock came again. "Reba?" said Tim, "are you ready?"

No. But she couldn't say that. She had to stand up and be calm and professional and controlled. She had to go downstairs and dance with strangers when the thought of being touched by any man but Chance made her want to cringe. He didn't want to touch her, though. All he wanted was the China Queen. What

could he hope to find in the Queen's cold, unloving
darkness to equal the living warmth of a woman's love?
Maybe he would be downstairs, waiting for her. Maybe
the time he had spent in the Queen's cold embrace
would make him understand that Reba loved him.

Reba stood up and went to the door, unlocking it.
Tim stepped into the room and stopped short, giving
her an appreciative male whistle.

Her dress was diagonally cut silk the color and
texture of gold dust. Its matte finish caught and held
light in subtle swirls that followed the lines of her body.
Elegant, sensuous, the silk bared her right shoulder and
flowed down her left shoulder to the floor, rustling
seductively with each tiny movement of her body. The
dress had only one fastening, a slanting row of three
teardrop diamonds set just below the left shoulder. A
matching diamond glittered in each earlobe. Her thick,
honey hair was piled in gleaming coils held by invisible
gold combs.

"It's a good thing I'm happily married," sighed Tim.
"You're more spectacular than anything we've auctioned off tonight."

Reba's mouth turned up in a brief, sad smile.
"Thanks." She had been going to wear the black silk
that was the Objet d'Art's trademark, but hadn't
wanted to be in funeral colors for Jeremy's ball. She put
her hand through Tim's arm. "Let's get it over with."

"Hey, you're going to a ball, not a burial."

Reba didn't say anything. Tonight was the last night
Jeremy's collection would ever be gathered in the same
place. She had even put the Tiger God and Green Suite
on display, complete with the silver-green diamond in
the rough. For it was a diamond, beyond doubt or
question, as she had known it would be. It gleamed
subtly among the other varied greens, showing its

quality in the way it transformed simple light into shimmering silver-green beauty, a crystal as unique as the man she loved.

The muted conversations of elegantly dressed people reached out from the del Coronado's gracious lobby, wrapping around Reba's silence. Tim escorted her into the George VII Ballroom, where the dance would be held. The room's ceiling was thirty feet high, covered in hand-rubbed, tongue-in-groove pine. Brocade wallpaper and heavy gold drapes added to the Victorian ambience that was at the core of the del Coronado's charm.

Normally a spacious dining area, tonight the room had been given over to the memory of Jeremy Sinclair. Arrayed in glass cases and velvet boxes, Jeremy's collection coiled through one-third of the room like an enormous glittering necklace. Women in glorious dresses glided among the cases, escorted by men in dinner jackets and black ties. Well-dressed men circulated unobtrusively in the crowd, their weapons concealed by tailored black silk jackets.

Reba couldn't help the depression that settled on her slender shoulders, dragging her down into darkness as she searched every part of the room for a man who had silver-green eyes and a tiger's untamed grace. Chance must know she would be here, a last tribute to Jeremy Bouvier Sinclair. If Chance wanted to see her, he would be here tonight.

But there was no man among all the men who could have been Chance Walker.

"What the hell!" said Tim, looking toward Jeremy's collection.

Reba glanced over and saw a huge redheaded man carrying an empty beveled glass case under one arm as though it were a lunch pail. Ignoring the curious looks from the crowd, the man set down the glass case and calmly opened it. Another man stood behind him, a sandy-haired man whose powerful shoulders and scarred hands proclaimed him to be a miner. The second man held a cardboard carton in his arms. A third man stood and watched the crowd with the assessing eyes of someone who had known a lot of trouble in his time.

The pressure of Tim's hand on Reba's arm wasn't what drew her toward the three men. There was something about their toughness and self-assurance that reminded her of Chance. She realized that she had seen all three of them before. In fact, since she'd arrived at the del Coronado with Jeremy's collection, she had seen them everywhere she turned. Not only had they covered the auction like a blanket, their room was just across the hall from hers.

"Want me to call a guard?" asked Tim softly.

Reba shook her head, compelled by the aura of tension and excitement that radiated out from the three men. The red-haired man opened the carton with thick, deft hands and reached inside.

"Wait," said Reba quietly. "Let's see what they—ohhh!"

Reba's gasp was lost in the larger gasp of the surrounding people. Held in the man's huge hands was a cluster of Pala tourmaline in a matrix of quartz crystals. The pink shafts had been fractured by the restless movements of the earth, yet the crystals were still intact, glorious in their resurrection and birth. Shafts of tourmaline as long as Reba's hand, longer, a sunburst of fiery pink capped by vibrant green.

The China Queen had come to life beneath Chance's hard and gentle hands.

The vision blurred and then resolved into tears burning Reba's eyes. She could never compete with the tourmaline's crystal mystery, its blazing glory. Chance had chosen well. The worst of it was that she couldn't blame him. To see that tourmaline—that luminous perfection—was to know finally, irrevocably, why men risked death in the dark passages of the earth. Beauty, not wealth. Beauty of the gods.

Next to that she was nothing, nothing at all.

She looked up and saw the red-haired man watching her. His hand came up in a curious salute, then he picked up the empty carton and left the room without speaking to her. He didn't have to. The tourmaline itself was the message. Chance had won. She had lost.

It was over.

Not until that moment did Reba realize that underneath her rage and fear she had been certain that her Tiger God would come back to claim her. So certain . . . and so wrong.

"There's no owner's name on it," said Tim, returning to Reba's side, "no identifying mark, just a small card in the corner that says 'nfs.' "

"Not for sale," murmured Reba. "As for an owner's name"—her lips turned down sadly—"do you have any doubt?"

"Chance?"

"Who else could have done it?" she asked, her voice husky. *"Tiger God."* No one listening to her would have known whether the words were endearment or epithet. At the moment, Reba herself wasn't sure.

She took a deep breath and let it out slowly. She would have given all but one specimen out of the Green Suite in order to be able to turn and walk out of the room, out of the hotel, out of her own skin. But that wasn't possible. If nothing else, she owed it to Jeremy's memory to drink champagne and dance and laugh at life and loss just as coolly as he had. And that was precisely what she would do for as long as her nerve held.

"Shall we open the ball?" she asked, turning to Tim, her back straight, her head erect, her cinnamon eyes brilliant with tears she refused to shed.

Tim lifted Reba's hand to his lips, bowed and led her onto the dance floor. She faced the platform where the musicians waited, nodded to the leader and turned back to Tim. As soon as he took her into his arms, the music began, a waltz as sophisticated as Reba's gown. For a few moments the dance floor belonged to them, then other couples appeared, called by rich music and the graceful movements of the woman in gold-dust silk.

At the end of the dance, Reba put her hand on Tim's arm and allowed herself to be led away, as proud as any queen. He seated her at one of the tables lining the wall where windows gave a view of the hotel's sweeping front lawn.

"Thank you, Tim. Go back to Gina now." She smiled, making it sound more like an invitation and less like an order.

He hesitated. "Are you sure you want to be alone?"

"I'm sure. Find Gina and dance and enjoy."

"What will you do?"

"Drink champagne," she said, signaling a passing waiter.

"Reba—"

"Go," she said softly.

Tim hesitated, then left, nearly bumping into the huge red-haired man as he turned. Reba looked at the man, realized he had been watching her and raised her dark honey eyebrows in silent query. He paused, then approached her.

"Red Day, ma'am. Glory's husband. Would you like to dance?"

"I think not," she said coolly, sipping her champagne, looking at the big man with distant curiosity. Though he must be fifty, he looked tough enough to bend sheet metal with his bare hands.

"Thank God," sighed Red, settling into the chair across from her. "I can't dance worth a handful of, er, dirt."

Reba stared at him for a moment longer, wondering where she had heard his name before. Not as Glory's husband, but in connection with tourmaline . . . Then she remembered the day when Chance had held a Chinese tear bottle in his hand, clear pink light pooling and shifting as he spoke in his deep voice about a Dowager Empress obsessed with Pala tourmaline.

"You're a collector. Rubellite, if I remember correctly."

"That's right," Red said, his blue eyes lighting with enthusiasm. "Do you—"

"Was that your tourmaline specimen?" she asked, cutting off whatever question he had been going to ask her.

"Wish it was. Bloody beauty, isn't it?"

"Bloody right," said Reba sardonically, saluting him with her champagne glass. She took another drink and grimaced. Tonight of all nights she wanted to get high, *numb,* and vintage champagne tasted like ashes. It was all she could do to swallow the stuff. "Maybe Chance will sell it to you."

Red shook his head slowly. "I offered him heaven and earth, and then threatened him with hell."

"If you need any help delivering on the threat," Reba said, smiling just enough to show the serrations of her even white teeth, "I have a few suggestions."

Red's laugh was as big as the rest of him. "Where did Chance find you, little lady?"

"Death Valley. Then," Reba added coolly, "a few

weeks later he swapped me for a mine called the China Queen."

Red looked startled. "But he said the mine wasn't his."

"He lied. He's good at that." She set down her champagne glass with a tiny snap that set the liquid to bubbling.

"Chance Walker doesn't lie," said Red, shifting his bulk in the small chair. "He doesn't steal or cheat, either. After that"—Red grinned—"I'll admit he's used up his share of the Commandments."

Reba had nothing to say to that except a silent *amen*. For a long time she and Red sat without speaking, listening to music as languid as moonlight on pearls, watching women held like precious, multi-colored gems in the dark settings of men's arms.

"Would you care to dance?" asked a voice at her elbow.

Reba's head snapped around. The man she saw standing at her elbow was even bigger than Red. At least six foot six inches, younger than Chance, built like Hercules and handsome as a god. She disliked the man on sight—not for what he was but for what he wasn't. He wasn't Chance.

"No," said Red, "she wouldn't like to dance."

"Wrong," snapped Reba, deciding instantly that she wanted to dance after all. "The lady would love to dance."

Red looked from Reba's angry face to the other man's inviting male smile. "Let me put it this way," said Red easily. "The lady will dance with you. Once. You listening, Melbourne?"

Melbourne shrugged indifferently and held his hand out to Reba. She came up out of her chair as gracefully as fire. He led her onto the dance floor. For a big man he moved very lightly, but it seemed that he held her much too close. Reba pushed delicately on his chest, politely hinting that she'd like more room. Melbourne's hand slid down her back to her hips, urging her closer. She pushed away hard, demanding more room.

"This is a waltz, not a wrestling match," she said tightly, looking up into Melbourne's eyes. They were very blue against his tan face and chestnut hair.

"Then stop wrestling," he said, smiling down at her patiently. "It's hard to dance at arm's length."

Reba bit off a hot retort, realizing that he was right; she was trying to keep at least eighteen inches between them. She was surprised by her reaction because it had been instinctive. Was she crazy? Here she was dancing with what had to be one of the most handsome men she'd ever seen and it was all she could do to fight down nausea when he put his hand on her hip. She had never been like this before.

"Sorry," she said, struggling to overcome her irrational distaste of being close to any man but Chance.

Melbourne sighed. "Where is he?"

"Who?"

"The man you belong to. It's not Red. He's got Glory, and God knows that's all the woman one man needs."

"What makes you think I 'belong' to any man at all?" she said coolly. "This is the twentieth century, remember?"

Melbourne shook his head and laughed. "That may be, but some things don't change. The second I put my hand on you I knew you belonged to someone else. Body language doesn't lie, as a man once taught me the hard way."

Reba went rigid. Chance had said that to her in Death Valley. Suddenly she was certain who had taught Melbourne about body language. On the heels of that certainty came the realization that Chance was right again. Body language didn't lie. She was his—and he didn't want her. With an effort that made her ache, she fought against her own deepest reflexes, forcing her body to relax in the arms of a man who wasn't Chance Walker.

Reba wasn't entirely successful, but at least she didn't force Melbourne to dance at arm's length. The dance ended and another one began. Melbourne looked down into her eyes and smiled. "Want to see if Red's temper matches his hair?"

Reba tried to smile in return, wishing that she were free to respond to Melbourne's teasing male presence. But she wasn't. She had been claimed by a Tiger God who didn't want her anymore. With a sad smile she shook her head. "No. I think I'll just turn you loose to brighten up the life of some lucky woman."

She felt the instant of denial that went through the big man's body. He looked at her speculatively before he led her off the dance floor to the table where Red waited with an obvious lack of patience.

"You're brighter than you look," said Red, smiling. Despite the gibe, it was obvious that he liked the younger man. He just didn't like Melbourne dancing with Reba.

"Who are you watching her for?" demanded Melbourne bluntly.

Red looked uneasily at Reba, accurately sensing that she wasn't as calm as she looked. "I'm not her keeper."

Melbourne said something beneath his breath that only Red caught. "Look mate," continued Melbourne in reasonable tones, "she says she doesn't belong to anyone. But you, Ted and Ian have been sticking to her like a bad reputation. You kicked the people out of the room across from hers, you follow her everywhere but the loo and you sleep across her doorstep at night like a faithful hound. You even try to tell me how many dances I can have, as though I were no better than a bloody wog."

"It wasn't me telling you," sighed Red, glancing ruefully at Reba before returning his attention to Melbourne. "It was Chance Walker."

Melbourne straightened, looking at Reba with a sudden interest that had nothing to do with her as a woman. "Bloody hell! He's never been the jealous type before."

Red shrugged. "He is now, Melbourne."

"I'll be goddamned." Melbourne turned and smiled at Reba. He bowed deeply, straightened and gave her a brotherly kiss on the forehead. "Thanks for the dance." After a long, considering look, he smiled slightly. "If it weren't for the body language, I'd be tempted to say to hell with Walker."

Red sat up quickly. "Melbourne—"

"Don't worry," said Melbourne, "I learned my lesson." He looked at Reba with a rueful smile. "I couldn't believe Walker was as confident as he looked, much less that he would fight a man my size bare-handed."

"You survived," grunted Red. "You got no complaints."

Melbourne laughed and strode away into the crowd. Reba looked at his vanishing back with a growing disbelief. She sank into the chair opposite Red. He watched her out of the corner of his eyes, seeing her temper rise in waves of color.

"Look at it this way, Reba," he said quietly. "Chance isn't being unreasonable. There are some people here tonight who aren't very nice under their clean silk shirts, and Chance knows every one of them. So long as they think you're Walker's woman, you and that fat collection of gems won't be bothered. Nobody gets in Chance's way. It just isn't bright."

Reba ignored Red's soothing words, feeling only her loneliness and anger and her nails digging into her palms. "Why is Chance doing this to me?" she said in a strained voice. "He won't let anyone else near me but he'll trade me for a few acres of dirt! He has the China Queen; he has the kind of strike miners dream about and live and die without ever finding. Why won't he let me try to find my own happiness? *Who the hell does he think he is?*"

"He's one unhappy man," said Glory from behind Reba.

The older woman sat next to Red, her vivid orange dress contrasting with his somber black evening clothes. She turned on Reba with hard green eyes. "When you gave Chance that mine, you gave him his grave. He's been digging it as fast as he can."

Reba went white. She held onto the table as the room spun darkly, becoming the ravenous black mouth of the China Queen, a kikituk with shattered pink crystal eyes. "That's not what I wanted, not what I meant," she whispered.

"That mine's a killer," said Red evenly. "Chance won't even let me down in it, and Christ knows we've dug some bloody awful holes together."

"And for what?" demanded Glory of Reba. "For money? Chance won't sell one bloody crystal! Not for love. Not for money. He just brings out sacks of tourmaline, turns it over to us and goes back down into that great she-bitch of a mine. What the hell for, Reba, if not to die?"

Reba pushed to her feet, swaying slightly, seeing nothing but her own nightmare coming true. She had to go to Chance, find him before the China Queen closed its mouth once and for all, devouring the man she loved. She pushed through the people in the enormous ballroom, oblivious to stares and greetings, hearing only Glory's brutal words.

By the time Reba reached the lobby she was running, holding her elegant dress high, taking stairs in graceful leaps because the elevator would be too slow. Ignoring the startled looks from other people, Reba flew down the long winding hallway to her second-floor suite. Once there, she pulled her dress above her knees, retrieving her room key from its place in a flat satin garter. Her hand was shaking enough that fitting the key into the lock was impossible.

"Damn!"

She took a steadying breath, jammed in the key and swept into the suite. Slamming the door behind her, she ran through the outer room, threw open the bedroom door—

—and found herself in the heart of beauty.

The black matte silk that was Reba's trademark had been put over every chair, every table, the bed, even the floor. Resting on the silk, illuminated with miner's lights, were clusters and mounds and sunbursts of Pala tourmaline. Only the bed was bare, its black silk shimmering with reflected light.

For an instant Reba felt as though she were inside a gem, a place of shattering beauty and brilliance, a faceted world as complex as the man who had turned the room into a fantasy of the China Queen. The key fell unnoticed from her hand as she turned slowly, looking for him, but she saw only the beauty of the tourmaline surrounding her, magnified by her own tears. Nowhere did she see the power and male grace of the man she loved.

"Chance," she whispered, holding out her hands blindly, "please be here."

She sensed his presence the instant before she heard

the bedroom door close behind her. A man's hands touched her shoulders, hands both hard and gentle, warm as sunlight. With a small sound she turned, seeking his warmth even as his arms pulled her close. She held him tightly, unable to speak, afraid that she would wake up and he would be gone. His lips moved over her, smoothing words and caresses over her fragrant skin.

"All my life treasure has been an obsession with me," Chance said, his voice deep, vibrant with emotion. "It was as though if I just looked hard enough I'd find something overwhelmingly wonderful, something surpassingly rare, something as powerful and beautiful and enduring as the earth itself. But nothing I found lived up to my expectations. No matter how beautiful, how precious, how rare . . ."

His lips gently found hers. His tongue traced the curves of her smile, tasting her tears, sharing her breath, filling the sweet softness of her mouth as she clung to him in a kiss that said more of hunger and searching than any words.

". . . and then I kissed you in Death Valley and my world turned inside out," said Chance, his fingers delicately tracing the line of her neck and arm. "I could take the China Queen from another Sylvie but not from the woman who trusted me enough to cry in my arms and then kiss me as though there had never been another man and never would be."

Chance's fingertip followed a single teardrop down Reba's cheek. "I never believed that you were another Sylvie. But I tried to. I wanted the China Queen more than I'd ever wanted anything in my life. I knew, I just *knew*, that I'd find what I was looking for in that mine. Then I walked into your office and saw that drunken bastard reaching for you." Chance's hands tightened as he remembered, all gentleness gone. "It's a good thing Todd hadn't touched you, *chaton*. I would have killed him."

Reba trembled, unable to breathe or speak for the emotions filling her. She watched Chance's silver-green eyes, listening to him with a stillness and intensity she had learned from him.

"I tried to tell you about the mine the second day," Chance continued, his fingers lingering over the three diamond teardrops on her left shoulder, "but Tim interrupted. Then you took me to your beach. You stood in the parking lot and you told me that no man had ever wanted you just for yourself. You were so beautiful and so proud. I knew if I told you about the Queen then you would hate me. So I told myself that if we had some time together I could make you understand that no matter why I had come to Death Valley, I came to Los Angeles for a different reason."

His hands caged her face. With an almost inaudible groan, Chance bent to take her lips once more. The restraint and heat and need in him were as shattering to her as the moment she had walked into her hotel bedroom and found herself surrounded by fantastic beauty. As he lifted her in his arms and carried her toward the silk-covered bed, she tried to tell him that she loved him but all she could do was respond to caresses which coaxed rather than demanded her passion. He set her gently on her feet, kissed her lips and her eyes as he continued speaking, his deep voice and words as seductive as his strength holding her close.

"Each minute I was with you I wanted you more," Chance murmured, his hand moving down her left shoulder, peeling away silk that shared the warmth and fragrance of her skin.

A tremor of need ran through Chance's body, telling

Reba that the wanting was still there, stronger than ever. She ran her fingers over the smooth pleats of his white dress shirt, wanting only to feel the heat of his skin next to hers. His shirt opened beneath her fingers. She buried her lips in the male textures of his hair as her dress slid to the floor, leaving her wearing only a satin garter and gold lace panties.

His lips moved just below her glittering earring. "Gold dust and diamonds," he said hoarsely, then invaded her mouth with his kiss before she could speak.

He possessed her mouth completely, his tongue moving slowly, deeply, while his hands caressed the beauty that had been concealed under the silk of her dress. When he felt her change beneath his touch, he made a deep sound and lifted her suddenly, bringing her breasts up to his hungry lips. She cried out as his mouth claimed her with savage restraint, tongue and teeth shaping her into hard peaks of desire.

A firestorm of passion swept over Reba, melting her. She no longer cared whether or not Chance loved her. He wanted her, and she loved him. He lowered her to the bed and shrugged out of his shirt with a muscular twist that made her hungry to touch him, hold him, love him. He took off everything but her earrings, then removed his clothes and stood looking down at her with hot silver eyes.

"After we dug our way out of that cave-in and you laughed and turned to me, sharing your joy in the sunlight and being alive, I knew that I couldn't risk telling you about the mine. I couldn't risk losing you. I thought if we were married, whatever had come before wouldn't matter. We'd start new from the moment we bathed each other in that spring.

"Then Glory came and blew my dream to hell."

Reba looked up and saw the pain beneath the harsh planes of Chance's face. She tried to speak, unable to bear seeing him hurt, but he was talking again, his voice urgent.

"I didn't believe you could walk away from what we had together. I knew you were furious. I knew I'd hurt you. But I thought if you'd just let me touch you, love you, I could make you understand that I never meant to deceive you."

Chance lay down beside her, not touching her despite the male hunger and need that gripped him, outlining each hard line of his body with urgency and restraint. His eyes closed for a moment, then opened again, silver-green, remote.

"And then you ran from me, leaving me nothing. So I went back into that she-bitch mine and dug as though if I dug deep enough, fast enough, long enough, I'd get it all back somehow, the woman and the love. All I got was crystal, cold and hard, a fool's ransom. But who wants to buy back a fool?"

The bitterness in Chance's voice made Reba ache.

"Chance—" she said, her voice breaking.

"You wouldn't talk to me, wouldn't see me," he continued, his voice husky and relentless. "But I knew you'd be here tonight. Jeremy's night. So I came."

Chance's hand moved but instead of touching Reba, his fingers closed over the piece of paper that lay between their bodies, a pale blur against black silk.

"I didn't understand why you asked me to give up the China Queen," he said quietly. "I do now. Once, I might have been satisfied with the Queen's cold treasure. But now I need your living warmth, your laugh, your hands touching me. You're the only thing I've found that is more beautiful the longer I look, more magic in sunlight than in darkness, precious beyond words or comparison or reason. All my life I've been digging through darkness, searching the earth for you, and I didn't even know it."

Reba breathed his name as her hands came up to his face. Gently he removed them, putting the piece of paper in her fingers.

"Read it," said Chance.

She tried, but there were too many tears. "I can't."

"It's a quit-claim to the China Queen. She's yours, Reba, one hundred percent yours. She has been since the day you left me."

"I don't want the Queen," Reba said despairingly, crumpling the paper and throwing it into the darkness beyond. "Don't you understand?" she cried.

Then Reba cried out again, but for a different reason. Chance's hands were moving over her, setting fire to her, bringing her a pleasure so great it was almost pain. She closed her eyes and made an incoherent sound, twisting beneath his touch, her hands seeking him. He moved swiftly, powerfully, covering her with his hard body.

"If you want, I'll give the China Queen to the first person who walks down the hall," Chance said, watching her, his voice savage. "I'll give it all away right now, every last bloody crystal. I'll give up anything you ask. Except you. Don't ask me to give you up. I won't. *I can't.* I finally know what love is. I'll never give that up. I love you, Reba."

Her eyes opened wide and wondering, incandescent with emotion. A shudder went through him, testing his strength as he watched the woman he loved.

"Say something, *chaton.* Don't make me guess whether I've lost your love."

"Keep the China Queen," she whispered.

His face changed, pain and vulnerability and despair.

"For our children," she added quickly, smiling and crying at the same time, realizing he had misunderstood. She buried her face in his hard shoulder, holding him until she ached. "You can't lose my love, Chance. I'll always love you."

His hands went to her hair, fingers seeking out the hidden gold combs. Honey strands tumbled smoothly from his fingers, whispering as sweetly as the words he kept saying over and over, as though having once spoken of love he could not stop, telling her with each breath, each caress, how infinitely precious she was to him. Her words mingled with his, her hands caressing him, telling him in return what he had told her.

Then he became a part of her, his body hot and gleaming, Tiger God in her arms to stay.

Silhouette

Intimate Moments

more romance, more excitement

—————————— $2.25 each ——————————

1 ☐ DREAMS OF EVENING
Kristin James

2 ☐ ONCE MORE WITH FEELING
Nora Roberts

3 ☐ EMERALDS IN THE DARK
Beverly Bird

4 ☐ SWEETHEART CONTRACT
Pat Wallace

5 ☐ WIND SONG
Parris Afton Bonds

6 ☐ ISLAND HERITAGE
Monica Barrie

7 ☐ A DISTANT CASTLE
Sue Ellen Cole

8 ☐ LOVE EVERLASTING
Möeth Allison

9 ☐ SERPENT IN PARADISE
Stephanie James

#10 ☐ A SEASON OF RAINBOWS
Jennifer West

#11 ☐ UNTIL THE END OF TIME
June Trevor

#12 ☐ TONIGHT AND ALWAYS
Nora Roberts

#13 ☐ EDGE OF LOVE
Anna James

#14 ☐ RECKLESS SURRENDER
Jeanne Stephens

#15 ☐ SHADOW DANCE
Lorraine Sellers

#16 ☐ THE PROMISE OF SUMMER
Barbara Faith

#17 ☐ THE AMBER SKY
Kristin James

#18 ☐ THE DANVERS TOUCH
Elizabeth Lowell

#19 ☐ ANOTHER KIND OF LOVE
Mary Lynn Baxter

#20 ☐ THE GENTLE WINDS
Monica Barrie

#21 ☐ RAVEN'S PREY
Stephanie James

#22 ☐ AGAINST THE RULES
Linda Howard

#23 ☐ THE FIRES OF WINTER
Beverly Bird

#24 ☐ FANTASIES
Pamela Wallace

#25 ☐ THIS MAGIC MOMENT
Nora Roberts

#26 ☐ OLD LOVE, NEW LOVE
Jane Clare

#27 ☐ DIANA'S FOLLY
Jillian Blake

#28 ☐ WALTZ IN SCARLET
Muriel Bradley

Silhouette
Intimate Moments

more romance, more excitement

READERS' COMMENTS ON
SILHOUETTE INTIMATE MOMENTS:

"About a month ago a friend loaned me my first Silhouette. I was thoroughly surprised as well as totally addicted. Last week I read a Silhouette Intimate Moments and I was even more pleased. They are the best romance series novels I have ever read. They give much more depth to the plot, characters, and the story is fundamentally realistic. They incorporate tasteful sex scenes, which is a must, especially in the 1980's. I only hope you can publish them fast enough."

S.B.*, Lees Summit, MO

"After noticing the attractive covers on the new line of Silhouette Intimate Moments, I decided to read the inside and discovered that this new line was more in the line of books that I like to read. I do want to say I enjoyed the books because they are so realistic and a lot more truthful than so many romance books today."

J.C., Onekama, MI

"I would like to compliment you on your new line of books. I will continue to purchase all of the Silhouette Intimate Moments. They are your best line of books that I have had the pleasure of reading."

S.M., Billings, MT

*names available on request